READ OVER TWO MILLION TIMES ONLINE AS *THE OFFICE* BY TBY789

Reworked and available in print for the first time
as *BEAUTIFUL BASTARD!*

"*Beautiful Bastard* has heart, heat, and a healthy dose of snark. Romance readers who love a smart plot are in for an amazingly sexy treat!"

—Myra McEntire, author of *Hourglass*

"Smart, sexy, and satisfying, Christina Lauren's *Beautiful Bastard* is destined to become a romance classic."

—Tara Sue Me, author of *The Submissive*

"*Beautiful Bastard* is the perfect mix of passionate romance and naughty eroticism. I couldn't, and didn't, put it down until I'd read every last word."

—Elena Raines, *Twilightish*

Praise for *The Office* by tby789

One of *TwiFic Reviews*'s Top 10 Fanfiction Classics

"*The Office* paved the way for *Fifty Shades* and a thousand other imitators."

—Anne Jamison, University of Utah

"Many fans consider *The Office* to be the best Twilight fanfic ever."

—*The Hollywood Reporter*

"Warning! *The Office* can be very addicting . . ."

—*Robstenation*

"*The Office* captivated me; I was *consumed*."

—Jennifer Grant, *PattinsonFilms*

"And if the amazing sex scenes weren't enough, *The Office* is actually really well written. *Really well*."

—*Twidiculous*

Beautiful BASTARD

A Novel

CHRISTINA LAUREN

GALLERY BOOKS

NEW YORK • LONDON • TORONTO • SYDNEY • NEW DELHI

Gallery Books
A Division of Simon & Schuster, Inc.
1230 Avenue of the Americas
New York, NY 10020

First Gallery Books trade paperback edition February 2013

GALLERY BOOKS and colophon are registered trademarks
of Simon & Schuster, Inc.

For information about special discounts for bulk purchases,
please contact Simon & Schuster Special Sales at 1-866-506-1949
or business@simonandschuster.com

The Simon & Schuster Speakers Bureau can bring authors to your
live event. For more information or to book an event contact
the Simon & Schuster Speakers Bureau at 1-866-248-3049 or
visit our website at www.simonspeakers.com.

Designed by Fine Design

Manufactured in the United States of America

20   19   18   17   16   15   14   13   12   11

Library of Congress Cataloging-in-Publication Data

Lauren, Christina.
    Beautiful bastard / Christina Lauren. — First Gallery Books trade
paperback edition.
      pages cm
    I. Title.
    PS3612.A9442273
    [B43 2013]
    813'.6—dc23   2012049975

ISBN 978-1-4767-3009-7
ISBN 978-1-4767-3010-3 (ebook)

To SM for unknowingly bringing us together,
to the fandom for making it official,
and to our husbands, for putting up with it all.

One

My father always said the way to learn the job you want is to spend every second watching someone do it.

"To get the job at the top, you've got to start at the bottom," he told me. "Become the person the CEO can't live without. Be their right-hand man. Learn their world, and they'll snatch you up the second you finish your degree."

I had become irreplaceable. And I'd definitely become the Right Hand. It just so happened that in this case, I was the right hand that most days wanted to slap the damn face.

My boss, Mr. Bennett Ryan. *Beautiful Bastard.*

My stomach clenched tightly at the thought of him: tall, gorgeous, and entirely evil. He was the most self-righteous, pompous prick I'd ever met. I'd hear all of the other women in the office gossip about his escapades and wonder if a nice face was all it took. But my father also said, "You realize early in life that beauty is only skin-deep, and ugly goes straight to the bone."

I'd had my fair share of unpleasant men in the past few years, dated a few in high school and college. But this one took the cake.

"Well, hello Miss Mills!" Mr. Ryan stood in the doorway to my office that served as an anteroom to his. His voice was laced with honey, but it was all wrong . . . like honey left to freeze and crack on ice.

After spilling water on my phone, dropping my earrings into the garbage disposal, being rear-ended on the interstate, and having to wait for the cops to come and tell us what we both already knew—that it was the other guy's fault—the last thing I needed this morning was a grumpy Mr. Ryan.

Too bad for me he didn't come in any other flavor.

I gave him my usual. "Good morning, Mr. Ryan," hoping he would give me his usual curt nod in return.

But when I tried to slip past him, he murmured, "Indeed? 'Morning,' Miss Mills? What time is it in your little world?"

I stopped and met his cold stare. He was a good eight inches taller than me, and before working for him I'd never felt so small. I'd worked for Ryan Media Group for six years. But since his return to the family business nine months ago, I'd taken to wearing heels I used to consider circus height just so I could approach him near eye level. Even so, I still had to tilt my head to look up at him, and he clearly relished it, hazel eyes flashing.

"I had a bit of a disaster morning. It won't happen again," I said, relieved that my voice came out steady. I had never been late, not once, but leave it to him to make a thing of it the first time it happened. I managed to slip past him, put my purse and coat in my closet, and power up my computer. I tried to act like he wasn't standing in the doorway, watching every move I made.

"'Disaster morning' is quite an apt description for what I've had to deal with in your absence. I spoke to Alex Schaffer personally to smooth over the fact that he didn't get the signed contracts when promised: nine a.m., East Coast time. I had to call Madeline Beaumont personally to let her know we were, in fact, going to proceed with the proposal as written. In other words, I've done your job and mine this morning. Surely, even with a 'disaster morning' you can manage eight a.m.? Some of us get up and start working before the brunch hour."

I glanced up at him, antagonizing me, glaring, arms crossed over his broad chest—and all because I was an hour late. I blinked away, very deliberately not staring at the way his dark tailored suit stretched across his shoulders. I had made the mistake of visiting the hotel gym during a convention the first month we worked together and walked in to find him sweaty and shirt-less next to the treadmill. He had a face that any male model would kill for and the most incredible hair I've ever seen on a man. Freshly fucked hair. That's what the girls downstairs called it, and according to them, it earned its title. The image of him wiping his chest with his shirt was forever burned into my brain.

Of course, he'd had to ruin it by opening his mouth: "It's nice to see you finally taking an interest in your physical fitness, Miss Mills."

Asshole.

"I'm sorry, Mr. Ryan," I said with just a hint of bite. "I understand the burden I placed on you by making you manage a fax machine and pick up a telephone. As I mentioned, it won't happen again."

"You're right, it won't," he replied, cocky smile firmly in place.

If only he would keep his mouth shut, he'd be per-fect. A piece of duct tape would do the trick. I had some in my desk that I'd occasionally pull out and fondle, hoping someday I could put it to good use.

"And just so you don't allow this incident to slip your memory, I'd like to see the full status tables for the Schaffer, Colton, and Beaumont projects on my desk by five. And then you're going to make up the hour lost this morning by doing a mock board presenta-tion of the Papadakis account for me in the conference room at six. If you're going to manage this account, you're going to prove to me that you know what the hell you're doing."

My eyes widened as I watched him turn away, slamming his office door behind him. He knew damn well that I was ahead of schedule with this project, which also served as my MBA thesis. I still had months to finish my slides once the contracts were signed . . . which they weren't—they hadn't even been fully drafted. Now, with everything else on my plate, he wanted me to put together a mock board presentation in . . . I looked at my watch. Great, seven and a half hours, if I skipped lunch. I opened the Papadakis file and got down to it.

❧

As everyone began filtering out for lunch, I remained glued to my desk with my coffee and a bag of trail mix I'd bought from the vending machine. Normally I'd bring leftovers or leave with the other interns to grab something, but time was not on my side today. I heard the outer office door open and looked up, smiling as Sara Dillon walked in. Sara was in the same MBA internship program at Ryan Media Group that I was, though she worked in accounting.

"Ready for lunch?" she asked.

"I'm going to have to skip it. This is the day from

hell." I looked at her apologetically, and her smile turned into a smirk.

"Day from hell, or *boss* from hell?" She took a seat on the edge of my desk. "I heard he was on a bit of a rampage this morning."

I gave her a knowing look. Sara didn't work for him, but she knew all about Bennett Ryan. As the youngest son of company founder Elliott Ryan, and with a notoriously short fuse, he was a living legend in the building. "Even if there were two of me, I wouldn't be able to get this finished in time."

"You sure you don't want me to bring you back something?" Her eyes moved in the direction of his office. "A hit man? Some holy water?"

I laughed. "I'm good."

Sara smiled and left the office. I'd just finished off the last of my coffee when I bent down, noting a run in my stockings. "And on top of everything else," I began, hearing Sara return, "I've already snagged these. Actually, if you're going somewhere there's chocolate, bring me back fifty pounds, so I can eat my feelings later."

I glanced up and saw that it wasn't Sara standing there. My cheeks flushed red and I pulled my skirt back down.

"I'm sorry, Mr. Ryan, I—"

"Miss Mills, since you and the other office girls have plenty of time to discuss problematic lingerie, in addition to putting together the Papadakis presentation, I need you to also run down to the Willis office and retrieve the market analysis and segmentation for Beaumont." He straightened his tie, looking at his reflection in my window. "Do you think you can manage that?"

Did he just call me an "office girl"? Sure, as part of my internship I often did some basic assistant work for him, but he knew damn well I had worked for this company for years before receiving a JT Miller scholarship to Northwestern. I was four months away from getting my business degree.

Getting my degree and getting the hell out from under you, I thought. I looked up to meet his blazing eyes. "I'll be happy to ask Sam if she—"

"It wasn't a suggestion," he cut me off. "I'd like you to pick them up." He gazed at me for a moment with a clenched jaw before turning on his heel and storming back to his office, pulling the door closed roughly behind him.

What the fuck was his problem? Was slamming doors like a teenager really necessary? I grabbed my blazer from the back of the chair and began making my way to our satellite office a few buildings down.

When I returned, I knocked on his door but there was no response. I tried the knob. Locked. He was probably having a late-afternoon quickie with some trust fund princess while I ran around Chicago like an insane person. I shoved the manila folder through the mail slot, hoping the papers scattered everywhere and he'd have to get down and sort them himself. Would serve him right. I rather liked the image of him on his knees on the floor, gathering scattered documents. Then again, knowing him, he would call me into that sterile hellhole to clean it up while he watched.

Four hours later I had the status updates complete, my slides mostly in order, and I was almost hysterically laughing with how awful this day was. I found myself plotting a very bloody and drawn-out murder of the kid at The Copy Stop. A simple job, that's all I had asked. Make some copies, bind some things. Should have been a piece of cake. In and out. But no. It had taken *two hours.*

I raced down the darkened hall of the now-empty building, the presentation materials clutched haphazardly in my arms, and glanced at my watch. Six twenty. Mr. Ryan was going to have my ass. I was twenty minutes late. As I experienced this morning, he hated late. "Late" was a word not found in the *Bennett Ryan Dickhead Dictionary.* Along with "heart," "kindness," "compassion," "lunch break," or "thank you."

So there I was, running through the empty halls in my stilt-like Italian pumps, racing to the executioner.

Breathe, Chloe. He can smell fear.

As I neared the conference room, I tried to calm my

breathing and slowed to a walk. Soft light shone from beneath the closed door. He was definitely in there, waiting for me. Carefully, I attempted to smooth my hair and clothing while tidying the bundle of documents in my arms. Taking a deep breath, I knocked on the door.

"Come in."

I walked into the warmly lit space. The conference room was huge; one wall was filled with floor-to-ceiling windows that gave a beautiful view of the Chicago cityscape from eighteen stories up. Dusk darkened the sky outside, and skyscrapers speckled the horizon with their lighted windows. In the center of the room stood a large heavy wood conference table, and facing me from the head of the table was Mr. Ryan.

He sat there, suit jacket hanging on the chair behind him, tie loosened, crisp white shirtsleeves rolled up to his elbows, and chin resting on his steepled fingers. His eyes were boring into mine, but he said nothing.

"I apologize, Mr. Ryan," I said, my voice wavering with my still labored breathing, "The print job took—" I stopped. Excuses wouldn't help my situation. And besides, I wasn't going to let him blame me for something I had no control over. He could kiss my ass. With my newfound bravery in place, I lifted my chin and walked over to where he sat.

Without meeting his gaze, I sorted through my papers and placed a copy of the presentation on the table before us. "Are you ready for me to begin?"

He didn't respond aloud, his eyes piercing my brave front. This would be a lot easier if he wasn't so gorgeous. Instead, he gestured toward the materials before him, urging me to continue.

I cleared my throat and began my presentation. As I moved through the different aspects of the proposal, he stayed silent, staring directly at his copy. Why was he so calm? His temper tantrums I could handle. But the eerie silence? It was unnerving.

I was leaning over the table, gesturing toward a set of graphs, when it happened.

"Their timeline for the first milestone is a little ambi—" I stopped midsentence, my breath caught in my throat. His hand pressed gently into my lower back before sliding down, settling on the curve of my ass. In the nine months I had worked for him, he had never intentionally touched me.

This was most definitely intentional.

The heat from his hand burned through my skirt and into my skin. Every muscle in my body tensed, and it felt like my insides were liquefying. What the hell was he doing? My brain screamed at me to push his hand off, to tell him to never touch me again, but my body had other ideas. My nipples hardened, and I clenched my jaw in response. *Traitor nipples.*

While my heart pounded in my chest, at least half a minute passed, and neither of us said anything as his hand moved down to my thigh, caressing. Our breathing and the muted noise of the city below were the only sounds in the still air of the conference room.

"Turn around, Miss Mills." His quiet voice broke the silence and I straightened my back, eyes facing forward. Slowly I turned, his hand skimming across me and sliding to my hip. I could feel the way his hand spread from his fingertips on my lower back all the way to where his thumb pressed against the soft skin just in front of my hipbone. I looked down to meet his eyes, which looked intently back at me.

I could see his chest rising and falling, each breath deeper than the last. A muscle twitched in his sharp jaw as his thumb began to move, slowly sliding back and forth, his eyes never leaving mine. He was waiting for me to stop him; there had been plenty of time for me to shove him away, or simply turn and leave. But I had too many feelings to sort out before I could react. I had never felt this way, and I had never expected to feel this about him. I wanted to slap him, and then pull him up by his shirt and lick his neck.

"What are you thinking?" he whispered, eyes somehow both mocking and anxious.

"I'm still trying to figure that out."

With those eyes still locked to mine, he began to

slide his hand lower. His fingers ran down my thigh, to the hem of my skirt. He moved it up so his fingertips traced the strap of my garter belt, the lace edge of one thigh-high stocking. A long finger slipped beneath the thin fabric and pulled it down slightly. I sucked in a sharp breath, feeling suddenly like I was melting from the outside in.

How could I let my body react like this? I still wanted to slap him, but now, more than that, I wanted him to keep going. The heavy ache between my legs was building. He reached the edge of my panties and slipped his fingers under the fabric. I felt him slide against my skin and graze my clit before pushing his finger inside me, and I bit my lip trying, unsuccessfully, to stifle my groan. When I looked down at him, beads of sweat were forming on his brow.

"Fuck," he growled quietly. "You're wet." His eyes fell closed and he seemed to be waging the same internal battle I was. I glanced down at his lap and could see him straining against the smooth fabric of his pants. Without opening his eyes, he withdrew his finger and fisted the thin lace of my panties in his hand. He was shaking as he looked up at me, fury clear in his expression. In one quick movement he tore them off, the rip of the fabric echoing in the silence.

He pulled my hips roughly, lifting me up onto the cold table and spreading my legs in front of him. I gave an involuntary groan as his fingers returned, sliding between my legs and pushing into me again. I despised this man in a singularly sharp way, but my body was betraying me; I craved more of what he was doing. Damn if he wasn't good at this. His weren't the gentle loving touches I was accustomed to. Here was a man used to getting what he wanted, and it turned out that right now, what he wanted was me. My head fell to the side as I leaned back on my elbows, feeling my impending orgasm approaching fast.

To my absolute horror I actually whimpered, "Oh, please."

He stopped moving, pulling his fingers back and holding them in a fist before him. I sat up, grabbing his silk tie and pulling his mouth roughly against mine. His lips felt as perfect as they looked, firm and smooth. I'd never been kissed by someone who clearly knew every single angle and dip and teasing move to make me almost completely lose my mind.

I bit his lower lip as my hands made quick work down to the front of his pants, whipping his belt free of the loops. "You better be ready to finish what you started."

He made a low, angry noise deep in his throat and took my blouse in his hands, ripping it open, the silver buttons skittering across the long conference table.

He slid his hands up my ribs and over my breasts,

thumbs slipping back and forth across my taut nipples, his dark stare fixated on my expression the entire time. His hands were big, and rough almost to the point of pain, but instead of wincing or backing off, I pushed into his palms wanting more, and harder.

He growled, fingers tightening. It occurred to me I might bruise, and for a sick moment I hoped I did. I wanted a way to remember this feeling, of being completely sure of what my body wanted, entirely unleashed.

He leaned close enough to bite my shoulder, whispering, "You fucking tease."

Unable to get close enough, I quickened my pace on his zipper, shoving his pants and his boxers to the floor. I gave his cock a hard squeeze, feeling him pulse against my palm.

The way he hissed my *last* name—"*Mills*"—should have sent a rush of fury through me, but I only felt one thing right now: pure, unadulterated lust. He forced my skirt up my thighs and pushed me back on the conference table. Before I could utter a single word, he took hold of my ankles, grabbed his cock, and took a step forward, thrusting deep inside me.

I couldn't even be horrified by the loud moan I let out—he felt better than anything.

"What's that?" he hissed through clenched teeth, his hips slapping against my thighs, driving him deep inside. "Never been fucked like this before, have you? You wouldn't be such a tease if you were being properly fucked."

Who did he think he was? And why the hell did it turn me on so much that he was right? I had never had sex anywhere but on a bed, and it never felt like this.

"I've had better," I taunted.

He laughed, a quiet mocking sound. "Look at me."

"No."

He pulled out just as I was about to come. At first I thought he was actually going to leave me this way, until he grabbed my arms and yanked me up off the table, lips and tongue pressing against mine.

"*Look* at me," he said again. And, finally, with him no longer inside me, I could. He blinked once, slowly, long dark lashes brushing against his cheek, and then said, "Ask me to make you come."

His tone was all wrong. It was almost a question, but his words were just like him—all bastard. I did want him to make me come. More than anything. But I'd be damned if I'd ever ask him for anything.

I dropped my voice and stared back at him. "You're an asshole, Mr. Ryan."

His smile told me that whatever he'd needed from me, he got. I wanted to slam my knees up into his balls, but then I wouldn't get more of what I really wanted.

"Say please, Miss Mills."

"*Please,* go fuck yourself."

The next thing I felt was the cold window against my breasts, and I groaned at the intense contrast in temperature between it and his skin. I was on fire; every part of me wanted to feel his rough touch.

"At least you're consistent," he snarled into my ear before biting my shoulder. He kicked at my feet. "Spread your legs."

I parted my legs and without hesitation he pulled my hips back and reached between us before thrusting forward into me.

"You like the cold?"

"Yes."

"Devious, filthy girl. You like being watched, don't you?" he murmured, taking my earlobe between his teeth. "You love that all of Chicago can look up here and see you getting fucked, and you loving every minute of it with your pretty tits pressed against the glass."

"Stop talking, you're ruining it." Though he wasn't. Not even close. His gravelly voice was doing wicked things to me.

But he just laughed in my ear and probably noticed the way I shivered at the sound. "You want them to see you come?"

I groaned in response, unable to form words with each repeated thrust into me, pressing me further against the glass.

"Say it. You want to come, Miss Mills? Answer me or I'll stop and make you suck me off instead," he hissed, driving himself deeper and deeper inside me with every thrust.

The part of me that hated him was dissolving like sugar on my tongue, and the part that wanted everything he had to give me was growing, hot and demanding.

"Just tell me." He leaned forward, sucked my earlobe between his lips and then gave it a sharp bite. "I promise I'll give it to you."

"Please," I said, closing my eyes to shut out everything else and just feel him. "Please. Yes."

He reached around, moving his fingertips across my clit with the perfect pressure, the perfect rhythm. I could feel his smile press into the back of my neck, and when he opened his mouth and pressed his teeth to my skin, I was done for. Warmth spread down my spine, around my hips, and between my legs, jerking me back into him. My hands slammed against the glass, my entire body quaking from the orgasm that was rushing over me, leaving me gasping for air. When it finally subsided, he pulled out and spun me around to face him, ducking his head to suck my neck, my jaw, my lower lip.

"Say thank you," he whispered.

I dug my hands into his hair and tugged hard, hoping I could get some reaction out of him, wanting to see if he was in control or delusional. *What are we doing?*

He groaned, leaning into my hands and kissing up and down my neck, pressing his erection into my stomach. "Now make me feel good."

I released one hand and brought it down to his cock and began stroking him. He was heavy, and long, and perfect in my palm. I wanted to tell him, but I'd be damned if I ever let him know how amazing he felt. Instead, I pulled away from his lips, staring at him with hooded eyes.

"I'm going to make you come so hard you forget that you're supposed to be the world's biggest asshole," I growled, sliding down the glass before slowly taking his entire cock in my mouth and back against my throat. He tensed and let out a deep moan. I looked up at him, his palms and forehead resting on the glass, his eyes closed tight. He looked vulnerable, and he looked gorgeous in his abandon.

But he *wasn't* vulnerable. He was the biggest jerk on the planet and I was on my knees in front of him. No fucking way.

So instead of giving him what I knew he wanted, I stood up, pulled my skirt back down, and met his eyes. It was easier now, without him touching me and making me feel things he had no business doing.

The seconds ticked by, neither of us looking away.

"What the fuck do you think you're doing?" he rasped. "Get on your knees and open your mouth."

"Not a chance."

I pulled the front of my buttonless shirt together and walked out, praying my shaky legs wouldn't betray me.

Grabbing my purse from my desk, I threw my blazer on, trying desperately to fasten the button with my trembling fingers. Mr. Ryan still hadn't come out, and I ran to the elevator praying to God it would get there before I had to face him again.

I couldn't even let myself think about what happened until I was out of there. I'd let him fuck me, give me the most amazing orgasm of my life, and then I'd left him with his pants around his ankles in the company conference room with the worst case of blue balls known to any man. If this was someone else's life I would be high-fiving them so hard. Too bad it wasn't.

Shit.

The doors opened and I entered, quickly pushing the button and watching as each floor counted down. As soon as the elevator reached the lobby I raced out and down the hall. I briefly heard the security guard say something about working late, but I just waved and sped past him.

With each step the ache between my legs reminded me of the events of the last hour. As I reached my car I unlocked it with the remote, pulled open the door, and collapsed into the safety of the leather seats. I looked up at myself in the rearview mirror.

What in the fuck was that?

Two

Christ. I am so fucking screwed.

I'd been staring at my ceiling since I woke up thirty minutes ago. Brain: a mess. Dick: hard.

Well, hard *again*.

I scowled at the ceiling. It didn't matter how many times I'd jerked off after she left me last night, it never seemed to go away. And though I didn't think it was possible, it was worse than the hundreds of other times I'd woken up this way. Because this time, I knew what I was missing. And she hadn't even let me come.

Nine months. Nine fucking months of morning wood, jacking off, and endless fantasies about someone I didn't even want. Well, that wasn't completely true. I wanted her. I wanted her more than any woman I'd ever seen. The big problem was I also hated her.

And she hated me too. I mean, she *really* hated me. In all my thirty-one years, I had never met someone who pushed my buttons like Miss Mills.

Just her name made my dick twitch. *Fucking traitor. I*

stared down at where I tented my sheets. This stupid appendage got me into this mess to begin with. I rubbed my hands across my face and sat up.

Why couldn't I just keep it in my pants? I'd managed for almost a year. And it had worked. I kept my distance, bossed her around, hell, even *I'll* admit I'd been a bastard. And then I just lost it. All it took was one moment, sitting in that quiet room, her smell all around me and that fucking skirt, her ass in my face. I snapped.

I was sure that if I just had her once, it would be disappointing and the wanting would be over. I'd finally have some peace. But here I was, in my bed, hard, as if I hadn't come in weeks. I looked at the clock, and it had only been four hours.

I took a quick shower, scrubbing myself roughly as if to remove any trace of her left from last night. This was going to stop, this *had* to stop. Bennett Ryan didn't act like some horny teenager, and I certainly did not fuck around in my office. The last thing I needed was a clingy woman ruining everything. I couldn't allow Miss Mills to have this control over me.

Everything was so much better before I knew what I was missing. For as awful as that was, this was million times worse.

———

I was making my way into my office when she walked in. The way she left last night, practically sprinting out the door, I figured one of two scenarios awaited me. Either she would be making eyes at me, thinking that last night meant something, that *we* meant something. Or she'd have my ass.

If word got out about what we'd done, not only could I lose my job, but I could lose everything I'd worked for. And yet, as much as I hated her, I couldn't see her doing something like that. If there was one thing I'd learned about her, it was that she was trustworthy and loyal. She might be a hateful shrew, but I didn't think she would throw me to the lions. She had worked for Ryan Media Group since college and was a valued part of the company for a reason. Now she was only months from obtaining her MBA and would have her pick of jobs when she was ready. No way would she jeopardize that.

But I'll be damned if she didn't completely ignore me. She walked in wearing a knee-length trench coat. It shielded whatever was beneath, but did a fantastic job showing off those amazing legs.

Oh shit . . . if she was wearing those shoes, there was a good chance . . . *No, not that dress. Please, for the love of God, not that dress.* I knew for a fact there was no way I had the willpower for that shit today.

I glared at her as she hung her jacket in her closet and sat down at her desk.

Well, fuck me running, that woman really was the biggest tease in the entire world.

It was the white dress. With a neckline that dipped down to accentuate the soft smooth skin of her neck and collarbone, and white fabric clinging perfectly to those gorgeous tits, the dress was the bane of my existence, my heaven and hell wrapped in one delicious package.

The hem fell just below her knees and it was the sexiest thing I had ever seen. It wasn't provocative in any way, but there was something about the cut and that goddamn virginal white that had me hard practically all day. And she always left her hair down when she wore it. One of my recurring fantasies was of taking all of the damned pins out of her hair before I grabbed a handful and fucked her.

God, she pissed me off.

When she still didn't acknowledge me, I turned and stormed into my office, slamming the door behind me. Why was she still affecting me this way? I'd never had anyone or anything distract me from work, and I hated her for being the first.

But part of me relished the memory of her victorious expression as she turned and left me gasping and practically begging her to suck me off. The girl had a spine made of steel.

I bit back a grin and focused instead on hating her.

Work. I would just focus on work and stop thinking about her. I walked over to my desk and sat down, trying to direct my attention to anything but thoughts of how amazing those lips felt around me last night.

Not conducive, Bennett.

I flipped open my laptop to check my schedule for the day. My schedule . . . shit. The bitch had the most up-to-date version in *her* computer. Hopefully I wasn't missing any meetings this morning, because I was not calling Ice Queen in here until I absolutely had to.

———

As I was going over a spreadsheet, a knock came at my door. "Come in," I called out. A white envelope was slammed down onto my desk. I looked up to see Miss Mills staring down at me with a defiantly crooked eyebrow. Without an explanation, she turned and walked out of my office.

I glared at the envelope, panicked. Likely it was a formal letter detailing my conduct and indicating her intent to file a harassment suit. I expected letterhead and her scribbled signature at the bottom of the page.

What I didn't expect was a sales receipt from an online clothing store . . . charged to the company credit card. I shot up out of the chair and raced out of my office after her. She was headed for the stairwell. Good. We were on the eighteenth floor, and nobody, besides maybe the two of us, ever used the stairs. I could scream at her all I wanted and no one would be the wiser.

The door closed with a heavy clang and her heels echoed their way down the stairs just in front of me.

"Miss Mills, where in the hell do you think you're going?"

She continued walking without turning back to look at me. "We're out of coffee," she hissed. "So as your *office girl*, I'm going down to the café on fourteen to retrieve some. Can't have you missing out on your caffeine fix."

How could someone so hot be such a bitch? I caught up to her on the landing between floors and grabbed her arm, pushing her against the wall. Her eyes narrowed contemptuously at me, her teeth clenched in a hiss. I whipped the receipt up in front of her face as I glared back at her. "What is this?"

She shook her head. "You know, for such a pompous know-it-all, you really are a stupid son of a bitch sometimes. What does it look like? It's a receipt."

"I can see that," I growled through my teeth, crumpling the paper into my clenched fist. I pressed the sharp tip of it into the delicate skin just above her breast and felt my cock twitch when she gasped and her eyes dilated. "Why are you making clothing purchases on your company credit card?"

"Some bastard tore my blouse." She shrugged her shoulders and then leaned her face closer to me and whispered, "*And* my panties."

Well, fuck.

I took a deep breath through my nose and threw the paper to the floor, leaning forward and pressing my lips against hers and digging my fingers into her hair, pinning her body against the wall. My dick throbbed against her abdomen as I felt her hand mirror my own and grip my hair, fisting it roughly.

I pulled her dress up along her thighs and groaned into her mouth as my fingers once again found the lace edge of her thigh highs. She did this to torment me, she *had* to. I felt her tongue run over my lips as my fingertips brushed the warm and wet material of her panties. I clenched my hold around the fabric and gave it a rough tug.

"Make a note to order another pair then," I hissed and then pressed my tongue between her lips and into her mouth.

She groaned deeply as I thrust two fingers inside of her, and if it was possible, she was even wetter than she'd been last night. *Seriously fucked-up situation we have going on here.* She broke away from my lips with a gasp as I fucked her hard with my fingers, my thumb rubbing vigorous circles on her clit.

"Get your cock out," she said. "I need to feel you in me. Now."

I narrowed my eyes at her, trying to hide the effect her words had on me.

"Say please, Miss Mills."

"Now," she said more urgently.

"Bossy much?"

She gave me a look that would shrivel the dick off a

lesser man and I laughed in spite of myself. Mills could hold her own. "Good thing I'm feeling generous."

I made quick work of my belt and pants before lifting her up and thrusting hard inside her. Christ, she felt amazing. Better than anything. It helped explain why I couldn't get her out of my head, and a small voice told me I might never get enough of this.

"Damn," I mumbled.

She gasped and I felt her clench around me, her breath ragged. She bit into the shoulder of my jacket and wrapped her leg around me as I began moving into her hard and fast against the wall. Any moment someone could enter the stairwell and catch me fucking her, and I couldn't care less. I needed to get her out of my system.

She lifted her head from my shoulder and bit her way up my neck before taking my bottom lip between her teeth.

"Close," she growled and tightened her leg around me to pull me deeper. "I'm close."

Perfect.

I buried my face in her neck and hair to muffle the groan as I came hard and suddenly inside her, squeezing her ass in my hands. Pulling out before she could rub herself against me anymore, I put her down on unsteady legs.

She gaped at me, her look thunderous. The stairwell filled with a leaden silence.

"Really?" she said, exhaling loudly. Her head fell back against the wall with a dull thud.

"Thanks, that was fantastic." I found my pants down around my knees.

"You're an asshole."

"You've mentioned this," I murmured, looking down as I pulled up my zipper.

When I looked back up, she had straightened her dress, but she still looked beautifully disheveled, and part of me ached to reach forward and slide my hand against her, to make her come. But a larger part of me relished the angry dissatisfaction in her eyes. "What goes around comes around, so to speak."

"It's too bad you're such a horrible lay," she replied calmly. She turned to continue down the stairs but stopped abruptly, spinning back to meet my eye. "And it's a good thing I'm on the pill. Thanks for asking, asshole."

I watched her disappear out of sight down the stairs and growled as I walked back to my office. I landed in my chair with a loud huff, raking my hands through my hair before removing her destroyed panties from my pocket. I stared at the white silk fabric between my fingers for a moment, then opened my desk drawer and dropped them in to join the pair from last night.

Three

How the hell I made it down those stairs without killing myself is beyond me. I ran out of there like I was on fire, leaving Mr. Ryan alone in the stairwell slack jawed, clothes askew, and hair standing on end like he'd been molested.

Blowing past the café on fourteen, and clearing the final floor landing in a leap—no easy task in these shoes—I pushed open the metal door and leaned against the wall, panting.

What just happened? Did I just fuck my boss on the stairs? I gasped and my hands flew over my mouth. Did I order him to? *Oh, Jesus.* What the hell was wrong with me?

Dazed, I stumbled away from the wall and up a few flights into the closest restroom. I did a quick check under all the stalls to make sure they were empty and then turned the lock on the main door. As I approached the bathroom mirror, I winced. I looked like I'd been ridden hard and put out to dry.

My hair was a nightmare. All my carefully styled waves were now a mass of wild tangles. Apparently Mr. Ryan liked my hair down. I'd have to remember that.

Wait. What? Where the hell did that come from? I most certainly would not remember that. I slammed my fist on the counter and moved closer to inspect the damage.

My lips were swollen, my makeup smudged; my dress was stretched out and practically hanging on me, and I was once again missing my panties.

Son. Of. A. Bitch. That was the second pair. What was he doing with them, anyway?

"Oh, God!" I said, panicked. They weren't lying in a pile in the conference room somewhere, were they? Maybe he picked them up and tossed them aside? I should ask him to be sure. But no. I wouldn't give him the satisfaction of even acknowledging this . . . this . . . what was this?

I shook my head, scrubbing my face with my hands. God, I'd made a mess of things. When I came in this morning, I'd had a plan. I was going to walk in there, throw that receipt in his pretty little face, and tell him to shove it. But then he'd looked so goddamn sexy in that charcoal Prada suit, and his hair stuck up like a neon sign screaming, Do Me, and I just lost all coherent thought. Pathetic. What was it about him that made my brain turn to mush and my panties wet?

This was not good. How was I going to face him without imagining him naked? Okay, well, not *naked*. I technically hadn't seen him completely undressed yet, but what I had seen caused a shiver to run through me.

Oh no. Did I just say "yet"?

I could quit. I thought about that for a minute but didn't like the way it felt. I loved my job, and Mr. Ryan might be the world's most epic douchebag, but I'd dealt with that for nine months and—the last twenty-four hours aside—I had him figured out and could handle him like no other. And as much as I hated to admit it, I loved watching him work. He was an asshole because he was both supremely impatient and an obsessive perfectionist; he held everyone to the same standards he set for himself and didn't put up with anything but the best effort. I had to admit I'd always appreciated the expectation that I would perform better, work harder, and do whatever it took to get the job done— even if I didn't always love his methods. He really was a genius in the marketing world; his whole family was.

And that was the other thing. His family. My dad was back home in North Dakota, and when I started as a receptionist while still in college, Elliott Ryan had been so good to me. They all had. Bennett's brother, Henry, was another senior executive and the nicest guy I'd ever met. I loved everyone here, so quitting was simply not an option.

The biggest issue was my scholarship. I needed to present my in-world experience to the JT Miller scholarship board before I completed my MBA, and I wanted my thesis to be a powerhouse. It's why I stayed on at RMG: Bennett Ryan offered me the Papadakis account—the marketing plan for the multibillionaire land developer—which was a bigger project than anything my peers were working on. Four months wasn't enough to start somewhere new and have anything good to show for it . . . was it?

No. Definitely couldn't leave Ryan Media.

With that decided, I knew I needed a plan of action. I had to remain professional and make sure Mr. Ryan and I never, ever happened again, even if this was by far the hottest, most intense sex I'd ever had in my life . . . even when he was withholding orgasms from me.

Ass.

I was a strong, independent woman. I had a career to build and had worked ridiculous hours to get where I was. My mind and body were not ruled by lust. I just had to remember what a jerk he was. He was a womanizing, arrogant, pigheaded asshat who assumed everyone around him was an idiot.

I smiled at myself in the mirror and reeled through a collection of my recent Bennett Ryan memories.

"I appreciate that you got me coffee when you made your own, Miss Mills, but if I'd wanted mud to drink I

would have scooped my mug through the garden soil this morning."

"If you insist on pounding your keyboard as if you're hammering gophers back home, Miss Mills, I'd appreciate it if you kept the door joining our offices closed."

"Is there a good reason it's taking you forever to take the contract drafts to legal? Does daydreaming about farm boys take up all your time?"

Hell, actually, this would be easier than I thought.

Feeling a new sense of determination, I straightened my dress, smoothed my hair, and marched pantiless and confident out of the bathroom. I quickly retrieved the coffee I was after and headed back to my office, making sure to avoid the stairs.

I opened the outer office door and stepped in. The door to Mr. Ryan's office was shut, and there was no noise coming from inside. Maybe he stepped out. *Like I could get so lucky.* Sitting in my chair, I pulled open my drawer and removed my cosmetic bag, fixing my makeup before getting back to work. The last thing I wanted to do was face him, but if I didn't plan on quitting, it would have to be done eventually.

When I looked through the calendar, I remembered Mr. Ryan had a presentation before the other executives on Monday. I grimaced when I realized this meant I would have to talk to him today to prepare materials. He also had a convention in San Diego next month, which meant I would have to be not only in the same hotel as him, but in the plane, the company car, and any meetings that came up as well. No, no awkwardness there at all.

For the next hour, I found myself glancing up at his door. And each time I did, my stomach began to flutter. This was ridiculous! What was wrong with me? I shut the file I was unsuccessfully reading and dropped my head into my hands just as I heard his door open.

Mr. Ryan walked out, not meeting my eyes. He'd straightened his clothes, slung his overcoat over his arm, and had a briefcase in hand, but his hair was still a crazy mess.

"I'm leaving for the rest of the day," he said, eerily calm. "Cancel my appointments and make any necessary adjustments."

"Mr. Ryan," I said, bringing him to a stop, his hand resting on the door. "Please don't forget you have a presentation to the executive committee on Monday at ten." I spoke to his back. He stood still as a statue, his muscles tensed. "If you like, I can have the spreadsheets, portfolios, and slide materials set up in the conference room by nine thirty."

Okay, I was actually kind of enjoying this. There was nothing about his posture that communicated *comfortable*. He nodded curtly and started to make his way out the door when I stopped him again.

"And, Mr. Ryan?" I added sweetly. "I need your signature on these expense reports before you leave."

His shoulders dropped and he exhaled harshly. Spinning on his heel to make his way to my desk, he never met my eyes as he leaned over and flipped through the forms to the Sign Here tabs.

I placed a pen on the desk. "Please sign where the tabs are, sir."

He hated being told to do what he was already doing, and I stifled a laugh. Snatching the pen from me, he slowly raised his chin, bringing his hazel eyes in line with my own. Our eyes locked for what seemed like minutes, neither of us looking away. For a brief moment I had an irresistible urge to lean in and suck on his pouty bottom lip and beg him to touch me.

"Don't forward my calls," he spat out, quickly signing the last form and tossing the pen onto my desk. "If there's an emergency, contact Henry."

"Bastard," I murmured to myself as I watched him disappear.

❧

To say my weekend sucked would be putting it mildly. I hardly ate, I hardly slept, and what little sleep I did get was interrupted by fantasies of my boss naked above me, beneath me, behind me. I almost wished for the return of classes just so I had something to distract me.

Saturday morning I awoke frustrated and crabby but managed to somehow get myself together and take care of housework and grocery shopping. Sunday morning, however, I was not so lucky. I woke with a start, panting and trembling, my body sweaty and twisted in a mass of cotton sheets. The dream I had was so intense it had actually brought me to orgasm. Mr. Ryan and I had been on the conference table again, but this time we were both completely naked. He was on his back and I straddled him, my body sliding back and forth, up and down his cock. He touched me everywhere: along the sides of my face, down my neck, across my breasts, to my hips, where he guided my movements. I fell to pieces when our eyes met.

"Shit," I groaned as I pulled myself out of bed. This was going from bad to worse, quickly. Who would have thought working for an angry jackass would result in my getting fucked up against a cold window at work and liking it?

I started the shower, and as I waited for the water to warm, my thoughts began to drift again. I wanted to see his eyes looking up from between my legs, wanted to see his expression as he climbed on top of me, pushed into me, felt how much I wanted him. I ached to hear the sound of his voice saying my name when he came.

My heart sank in my chest. Fantasizing about him was a one-way ticket to trouble. I was on the cusp of getting my graduate degree. He was an executive. He had nothing to lose, and I stood to lose it all.

I showered and dressed quickly to meet Sara and Julia for brunch. Sara and I got to see each other every day at work, but Julia, my best friend since middle school, was tougher to nail down. She was a buyer for Gucci and dutifully filled my closet with samples and overstock. Thanks to her and her discount, I owned some of the most beautiful clothes money could buy. I still paid a pretty penny for them, but it was worth it. I made decent money at Ryan Media, and my scholarship covered all of my school costs, but even I couldn't spend nineteen hundred dollars on a dress and not want to off myself.

I'd sometimes wondered if Elliott paid me so well because he knew I was the only one who could handle his son. Oh, if only he knew.

I decided that it would be a bad idea to talk to the girls about what was going on. I mean, Sara worked for Henry Ryan and saw Bennett around the building all the time. There was no way I could ask her to keep that kind of secret. Julia on the other hand would kick my ass. For almost a year she'd listened to me complain about what a dick he was, and she would not be happy to find out I was screwing him.

Two hours later I was sitting with my two best friends, drinking mimosas on the patio of our favorite restaurant, talking about men and clothes and work. Julia had surprised me with a dress made from the most sumptuous fabric I'd ever felt. It sat in a garment bag slung over the chair next to me.

"So how's work going?" Julia asked between bites of her melon. "That douche of a boss still giving you a hard time, Chloe?"

"Oh, Beautiful Bastard." Sara sighed, and I carefully studied the condensation on my champagne flute. She popped a grape into her mouth and spoke around it. "God, you should see him, Julia. It's the most perfect nickname I've ever heard. He is a god. And I mean that. There's nothing wrong with him, physically. Perfect face, body, clothes, hair . . . Oh, God, the hair. He's got that artfully arranged messy thing going on," she said, motioning above her head. "Looks like he just banged the hell out of someone."

I rolled my eyes. I never needed a reminder about the hair.

"But—and I don't know what Chloe has told you— he really is awful," Sara continued, growing serious. "I mean, I wanted to shove a pocket knife into each of his tires within the first fifteen minutes of meeting him. He is the biggest dick I've ever met."

I almost choked on a piece of pineapple. If Sara only knew. Truly, the man was blessed in the man-parts department. It was unfair.

"Why is he such a jerk?"

"Who knows?" Sara said, and then blinked away as if she was really considering whether he had a good excuse. "Maybe he had a hard childhood?"

"Have you *met* his family?" I asked, skeptical. "Hello, Norman Rockwell."

"True," she conceded. "Maybe it's some sort of defense mechanism. Like, he's bitter and feels like he has to work harder and prove himself to everyone all the time because he's so damn pretty?"

I snorted. "There isn't a deep reason. He thinks everyone should care as much and work as hard as he does, and most people don't. It pisses him off."

"Are you *defending* him, Chloe?" Sara asked with a surprised grin.

"Definitely *not*."

I noticed Julia's blue eyes were trained on me and had narrowed in silent accusation. I'd done my share of complaining about my boss in the past several months, but maybe I'd never mentioned that he was gorgeous?

"Chloe, have you been holding out on me? Is your boss a hot piece?" she asked.

"He *is* gorgeous, but his personality makes it pretty hard to appreciate." I tried to be as nonchalant as I could. Julia had a way of reading every thought I had.

"Well," she said, shrugging her shoulders and tak-

ing a long sip of her drink, "maybe he's pissed off because he's got a tiny dick."

I tipped back my champagne flute as my two friends
howled in fits of laughter.

❧

Monday morning, I was a bundle of nerves as I made
my way into the building. I'd made my decision: I
wasn't going to sacrifice my job because of our lack of
judgment. I wanted to finish this position with a stellar
presentation for the scholarship board and then leave
and start my career. No more sex, no more fantasizing.
I could easily work—*business only*—with Mr. Ryan for
another few months.

Feeling the need for a boost of confidence, I wore
the new dress Julia had given me. It hugged my curves
without looking too provocative. But my secret confidence weapon was my underwear. I'd always had a
thing for expensive lingerie, and early on had learned
where to hunt for the best sales. Wearing something
sexy under my clothes was empowering, and the pair
I had on would most certainly do the trick. They were
black silk in front, embellished with embroidery, and
the back consisted of a series of delicate tulle ribbons,
crisscrossing to meet in the center near my tailbone
with a dainty black bow. With each step, the fabric of

my dress caressed my bare skin. I could take whatever Mr. Ryan had to say today, and I could dish it right back to him.

I'd arrived early to have time to prepare for the presentation. It wasn't strictly my job, but Mr. Ryan refused to have a dedicated assistant, and when left to his own devices, he was a disaster at making meetings pleasant: no coffee, no pastries, just a room full of people, pristine slides and handouts, and, as always, endless work.

The lobby was empty; the wide space opened three stories up and gleamed with polished granite flooring and travertine walls. As the elevator doors closed behind me, I gave myself a mental pep talk, recounting all the arguments we'd had and the jackass comments he'd made.

"Type, don't write anything longhand. Your handwriting looks like a third grader's, Miss Mills."

"If I wanted to enjoy your entire conversation with your graduate advisor, I'd leave my office door open and get some popcorn. Please, keep your voice down."

I could do this. That bastard had picked the wrong woman to mess with, and I'd be damned if I would let him intimidate me. I lowered my hand to my ass and smiled wickedly . . . *power panties.*

As I expected, the office was still empty when I ar-

rived. I gathered everything he would need for his presentation and headed to the conference room to set up.
I tried to ignore the Pavlovian response I had to seeing
the wall of windows, the gleaming conference table.

Stop it, body. Engage now, brain.

Glancing around the sun-filled room, I set the files
and laptop on the large conference table and helped the
catering staff set up the breakfast spread along the back
wall.

Twenty minutes later the proposals were set out, the
projector was prepared, and refreshments were ready.
With time to spare I found myself wandering over to
the window. I reached out and touched the smooth
glass, overwhelmed by the sensations it brought; the
heat of his body against my back, the feel of the cool
glass against my breasts, and the raw animalistic sound
of his voice in my ear.

"Ask me to make you come."

I closed my eyes and leaned in, pressing my palms
and forehead against the window, and let the power of
the memories overtake me.

I was startled from my fantasy by a throat clearing
behind me. "Daydreaming on the clock?"

"Mr. Ryan," I gasped, spinning around. Our eyes
locked and I was once again struck by how beautiful he
was. He broke eye contact to survey the room.

"Miss Mills," he said, each word sharp and clipped. "I'll be giving the presentation on the fourth floor."

"Excuse me?" I asked, irritation flooding me. "Why? We always use this room. And why did you wait until the last minute to tell me?"

"Because," he growled, leaning on his fists on the table, "I am the boss. I make the rules, and I decide when and where things happen. Maybe if you weren't intent on staring out windows, you would have taken the time this morning to come confirm the details with me."

My mind flooded with white-hot images of my fist connecting with his throat. It took every bit of control I had not to jump across the table and strangle him. A smug smile crept over his face.

"Fine by me," I said, swallowing my annoyance. "No good decisions are ever made in this room anyway."

❧

When I turned the corner into the new conference room, my eyes immediately met Mr. Ryan's. Sitting in his chair, his hands predictably tented in front of him, he was the portrait of barely contained patience. *Typical.*

Then I noticed the person beside me: Elliott Ryan.

"Here, let me help you with that, Chloe," he said, taking a stack of folders from my arms so I could more easily maneuver the cart full of food into the room.

"Thank you, Mr. Ryan." I shot a pointed look at my boss.

"Chloe," the elder Mr. Ryan said, laughing. He took some handouts and sent the stack around the table for the attendees to take. "How many times do I need to tell you to call me Elliott?" He was every bit as handsome as both of his sons. Tall and muscular, all three Ryan men shared the same chiseled features. Elliott's salt-and-pepper hair had turned silver over the years since I'd first met him, but he was still one of the most handsome men I'd ever met.

I smiled gratefully at him as I sat down. "How is Susan doing?"

"She's doing fine. She keeps bugging me about having you over," he added with a wink. It didn't escape my attention that the youngest Mr. Ryan snorted in annoyance beside me.

"Please tell her hi from me."

Footsteps sounded behind me and a hand reached out to gently tug my ear. "Hey, kiddo," Henry Ryan said, giving me a wide grin. He turned to address the rest of the room. "Sorry I'm late, guys. I guess I thought we were meeting up on your floor."

I chanced a smug look out of the corner of my eye, meeting my boss' gaze. The stack of handouts came back to me and I handed a copy to him. "Here you are, Mr. Ryan."

Without so much as a glance, he snatched the stack and began leafing through them.

Dick.

Just as I was taking my seat, Henry's boisterous voice called out, "Oh, Chloe, while I was up there waiting, I found these on the floor." I walked over to him and saw two antiqued silver buttons sitting in his palm. "Would you ask around and see if anyone's lost these? They look kind of expensive."

I felt my face heat. I had completely forgotten about my ruined shirt. "Um . . . sure."

"Henry, can I see those for a minute?" Jackass suddenly chimed in, taking them from his brother. He turned to me with a wicked smirk in place. "Don't you have a blouse with buttons like these?"

I glanced quickly around the room; Henry and Elliott were already absorbed in another conversation, oblivious to what was happening between us.

"No," I said, trying to sound as disinterested as possible. "I don't."

"Are you sure?" Taking my hand, he ran a finger from the inside of my arm to my palm before dropping the buttons and closing my hand around them. My breath caught in my throat and my heart pounded fiercely against my chest.

I jerked my hand back as if I'd been burned. "I'm sure."

"I could have sworn the blouse you wore the other day had little silver buttons. The pink one? I remember because I noticed one of them was loose when you came looking for me upstairs."

If possible, I felt my face heat further. What was he playing at? Was he trying to insinuate that I had orchestrated a way to get him alone in the conference room?

Leaning in closely, his breath hot on my ear, he whispered, "You really should try to be more careful."

I attempted to maintain my calm as I lowered my hand from his. "You bastard," I replied through gritted teeth before he pulled away, looking taken aback.

How could he look surprised, as if I'd been the one to break the rules? It was one thing to be a dick to me, but to jeopardize my reputation in front of other executives—he was going to get an earful later.

Throughout the meeting we cast glances at each other, mine fueled with anger and his with increasing uncertainty. I looked down at the spreadsheets in front of me as much as possible to avoid looking at him.

As soon as it was all over, I gathered my things and got the hell out of there. But as expected, he was hot on my tail all the way to the elevator until we were both seething silently in the back, on our way up to the office.

Why wouldn't this thing hurry up, and why did

someone on every floor decide they needed to use it *now*? People all around us were talking on phones, shuffling files, discussing lunch plans. The noise grew to a heavy buzz, nearly drowning out the verbal ass-kicking I was giving Mr. Ryan in my head. By the time we reached the eleventh floor, the elevator was almost at capacity. When the door opened and three more people decided to squeeze in, I was pushed farther into him, my back against his chest and my ass against his . . . *oh*.

I felt the rest of his body stiffen subtly and heard him take a sharp breath. Instead of pressing into him, I stepped as far away as I could. He reached forward and gripped my hip, pulling me back again.

"I liked that ass against me," he murmured, low and warm into my ear. "Where do you—"

"I'm two seconds away from castrating you with my heel."

He leaned even closer. "Why are you suddenly more pissy than usual?"

I turned my head and said, in barely a whisper, "It would be just like you to make me look like a career-climbing whore in front of your father."

He dropped his hand, slack jawed. "No." Blink. Blink. *"What?"* Confused Mr. Ryan was surprisingly hot. *Bastard.* "I was just playing around."

"What if they'd heard you?"

"They didn't."

"They could have."

He genuinely looked like the thought had never occurred to him, and it probably hadn't. It was easy for him to play games from his perch at the top. He was the workaholic executive. I was the girl halfway up the ladder.

The person on our left glanced over and we both stood straight, looked forward. I elbowed him sharply in the side, and he pinched my ass hard enough to make me gasp.

"I won't apologize," he said under his breath.

Of course you won't. Dick.

He pressed into me again, and I felt the length of him grow even harder, the traitor warmth spreading between my legs.

We reached the fifteenth floor and a few more people filed out. I reached behind me, slid my hand between us, and palmed him. He exhaled a warm puff against my neck, whispering, "Fuck yes."

And then I squeezed.

"Fuck. *Sorry!*" he hissed into my ear. I let go, dropping my hand and grinning to myself. "Christ, I was just playing around with you."

The sixteenth floor. The rest of the crowd exited in a single rush, apparently headed to the same meeting.

As soon as the doors closed and the elevator began to move, I heard a growl from behind me and caught a quick, sudden movement as Mr. Ryan slammed his hand against the stop button on the control panel. His eyes turned on me and they were darker than I had ever seen them. In one fluid motion, he pinned me against the wall of the elevator with his body. He pulled away just long enough to give me an angry glare and mutter, "Don't move."

And even though I wanted to tell him to fuck off, my body begged me to do whatever he said.

Reaching over to my discarded files, he plucked a sticky note off the top and placed it over the camera lens set into the ceiling.

His face was only a couple of inches from mine, his breath coming out in sharp bursts against my cheek. "I would never imply you're trying to fuck your way to the top." He exhaled, bending into my neck. "You're thinking too much."

I pulled back as much as I could, gaping at him. "You're not thinking *enough*. This is my career we're talking about. You have all of the power here. You have nothing to lose."

"I have the power? You're the one who pressed into my dick in the elevator. You're the one *doing* this to me."

I felt my expression soften; I wasn't used to seeing him be vulnerable with me, even a little. "Then don't blindside me."

After a long pause, he nodded.

The sound of the building all around us filled the elevator as we continued to stare at each other. The ache for contact began to build, first in my navel and spreading lower, between my legs.

He bent forward, licking my jaw before covering my lips with his, and an involuntary groan rumbled in my throat as his hardened cock pressed against my stomach. My body began acting on instinct and my leg wrapped around his, pressing me closer against his arousal, my hands finding their way to his hair. He pulled back just long enough for his fingers to flick at the clasp at my waist. My dress drifted apart in front of him.

"Such an angry kitty," he whispered. Placing his hands on my shoulders, he looked into my eyes and slid the fabric to the floor. Goose bumps spread along my skin as he took my hands, turned me around, and pressed my palms against the wall.

Reaching up, he removed the silver comb from my hair, letting it fall down my naked back. Taking my hair in his hands, he roughly pulled my head to the side, giving him access to my neck. Hot, wet kisses rained down my spine and across my shoulders. His touch left a spark of electricity over every inch of skin he touched. On his knees behind me, he grabbed my ass and pressed his teeth into the flesh, eliciting a sharp gasp from me before he stood back up.

Holy hell, how does he know to do these things to me?

"Did you like that?" His fingers pressed and pulled at my breasts. "Being bitten on the ass?"

"Maybe."

"You're such a filthy fucking girl."

I yelped out in surprise as I felt his hand smack hard where his teeth had just been, and my only response was a moan of pleasure. I breathed in another sharp gasp as his hands clasped the delicate ribbons of my underwear and ripped it off.

"Expect another bill, asshole."

He chuckled darkly and pressed up against me again, the cool wall against my breasts sending shivers through my body and pulling forward the memory of the window that first time. I'd forgotten how good the contrast—cold versus warm, hard versus *him*—felt against me. "Worth every penny." His hand slid around my waist and down my abdomen, slipping lower until his finger rested on my clit. "You know, I think you wear those things just to tease me."

Was he right? Was I delusional, thinking they were for me?

The pressure from his touch caused me to ache, his fingers pressing and releasing, leaving me wanting. Moving lower, he stopped right at my entrance. "You're so wet. God, you must have been thinking about this all morning."

"Fuck you," I groaned, gasping as his finger finally pushed inside, pressing me back into him.

"Say it. Say it and I'll give you what you want." A second finger joined the first, and the sensation caused me to cry out.

I shook my head, but my body betrayed me again. He sounded so needy; his words were teasing and controlling, but it felt like he was begging too. I closed my eyes, trying to clear my thoughts, but everything was just too much. The feel of his clothed body against my naked skin, the sound of his rough voice, and the feeling of his long fingers plunging in and out of me had me teetering on the edge. His other hand reached up, firmly pinching my nipple through the sheer fabric of my bra, and I moaned loudly. I was so close.

"Say it," he grunted into my ear as his thumb rolled over my clit. "I won't have you angry with me all day."

I gave in, finally, whispering, "I want you inside me." He let out a low, strangled moan and his forehead rested on my shoulder as he began moving faster, plunging and circling. His hips ground against my ass, his erection rubbing against me. "Oh, God," I moaned, the coil tightening deep inside, my every thought focused on the pleasure begging to break free.

And then the rhythmic sounds of our panting and groans were suddenly interrupted by the shrill ringing of a phone.

We stilled as the realization of where we were crashed down on us. Mr. Ryan cursed as he moved away from me and took the elevator's emergency receiver.

Turning, I grabbed my dress, slipped it over my shoulders, and began fastening it with shaking hands.

"Yes." He sounded so calm, not even a little out of breath. Our eyes locked across the elevator. "I see . . . No, we're fine . . ." He bent over slowly, removing my torn and discarded panties from the elevator floor. "No, it just stopped." He listened to the person on the other end, while rubbing the silky fabric between his fingers. "That's fine." He finished, hanging up the phone.

The elevator jerked as it began ascending again. He looked down at the lace in his hand and then back to me. And then he smirked, stepping away from the wall and stalking toward me. Placing one hand next to my head, he leaned in, running his nose along my neck and whispering, "You smell as good as you feel."

A small gasp escaped me.

"And these," he said, motioning to my panties in his hand, "are mine."

The elevator chimed as we stopped at our floor. The doors opened and without a single glance back in my direction, he slipped the delicate fabric into the pocket of his suit jacket and strode out.

FOUR

Panic. The emotion gripping me as I all but sprinted to my office could only be described as pure panic. I couldn't believe what was happening. Being alone with her in that tiny steel prison—her smell, her sounds, her skin—made my self-control evaporate. I was unraveling. This woman had a hold on me unlike anything I'd ever experienced.

Finally in the relative safety of my office, I collapsed on the leather sofa. Leaning forward, I gripped my hair tightly, willing myself to calm and my erection to subside.

Things were going from bad to worse.

I'd known from the minute she reminded me of the morning's meeting that there was no way in hell I could form one coherent thought, let alone give an entire presentation in that fucking conference room. And forget sitting at that table. Walking in there to find her leaning up against the glass, deep in thought, was enough to make me hard again.

I'd made up some bullshit story about the meeting being moved to a different floor, and of course she called me on it. Why did she always have to antagonize me? I made a point of reminding her of who was in charge. But as with every other argument we'd ever had, she threw it right back in my face.

I jumped slightly at a loud thud in the outside office. Followed by another one. And yet another. What the hell was going on out there? I stood and made my way to the door, opening it to find Miss Mills slamming down her folders in different piles. I folded my arms and leaned against the wall, watching her for a moment. The sight of her so angry was not diminishing the problem in my trousers in the slightest.

"Would you mind telling me what your problem is?"

She looked up at me as if I'd sprouted an extra head. "Are you out of your mind?"

"Not even a little."

"Pardon me if I feel a touch edgy," she hissed, grabbing a stack of folders and roughly shoving them into a drawer.

"I'm not exactly thrilled with the—"

"Bennett," my dad said, walking briskly into my office. "Great job in there. Henry and I just spoke with Dorothy and Troy and they were—" He stopped and stared at where Miss Mills stood, white-knuckling the edge of her desk.

"Chloe, dear, are you okay?"

She straightened and stretched her fingers, nodding. Her face was beautifully flushed, her hair a little wild. From me. I swallowed and turned to look out the window.

"You don't look well," Dad said, walking to her and putting his hand on her forehead. "You're hot."

I clenched my jaw as I watched their reflection in the glass, a strange feeling clawing its way up my spine. *Where is this coming from?*

"Actually," she said, "I do feel a little off."

"Well, you should head home. With your work schedule and having just finished the semester at school, no doubt you're—"

"We have a full calendar today, I'm afraid," I said, turning to face them. "I was expecting to finish Beaumont, Miss Mills," I growled through clenched teeth.

My father turned his steely gaze on me. "I'm sure you can handle whatever needs to be done, Bennett." He turned back to her. "You go on ahead."

"Thank you, Elliott." She looked at me, arching a perfectly sculpted brow. "See you tomorrow morning, Mr. Ryan."

I watched her walk out and my father closed the door behind her, turning to look at me with fire in his eyes.

"What?" I asked.

"It wouldn't kill you to be a little nicer, Bennett." He moved forward and sat on the corner of her desk. "You're lucky to have her, you know."

I rolled my eyes and shook my head. "If her personality were as appealing as her PowerPoint skills, we wouldn't have a problem."

He cut me off with a glare. "Your mother called and told

me to remind you about dinner tonight at the house. Henry and Mina are coming over with the baby."

"I'll be there."

He made his way over to the door, stopping to look back at me. "Don't be late."

"I won't. Christ!" He knew as well as anyone that I don't show up late for anything, even something as simple as a family dinner. Henry, on the other hand, would be late to his own funeral.

Finally alone, I stepped back into my office and collapsed into my chair. Okay, so maybe I was a little on edge.

I reached into my pocket and pulled out what remained of her underwear, ready to discard them into my drawer with the others, when I noticed the tag. Agent Provocateur. She dropped a pretty penny on these. And it sparked my curiosity. I opened the drawer to examine the other two pair. La Perla. Damn, this woman was serious about her underwear. Maybe I should stop into the La Perla store downtown sometime and at least see how much my little collection was costing her. I ran my free hand through my hair and tossed them all back in the drawer slamming it shut.

I was officially out of my mind.

———

As hard as I tried, I couldn't focus on a damn thing all day. Even after a vigorous lunchtime run, I still couldn't get my mind past the morning's events. By three, I knew I had to get out of there. I reached the elevator and groaned slightly, opting for the stairs and then realizing that was an even worse mistake. I sprinted down eighteen flights.

Pulling up to my parents' home later that evening, I felt some of my tension slip away. As I walked into the kitchen, I was immediately engulfed by the familiar smell of Mom's cooking, and my parents' happy chatter coming from the dining room.

"Bennett," my mom sang as I stepped into the room. I bent down and kissed her cheek, allowing her a brief moment to try and fix my unruly hair. Finally swatting her hands away, I grabbed a large bowl from her and placed it on the table, snatching a carrot as commission. "Where's Henry?" I asked, looking out toward the living room.

"They're not here yet," answered my dad as he walked in. Henry was bad enough, but throw in his wife and daughter and they were lucky to even make it out of the house at all. I walked to the bar outside to make my mother a dry martini.

Twenty minutes later, the sounds of chaos came from the foyer, and I stepped in to meet them. A small, unstable body with a toothy grin hurled itself at my knees. "Benny!" the little girl squealed.

I snatched Sofia up and smothered her cheeks with kisses.

"God, you're pathetic," Henry groaned as he walked past me.

"As if you're any better."

"You should both shut up, if anyone wants my opinion," Mina added, following her husband into the dining room.

Sofia was the first grandchild and the princess of the family. As usual, she preferred to sit on my lap during dinner and I tried to eat around her, doing my best to avoid her "help." She definitely had me completely wrapped around her finger.

"Bennett, I've been meaning to ask you," my mother began, handing me the bottle of wine. "Would you invite Chloe to dinner next week, and do your best to convince her to actually come?"

I groaned in response and received a quick kick in the shin from my father. "Christ. Why is everyone so insistent on getting her over here?" I asked.

Mom straightened, wearing her best Firm Mother face. "She's in a strange city all alone, and—"

"Mom," I interrupted, "she's lived here since college. She's twenty-six. It's not a strange city to her anymore."

"Actually, Bennett, you're right," she answered with a rare edge in her voice. "She came here for college, graduated summa cum laude, worked with your father for a few years before moving to your department and being the best employee you've ever had—all while she attends night school to get her degree. I think Chloe is pretty amazing, so I have someone I'd like her to meet."

My fork froze in midair as those words sank in. Mom

wanted to set her up with someone? I tried to mentally file through all of the single men we knew and had to discount each of them immediately. *Brad: too short. Damian: fucks anything that moves. Kyle: gay. Scott: dumb.* Well, this was odd. I felt something constrict in my chest, but I wasn't sure what it was. If I had to put a name on it, I'd call it . . . anger?

Why would I be angry that my mom wanted to set her up? *Probably because you're sleeping with her, dumb ass.* Well, not really sleeping with her so much as fucking her. Okay, fucked her . . . twice. "Fucking her" would imply an intent to continue.

Oh, also, I felt her up her in an elevator and was hoarding her shredded panties in my desk drawer.

Creeper.

I pressed my hands to my face. "Fine. I'll talk to her. But don't get your hopes up. She's about as charm-free as they come, so that's a hard deal to close."

"You know, Ben," my brother chimed in, "I think everyone here would agree that you are literally the only one who has a hard time getting along with her."

I looked around the table, frowning at the heads bobbing up and down, agreeing with my idiot brother.

The rest of the night consisted of more talk about how I needed to try and be nicer to Miss Mills, and about how great they all thought she was, and about how much she

would like my mom's best friend's son, Joel. I had completely forgotten about Joel. He was nice enough, I guess.
Except he'd played Barbies with his little sister until he was
fourteen and cried like a baby when he took a baseball to
the shin in tenth grade.

Mills would eat him alive.

I laughed to myself at the thought.

We also talked about the meetings we had lined up for
this week. A big one was planned for Thursday afternoon,
and I would be accompanying my father and brother. I knew
that Miss Mills already had everything all planned and ready
to go. Much as I hated to admit it, she was always two
steps ahead and anticipated everything I needed.

I left with the promise that I would do my best to convince her to come, although to be honest I didn't even know
when I would see her in the next few days. I had meetings
and appointments all over the city, and I doubted that in
those brief moments I was actually in the office I would
have much good to say.

———

Glaring out the window as we crawled down South Michi-
gan Avenue the next afternoon, I wondered if my day would
ever improve. I hated sitting in traffic. The office was only a
few blocks away, and I was seriously considering just having
the driver take the car back and getting out and walking.

It was already after four, and we'd managed to travel only three blocks in twenty minutes. Perfect. Closing my eyes, I rested my head on the seat and recalled the meeting I had just left.

Nothing in particular had gone wrong; in fact, quite the opposite. The clients had been thrilled with our proposals, and everything had gone off without a hitch. I just couldn't shake my horrible mood.

Henry had made a point of telling me every fifteen minutes of the last three hours that I was behaving like a moody teenager, and by the time the contracts were signed, I wanted to beat the shit out of him. Every chance he got he asked what the hell my problem was, and frankly, I couldn't say I blamed him. Even I had to admit I'd been a prick the last couple of days. And for me, that was saying something. Of course Henry declared as he left to head home that my problem was I needed to get laid.

If he only knew.

It had been one day. Just one day since the event in the elevator left me rock hard and with an itching desire to touch every inch of her skin. The way I was acting you'd think I hadn't had sex in six months. But no, nearly two days of not touching her and I felt like a lunatic.

The car stopped again and I thought I would scream. My driver lowered the separator between the front and back seats, tossing me an apologetic smile. "Sorry, Mr. Ryan. I'm sure you're going crazy back there. We're only four blocks away; would you rather walk?" Glancing out the tinted windows, I noticed we'd stopped right across the street from La Perla. "I can pull over just—"

I was out of the car before he had a chance to finish his sentence.

Standing on the curb waiting to cross, it occurred to me that I didn't have a clue what point there would be to going inside. What was I planning on doing? Was I buying something or just torturing myself?

I stepped into the store and stopped in front of a long table covered with frilly lingerie. The floors were a warm honey wood, the ceilings littered with long cylindrical light fixtures, clustered into groups throughout the large room. The dim lighting cast the entire space in a soft intimate glow, illuminating the tables and racks of expensive lingerie. Something about the delicate lace and satin brought on that all-too-familiar desire for her.

Running my fingers along a table set near the front of the store, I became aware that I had already garnered the attention of the sales staff. A tall blonde walked toward me.

"Welcome to La Perla," she said, looking me up and down like a lion eyeing a steak. It occurred to me that a woman in this business would know how much I paid for my suit, and that my cuff links were real diamonds. Her eyes practically turned into flashing dollar signs. "Is there something I can help you find today? Maybe a gift for your wife? Your girlfriend perhaps?" she added, a hint of flirtation in her voice.

"No, thank you," I answered, suddenly feeling ridiculous for even being here. "I'm just looking."

"Well, if you change your mind, let me know," she said with a wink, before turning and making her way back to the sales counter. I watched her walk away and was immediately disgusted that I hadn't even considered getting her number. Fuck. I wasn't a total manwhore, but a beautiful woman in a lingerie store, of all places, had just flirted with me and it hadn't even occurred to me to flirt back. Christ. What the hell was wrong with me?

I was just about to turn and leave when something caught my eye. I let my fingers run across the black lace garter belt hanging on a rack. I hadn't realized women really wore these outside of *Playboy* photo shoots until I'd started working with *her.* I remembered a meeting our first month working together. She had crossed her legs beneath the table and shifted in just the right way that her skirt rode up, revealing the delicate white strap attached to her stockings. It was the first time I'd seen evidence of her penchant for lingerie, but it wasn't the first time I'd had to spend the lunch hour beating off in my office thinking about her.

"See something you like?"

I turned, startled to hear a familiar voice behind me.

Shit.

Miss Mills.

But I'd never really seen her like this before. She looked stylish as always, but completely casual. She was wearing dark fitted jeans and a red tank top. Her hair was in a sexy ponytail, and without makeup or the glasses she sometimes wore around the office, she didn't look much older than twenty.

"What the hell are you doing here?" she asked, her fake smile slipping from her face.

"How is that any of your business?"

"Just curious. You don't have enough of my underwear that you have to start a collection of your own?" She glared at me, motioning to the garter belt still in my hands.

I let go of it quickly. "No, no, I—"

"What exactly do you do with them, anyway? Do you have them tucked away somewhere like little mementos of your conquests?" She folded her arms across her chest, causing her breasts to push together. My eyes fell straight to her cleavage and my dick stirred in my pants.

"Jesus," I said, shaking my head. "Why do you have to be such a bitch all the time?" I could feel the adrenaline trickling into my veins, feel my muscles tensing as I literally shook with lust and rage.

"I guess you just bring out the best in me," she said. She was leaning forward, her chest nearly touching mine. Looking around, I noticed we were drawing attention from the other people in the store.

"Look," I said, trying to compose myself. "How about you calm down and lower your voice." I knew I had to get out of here soon, before something happened. For some sick reason, fighting with this woman always ended with her panties in my pocket. "What are you doing here anyway? Why aren't you at work?"

She rolled her eyes. "I've been working for you for almost a year, so you'd think you'd remember that I check in with my advisor every other week. I just finished and wanted to do some shopping. Maybe you need to put an ankle bracelet on me so you can creepily stalk me full time. Though, hey, you managed to find me here without one."

I glared at her, struggling to find something to say. "You're always so fucking pissy with me."

Nice one, Ben. Really clever.

"Come with me," she said, and grabbed hold of my arm, dragging me to the back of the store. She pulled me around a corner and into a dressing room. She had obviously been here awhile; there were piles of lingerie on the chairs and hangers full of unidentifiable scraps of lace. Music was being piped through overhead speakers, and I was glad I wouldn't have to worry about keeping my voice down as I strangled her.

Closing the large mirrored door opposite a silk-covered chaise, she stood with her eyes locked on mine. "Did you follow me here?"

"Why the hell would I do that?"

68

"So you just happened to be browsing around a women's lingerie store. Just some pervy thing you do in your spare time?"

"Get over yourself, Miss Mills."

"You know, it's a good thing you've got that big dick to make up for that mouth of yours."

I found myself leaning forward, whispering, "I'm pretty sure you'd be thrilled with my mouth too."

Suddenly everything felt too intense, too loud, too vivid. Her chest was heaving, and her gaze shifted to my mouth as she bit her bottom lip. Slowly wrapping my tie around her fist, she pulled me to her. I opened my mouth, feeling her soft tongue press forward.

I couldn't pull back now, and slid one hand to her jaw and the other up to her hair. I removed the clip holding her ponytail and soft waves fell around my hand. I fisted the mass tightly, jerking her head to better accommodate my mouth. I needed more. I needed all of her. She moaned and I pulled it tighter. "You like that."

"God, yes."

At that moment, hearing those words, I didn't care about anything else: where we were, who we were, or how we felt about each other. Never in my life had I felt such raw chemistry with anyone. When we were together like this, nothing else mattered.

My hands ran down her sides and I gripped the hem of her shirt, bringing it up and over her head, breaking our kiss for only a second. Not to be left behind, she pushed my jacket from my shoulders and it dropped to the floor.

My thumbs ran circles across her skin as I moved my hands to the waist of her jeans. Quickly undone, they fell to the floor, and she kicked them off along with her sandals. I kissed down her neck and shoulders.

"Damn," I growled. Looking up I could see her perfect body reflected back at me in the full-length mirror. I had fantasized about her undressed more times than I could probably admit, but reality, in daylight, was better. So much better. She was wearing sheer black panties that only covered half her ass, and a matching bra, her silky hair spilling down across her back. The muscles in her long, toned legs flexed as she pushed up on her toes to reach my neck. The visual, along with the feeling of her lips, made my dick push painfully against the confines of my pants.

She bit my ear hard as her hands went to the buttons of my shirt. "I think you like it rough too."

I undid my pants and belt, pushing them and my boxers to the floor, and then pulled her with me to the chaise.

A thrill shot through me as my hands moved around her ribs to the clasp of her bra. Her breasts pressed against me as if urging me on, and I kissed along her neck as my fingers quickly unhooked her bra and I slipped the straps from her shoulders. I pulled back slightly to allow the garment to fall and for the first time took in the full view of her breasts completely bared to me. *Fucking perfect.* In my fantasies

I'd done everything to them: touched them, kissed them, sucked them, fucked them, but nothing compared to the reality of just staring at them.

Her hips rolled over me, and nothing but her tiny panties separated us. I buried my face in her chest and her hands ran through my hair, pulling me closer.

"You want to taste me?" she whispered, staring down at me. She pulled my hair hard enough to yank my head away from her skin.

I had no smart-ass remark, nothing biting to get her to stop talking and just fuck me. I did want to taste her skin. I wanted it more than I think I'd ever wanted anything. "Yeah."

"Ask nicely, then."

"Fuck asking nicely. Let me go."

She whimpered, leaning forward to let me suck a perfect nipple into my mouth, causing her to pull harder on my hair. Damn that felt good.

So many thoughts ran through my mind. There was nothing in this world I wanted more than to bury myself in her, but I knew when it was over, I would hate us both. Her for making me weak, and myself for allowing lust to override my common sense. But I also knew I couldn't stop. I had turned into a junkie, living for my next fix. My perfectly constructed life was crashing around me and all I cared about was feeling her.

Sliding my hands down her sides, I let my fingers run along the waist of her underwear. A shiver went through her, and I closed my eyes tightly as I bound the material in my hand, willing myself to stop.

"Go ahead and rip them . . . you know you want to," she murmured into my ear and then bit down hard. A half-second later, her panties were nothing but a mess of lace in the corner of the room. Grabbing her hips roughly, I lifted her and held the base of my dick with the other hand, and pulled her down onto me.

The feeling was so intense that I had to forcefully still her hips to keep from exploding. If I lost it now, she would only throw it back in my face later. And I wouldn't give her the satisfaction.

Once I felt in control again, I began moving her hips. We hadn't been in this position yet—her on top, face-to-face—and even though I hated to admit it, our bodies fit together perfectly. Bringing my hands down her hips to her legs, I gripped one in each hand and wrapped them around my waist. The change of position brought me deeper inside her, and I buried my face in her neck to keep from groaning out loud.

I was aware of the sounds of voices all around us as people entered and left the other dressing rooms. The thought that we could get caught at any moment only made this better.

Her back arched as she stifled a moan, and her head fell back. The deceptively innocent way she bit her lip was driving me crazy. Once again I found myself looking over her shoulder, to watch us in the mirror. I had never seen any-thing so erotic in my entire life.

She pulled my hair once again, guiding my mouth back to hers, our tongues gliding together, matching the motion of our hips. "You look so good over me," I whispered into her mouth. "Turn around, you need to see something." I pulled her up and turned her to face the mirror. With her back against my chest, she lowered herself back onto me.

"Oh, God," she said. She breathed out heavily as her head fell back against my shoulder, and I was unsure if it was from the feeling of me inside her or the image reflected in the mirror. Or both.

I gripped her hair and forced her head back up, "No, I want you to look right there," I growled in her ear, meeting her gaze in the mirror. "I want you to watch. And tomorrow when you're sore, I want you to remember who did it to you."

"Stop talking," she said, but she shivered and I knew she loved every word. Her hands ran up her body and be-hind her until they dug into my hair.

I touched every inch of her body and I trailed biting kisses along the back of her shoulders. In the mirror I could see myself sliding in and out of her; and as much as I didn't want these memories in my head, I knew that was a sight I would never forget. I moved one hand down to her clit.

"Oh, shit," she whispered. "Please."

"Like this?" I asked, pressing, circling.

"Yes, please, more, please, please."

Our bodies were now covered in a thin sheen of sweat, leaving her hair sticking slightly to her forehead. Her gaze never left where we came together as we continued to move against each other, and I knew we were both close. I wanted her to meet my eyes in the mirror—and then immediately knew it would show her too much. I didn't want her to see so plainly what she was doing to me.

The voices around us continued, completely unaware of what was going on in this tiny room. If I didn't do something, our little secret would not be kept for long. As her movements became more frenzied and her hands gripped my hair tighter and tighter, I pressed my hand against her mouth, stifling her scream as she came apart around me.

I muffled my own moans against her shoulder and with a few more thrusts, I exploded deep inside her. Her body slumped into me as I leaned back against the wall.

I needed to get up. I needed to get up and dress, but I didn't think my shaky legs could carry me. Any hope I'd had that the sex would become less intense, and that I would get over this obsession, was quickly being crushed.

Reason was slowly beginning to seep back into my consciousness, along with the disappointment that I had once again succumbed to this weakness. I shifted her up and off my lap before bending to reach for my boxers.

When she turned and looked at me, I expected hatred or indifference, but there was something vulnerable in her eyes before they snapped shut and she looked away. We both dressed in silence; the fitting room area suddenly seemed too quiet and too small, and I was overly aware of each breath she took.

Straightening my tie, I picked up the torn panties from the floor, depositing them in my pocket. I went to grab the door handle and stopped. Reaching out, I ran my hands slowly along the lacy fabric hanging from one of the hooks on the wall.

I met her eyes and said, "Get the garter belt too." And without looking back, I walked out of the dressing room.

Five

There were eighty-three vents, twenty-nine screws, five blades, and four bulbs on the ceiling fan above my bed. I rolled to my side, certain muscles mocking me and providing undeniable proof of why I was unable to sleep.

"I want you to watch. And tomorrow when you're sore, I want you to remember who did it to you."

He wasn't kidding.

Without realizing it, my hand had traveled to my breast, absently twisting my nipple beneath my tank top. Closing my eyes, the touch of my own hands turned into his in my memory. His long, graceful fingers ghosting along the undersides of my breasts, his thumbs brushing my nipples, cupping me in his large palms . . . *damn it*. I let out a loud sigh and kicked a pillow off my bed. I knew exactly where this train of thought was headed. I had done this exact same thing three nights in a row and it had to stop now. With a huff I rolled over onto my stomach and closed my eyes tight, willing sleep to come. As if that ever worked.

I still remembered, with perfect clarity, the day almost a year and a half ago when Elliott asked me up to his office for a talk. I'd started at RMG working as a junior assistant for Elliott when I was in college. When my mother died, Elliott had taken me under his wing; not so much a father figure, but certainly as a caring and warm mentor who had me to his home for dinner to keep an eye on my emotional state. He'd insisted his door would always be open for me. But on that particular morning, when he phoned my office, he sounded uncharacteristically formal, and frankly I was scared shitless.

In his office, he'd explained how his youngest son had lived in Paris for the past six years, working as a marketing executive for L'Oréal. This son, Bennett, was finally coming home, and in six months would take over the position of chief operating officer at Ryan Media. Elliott knew I was a year into my business degree and was looking into internship options that would give me the critical hands-on experience I needed. He insisted I complete my master's internship at RMG and that the youngest Mr. Ryan would be more than thrilled to have me on his team.

Elliott handed me the company-wide memo that

would circulate the following week to announce Bennett Ryan's arrival.

Wow. That was my only thought as I looked over the paper on my way back to my office. Executive VP of product marketing at L'Oréal in Paris. Youngest nominee ever featured in the *Crain's* "Forty Under 40" list, published several times in the *Wall Street Journal.* A dual MBA from NYU-Stern School of Business and HEC Paris, where he specialized in corporate finance and global business, graduating summa cum laude. All by the age of thirty. Christ.

What was it Elliott had said? *Extremely driven?* That was an understatement if I'd ever heard one.

Henry had hinted that his brother didn't quite share his laid-back personality, but when I'd seemed concerned he quickly put my mind at ease. "He has a tendency to be a bit stiff and completely anal retentive at times, but don't worry about it, Chloe. You can handle his bark; you guys are going to be a great team. I mean, come on," he said, wrapping his large arm around me. "How could he not love you?"

I hated to admit it now, but by the time he was set to arrive, I had developed a bit of a crush on Bennett Ryan. I was extremely anxious about working with him, but I was also impressed with everything he'd accomplished in his relatively short life. Looking up his picture online didn't hurt either: the man was a specimen. We communicated through e-mail leading up to his arrival, and although he seemed nice enough, he was never overly friendly.

On the big day, Bennett wasn't due in until after the board meeting that afternoon, when he would be officially introduced. I had the entire day to work myself up into a ball of nerves. Being the good friend she is, Sara came upstairs to distract me. She sat in my chair and we spent over an hour discussing the merits of the *Clerks* movies.

Soon I was laughing so hard I had tears running down my face. I didn't notice that Sara stiffened when the outer office door opened, and I didn't notice that someone was now standing behind me. And though Sara tried to warn me with a swift hand across the throat—the universal sign for "shut the fuck up"—I ignored her.

Because, apparently, I'm an idiot.

"And then," I said, giggling and holding onto my sides, "she says, 'Fuck, I had to take a fucking order off a guy I blew after junior prom once.' And then he says, 'Yeah, I've waited on your brother too.'"

Another bout of laughter hit me, and I stumbled backward a bit until I collided with something hard and warm.

Spinning around, I was mortified to see that I had just ground my ass onto my new boss' thigh.

"Mr. Ryan!" I said, recognizing him from his photographs. "I'm so sorry!"

He did not look amused.

In an attempt to ease the tension, Sara stood and extended her hand. "It's a pleasure to finally meet you. I'm Sara Dillon, Henry's assistant."

My new boss simply glanced at her hand without returning the gesture and raised one of his perfect eyebrows. "Don't you mean 'Mr. Ryan'?"

Sara's hand slowly fell as she watched him, obviously flustered. Something about his physical presence was so intimidating she was at a loss for words. When she recovered, she stuttered, "Well . . . we are fairly casual around here. We're all on a first-name basis. This is your assistant, Chloe."

He nodded to me. "Miss Mills. You will refer to me as Mr. Ryan. And I expect you in my office in five minutes so that we may discuss proper workplace decorum." His voice was serious when he spoke, and he nodded curtly to Sara. "Miss Dillon."

Sliding his gaze to mine for another moment, he turned on his heel toward his new office and I watched in horror as the first of his infamous door slams took place.

"What a *bastard*!" Sara mumbled between tight lips.

"A beautiful bastard," I replied.

Hoping to smooth things over, I went down to the

café to get him a cup of coffee. I'd even asked Henry
how he took it—black. When I nervously made it back
to his office door, my knock was followed by an abrupt
"come in," and I willed my hands to stop shaking. I
curved my lips into a friendly smile, intent on making
a better impression this time, and opened the door to
him talking on the phone and writing furiously on the
notepad in front of him. My breath caught when I heard
his smooth, deep voice speaking in flawless French.

"Ce sera parfait. Non. Non, ce n'est pas nécessaire.
Seulement quatre. Oui. Quatre. Merci, Ivan."

He ended the call but never lifted his eyes from his
papers to greet me. Once I was standing in front of his
desk, he addressed me in the same stern tone as before. "In the future, Miss Mills, you will keep all non-
workplace-related conversations outside of the office.
We're paying you to work, not gossip. Do I make myself clear?"

I stood speechless for a moment until he lifted his
eyes to meet mine, raising an eyebrow. I shook myself
out of my trance, all at once realizing the truth about
Bennett Ryan: although he was even more breathtak-
ingly gorgeous in person than in photos, he was not at
all like I had imagined. And he was absolutely nothing
like his parents and brother.

"Very clear, sir," I said as I walked around his desk
to set his coffee in front of him.

But just as I was about to reach his desk, my heel caught on the rug and I lunged forward. I heard a loud "Shit!" escape his lips—the coffee now nothing more than a scorching stain on his expensive suit.

"Oh my God, Mr. Ryan, I am *so* sorry!"

I rushed over to the sink in his bathroom to grab a towel and ran back, falling to my knees in front of him and attempting to wipe off the stain. In my haste, and in the midst of humiliation I didn't think could get any worse, it suddenly occurred to me that I was furiously rubbing the towel against his crotch. I averted my eyes and hand, feeling a heated blush spread from my face down my neck as I caught a glimpse of the noticeable bulge in the front of his pants.

"You may go now, Miss Mills."

I nodded, rushing out of the office, mortified that I'd made such a horrible first impression.

Thankfully, I proved myself pretty quickly after that. There were times when he even seemed impressed with me, although he was always short and on edge. I chalked it up to his being a giant asshat, but I had always wondered if there was something specific about me that rubbed him the wrong way.

Besides that towel, of course.

When I arrived at work, I bumped into Sara on my way to the elevator. We made plans to have lunch next week and said good-bye as she reached her floor. Arriving at the eighteenth floor, I noticed Mr. Ryan's office door was closed as usual, so I couldn't tell if he was here yet. I turned on the computer and tried to mentally prepare myself for the day. Lately, anxiety hit every time I sat in this chair.

I knew I would see him this morning; we went over the schedule for the coming week every Friday. But I never knew what kind of mood he would be in.

Although his temper had been even worse lately, his last words to me yesterday had been, "Get the garter belt too." And I had. In fact, I was wearing it now. Why? I had no idea. What in the hell had he meant by that? Did he think he was going to see it? No fucking way. Then why had I worn it? *I swear to God, if he rips it* . . . I stopped myself before I could finish.

Of course he wouldn't rip it. I was never going to give him the chance.

Keep telling yourself that, Mills.

Answering some e-mails, editing the Papadakis contract for intellectual property issues, and making a few hotel inquiries took my mind off the situation for a bit, and about an hour later his office door opened. Looking up, I was met with a very businesslike Mr. Ryan.

His dark, two-button suit was impeccable, comple-
mented perfectly by the pop of color in his red silk tie.
He looked calm and completely at ease. No trace remained of the wild man who had fucked me in the La
Perla dressing room approximately eighteen hours and
thirty-six minutes ago. Not that I was counting.

"Are you ready to begin?"

"Yes, sir."

He nodded once and turned back to his office.

Okay, so that's how this was going to play out. Fine
by me. I wasn't sure what I'd been expecting but was
somewhat relieved that things weren't different. Things
between us were getting more and more intense, and
it would mean a harder crash when it all stopped and I
was left to pick up the pieces of my career. I hoped we
could limp through this without further disaster until I
finished my degree.

I followed him into his office and took a seat. I began going over the list of tasks and appointments that
needed his attention. He listened without comment,
jotting things down or entering them into his computer when needed.

"There's a meeting with Red Hawk Publishing
scheduled for three this afternoon. Your father and
brother are also planning to attend. It will probably
take up the rest of the afternoon, so your calendar has

been cleared . . ." And so it went, until eventually we got to the part I'd been dreading.

"Lastly, the JT Miller Marketing Insight Conference is in San Diego next month," I said, suddenly becoming interested in what I was doodling in my calendar. The pause that followed seemed to drag forever, and I glanced up to see what was taking so long. He was staring at me, tapping a gold pen on the desk, his face completely void of any expression.

"Will you be accompanying me?" he asked.

"Yes." My one word created a suffocating silence in the room. I had no idea what he was thinking as we looked at each other. "It's in the terms of the scholarship that I attend. I, uh, also think it'd be good to have me there to, um, help manage your affairs."

"Make all the necessary arrangements," he said with an air of finality as he resumed typing on his computer. Assuming I had been dismissed, I stood and began walking toward the door.

"Miss Mills."

I turned to look at him, and even though he didn't meet my gaze, he almost seemed nervous. Well, *that* was different.

"My mother has asked me to extend an invitation to you for dinner next week."

"Oh." I felt heat bloom across my cheeks. "Well,

please tell her I'll look at my schedule." I turned to leave again.

"I was told I must . . . *strongly* encourage you to attend."

Turning back slowly, I saw he was now staring at me, and he definitely looked uncomfortable. "And why exactly should you do that?"

"Well," he said before clearing his throat, "apparently she has someone she would like you to meet."

This was new. I'd known the Ryans for years, and although Susan might have mentioned a name in passing, she'd never actively tried to fix me up with anyone.

"Your mother is trying to set me up?" I asked walking back toward his desk and folding my arms over my chest.

"So it seems." Something in his face didn't quite fit his nonchalant answer.

"Why?" I asked with a raised eyebrow.

His brow furrowed in obvious annoyance. "How the hell would I know? It's not like we sit around discussing you," he growled. "Maybe she's worried that with that sparkling personality of yours you'll end up an old spinster wearing muumuus and living in a house full of cats."

Leaning forward with my palms on his desk I glared at him. "Well, maybe she should be more worried that her son will turn into a dirty old man who

spends his time hoarding panties and stalking girls in lingerie stores."

Jumping out of his chair, he leaned toward me, his face furious. "You know, you are the most—" He was cut off as the phone rang. We stared fiercely at each other from across the desk, both of us breathing heavily. For a moment, I thought he would throw me across the desk. For another moment, I wanted him to. Still glaring at me, he reached for the phone.

"Yes," he barked sharply into the receiver, his eyes never leaving mine. "George! Hello. Yes, I have a minute."

He lowered himself back into his desk chair, and I lingered to see if he needed anything from me while he talked to Mr. Papadakis. He held up his index finger for me to wait before he slid it over his pen, rolling it across his desk as he listened to the call.

"You need me to stay?" I asked.

He nodded once before speaking into the phone, "I don't think you'd need to be that specific at this stage, George." The deep tenor of his voice vibrated down my spine. "Just a general outline is fine. We need to know the scope of this proposal before we can move into drafting."

I shifted where I stood. He was such an egomaniac, making me stand here like I was holding a plate of grapes and fanning him while he spoke to a colleague.

He looked up at me and did a slight double take, his eyes dropping to my skirt. When he looked back up, his lips opened slightly, as if he would ask me something were he able. And then he reached forward, pen poised between his finger and thumb, and used the tip of it to lift the hem of my skirt up my thigh.

His eyes widened when he saw the garter.

"I understand," he murmured into the phone, letting my skirt fall. "I think we can agree that's a positive development."

His eyes moved up my body, darkening as they traveled. My heart began to pound. When he looked at me like that, I wanted to slip onto his lap and bind him to the chair with his tie.

"No, no. Nothing so broad at this point. As I said, this is only a preliminary outline."

I slipped around his desk and sat in the chair across from him. He raised an eyebrow, interested, and then slipped the tip of the pen between his teeth, biting down.

Heat bloomed between my legs and I reached for the hem of my skirt, sliding the fabric up my thighs, exposing my skin to the cool air in his office, and to the hungry eyes across the desk from me.

"Yes, I see," he said, but his voice was deeper even still, hoarse now.

My fingertips trailed over the lines of the garters,

along skin and to the satin of my underwear. Nothing—and no one—had ever made me feel as sexy as he did. It was as if he took all my thoughts of my job, my life, and my goals and said, *"These are all well and good, but look at this other thing I'm offering you. It will be twisted and very dangerous but you'll crave it. You'll crave me."*

And if he'd said that out loud, he would have been right.

"Yes," he said again. "I think that's the ideal path forward."

You do, do you? I smiled at him, chewing my lip, and he gave me a devilish half smile in return. The fingers of one hand traveled higher, cupping my breast and squeezing. With my other hand, I pushed the center of my panties aside and ran two fingers across my wet skin.

Mr. Ryan coughed and fumbled for his water glass. "That's fine, George. We'll take that over when we receive it. We can handle that timeline."

I began moving my hand, thinking of his long fingers rolling the pen, those very hands grabbing my hips and waist and thighs when he drove into me in the lingerie store.

I moved faster, my eyes falling closed and head dropping back against the chair. I tried to be quiet, biting down on my lip when a tiny moan escaped. I imagined his hands and taut forearms, muscles tensing beneath skin as his fingers moved inside me. His legs in front of my face the night in the conference room, tight and sculpted, struggling to keep from thrusting.

Those eyes, on me, dark and pleading.

I looked up to see them exactly as I imagined, not watching my hand but seeing his hungry expression trained on my face as I fell and fell and fell. My climax was both overwhelming and unsatisfying: I wanted it to be his touch doing this to me instead of my own.

At some point, his call had ended, and my breath sounded too loud in the silent room. He sat across from me, sweat beading his brow, his hands gripping the arms of his desk chair as if he'd been thrown into the wind.

"What are you doing to me?" he asked quietly.

I grinned, blowing my bangs out of my eyes. "I'm pretty sure I just did that to myself."

His brow lifted. "Indeed."

I stood, smoothing my skirt back down my thighs. "If that will be all, Mr. Ryan, I'll get back to work."

❧

By the time I returned from freshening up in the restroom, I had a text message from Mr. Ryan, informing me that he would meet me in the parking garage to head downtown. Thank God the other executives and their assistants would be going to the Red Hawk meeting. I knew from our history that if I had to sit in a limo with that man alone for twenty minutes— especially after what I just did—there were only two possible outcomes. And only one of them ended with his balls intact.

The limo was waiting right outside, and as I made my way to it our driver smiled widely to me and opened the door. "Hey, Chloe, how's work?"

"Busy, fun, never-ending. How's school?" I smiled back. Stuart was my favorite driver, and although he had a tendency to be a bit of a flirt, he always made me smile.

"If I could drop physics and still graduate with a degree in biology, I would. Too bad you aren't a scientist or you could tutor me," he said, wiggling his eyebrows.

"If you two are finished, we actually have somewhere important to be. Maybe you can flirt with Miss Mills on your own time." Mr. Ryan was apparently already inside waiting for me, and he glared at the two of us as he retreated back into the car. I grinned and rolled my eyes at Stuart before stepping inside.

Aside from Mr. Ryan, the car was empty. "Where are the others?" I asked, confused, as we pulled away.

"They have a dinner meeting later this evening and

decided to drive separately." He busied himself with his printouts. I couldn't help but notice the way he was nervously tapping his fancy Italian oxfords.

I eyed him suspiciously. He didn't look any different. In fact, he looked sexier than hell. His hair was its usual perfect mess. As he absentmindedly lifted his gold pen to his lips, just as he had in his office earlier, I actually had to shift in my seat to ease my discomfort.

When he looked up, the smirk on his face let me know I had been caught ogling him. "See something you like?" he asked.

"Not back here," I replied with a smirk of my own. And just because I knew it would get to him, I purposely recrossed my legs, making sure my skirt rode up a bit more than was appropriate. Maybe he needed to remember who could win at this game. The scowl was back in an instant. Mission accomplished.

The eighteen and a half minutes left of our twenty-minute drive were spent trading dirty looks across the car while I tried to pretend I wasn't fantasizing about having his pretty head between my legs.

Needless to say, by the time we got there, I was in a bad mood.

The next three hours passed at a snail's pace. The other executives arrived and introductions were made all around. A particularly striking woman named Lila seemed to take an immediate interest in my boss. She was in her early thirties with thick red hair, luminous dark eyes, and a body to die for. And of course, the panty-dropping smile was in full force as he nearly charmed her unconscious the entire afternoon.

Asshole.

When we walked into the office at the end of the day, after an even more tense drive back, it still seemed like Mr. Ryan had something to say. And if he didn't do it soon, I was going to explode. When I wanted him to be quiet, he couldn't keep his mouth shut. But when I needed him to say something, he became a mute.

A sense of déjà vu and dread filled me as we made our way through the semideserted building and toward the elevator. The second those gold doors closed I wished I were anywhere but standing next to him. *Was there suddenly less oxygen in here?* As I glanced at his reflection in the polished doors, it was hard to tell how he felt. He'd loosened his tie and his suit jacket was slung over his arm. During the meeting, he'd rolled the sleeves of his dress shirt partway up his forearms and I tried not to stare at the lines of muscle beneath his skin. Other than the constant clenching of his sharp jaw and his downcast eyes, he looked completely calm.

When we reached the eighteenth floor, I let out a giant breath. That had to have been the longest forty-two seconds of my life. I followed him through the door, trying to keep my eyes off him as he quickly entered his own office. But to my surprise, he didn't close the door behind him. He always closed his door.

I quickly checked my messages and wrapped up a few last-minute details before I could leave for the weekend. I don't think I'd ever been in more of a hurry to get out of here. Well, that wasn't exactly true. The last time we were alone on this floor I had made a pretty quick getaway. Damn, if there was ever a time to not think about that, it would be now, in the empty office. Just me and him.

He left his office right as I was gathering my things, placing an ivory envelope on my desk and continuing to the door without pausing. *What the hell was this?* Quickly opening the envelope, I saw my name on several pieces of elegant ivory paper. It was paperwork for a private credit account at La Perla, with Mr. Bennett Ryan as the account holder.

He opened a credit account for me?

"What the hell is this?" I said, seething. I jumped from my chair and asked, "You got me a line of credit?"

Stopping midstride and hesitating slightly, he turned to face me. "After your little show today, I made a phone call and arranged for you to purchase whatever you . . . need. Of course there's no limit on the account," he stated flatly, having wiped all trace of discomfort from his face. This is why he was such a master at what he did. He had an uncanny ability to regain control of any situation. But did he honestly think he could control me?

"So, to be clear," I said, shaking my head and trying to keep some semblance of calm, "you arranged to buy me *underwear*."

"Well, just to replace the things that I—" he stopped, possibly rethinking his response. "The things that have been damaged. If you don't want it, *don't fucking use it*," he hissed before turning to leave again.

"You son of a bitch." I moved to stand in front of him, the crisp stationery now a mangled ball of paper in my clenched fist. "Do you think this is funny? Do you think I'm some plaything you can just dress up for your amusement?" I didn't know who I was angrier with: him for thinking of me that way, or me for allowing this thing to start in the first place.

He scoffed, "Oh yes. I find this absolutely hilarious."

"Take this and stick it up your ass." I shoved the ivory paper into his chest and grabbed my purse, turning and literally sprinting to the elevator. *What an egotistical, womanizing ass.*

Logically I knew that he hadn't meant to insult me, at least I hoped not. But this? This was exactly why you don't fuck your boss, why you definitely don't get off and give him a little show in his office.

Apparently, I missed that part of orientation.

"Miss Mills!" he shouted, but I ignored him and stepped into the elevator. *Come on,* I said to myself as I repeatedly pushed the button for the parking garage. His face appeared just as the doors closed and I smiled to myself as I flipped him off. *Real mature, Chloe.*

"Shit. Shit. Shit!" I yelled into the empty elevator, practically stomping my feet. That bastard had ripped his last pair of panties.

The elevator chimed, signaling that I'd reached the garage, and, muttering to myself, I made my way to my car. The garage was dimly lit and mine was one of the only cars left on this level, but I was too furious to even give it a second thought. I'd hate to see the unlucky prick who dared mess with me right now. Just as that thought entered my mind, I heard the stairwell door burst open and Mr. Ryan call out from behind me.

"Christ! Will you fucking wait?" he shouted. It did not escape my attention that he was out of breath. I suppose sprinting down eighteen flights of stairs would do that to a person.

Unlocking my car, I jerked open the door and threw my purse onto the passenger seat. "What the hell do you want, Ryan?"

"God, can you take it out of bitch mode for two seconds and listen to me?"

I spun around to face him. "Do you think I'm some kind of *whore*?"

A hundred different emotions flashed across his face: anger, shock, confusion, hate, and fuck me if he didn't look delicious. He'd opened the collar of his shirt, his hair was an absolute mess, and the bead of sweat running down the side of his jaw was not helping the situation. I was determined to stay mad.

Keeping a careful distance, he shook his head. "Jesus," he said, looking around the garage. "You think I see you as a *whore*? No! It was just in case—" He stopped, trying to organize his thoughts. He seemed to finally give up, jaw clenched.

The rage was coursing through me so strongly that before I could stop myself, I stepped forward and slapped him hard across the face. The sound cracked through the empty garage. With a shocked and furious glare, he reached up and touched the spot where I had struck him.

"You may be my boss, but you do *not* get to decide how this works."

The silence stretched before us, the sounds of the traffic and the outside world barely registering in my consciousness. "You know," he began with a dark stare, taking a single step toward me, "I didn't hear you complaining."

Oh, that smooth fucker.

"Against the window." Another step. "In the elevator and stairwell. In the dressing room while you watched me fuck you." And another. "When you spread your legs in my office today, I didn't hear one word of protest out of that fucking mouth of yours."

My chest was heaving, and I could feel the cool metal of my car through the thin material of my dress. Even with my shoes, he still stood a full head above me, and when he leaned down, I could feel his warm breath against my hair. All I had to do was look up, and our mouths would meet.

"Well, I'm over it," I said through clenched teeth, but each labored breath brought me a brief moment of relief as my chest grazed against his.

"Of course you are," he whispered, shaking his head and moving even closer, his erection pressing into my stomach. He braced his hands against the car, trapping me. "Completely over it."

"Except . . . maybe . . ." I said, not sure whether I meant to say it out loud.

"Maybe just one more time?" His lips barely brushed mine.

It was too gentle, too real.

Turning my face up, I whispered against his mouth, "I don't want to want this. It's not good for me."

His nostrils flared slightly and just when I thought I would go insane, he took my lower lip roughly between his and pulled me to him. Growling into my mouth, he deepened the kiss and pushed me forcefully against the car. Like last time, he reached up and removed the pins from my hair.

Our kisses were teasing then rough, coming together and pulling apart, hands fisting in hair and tongues sliding against each other. I gasped as he bent his knees slightly, grinding his cock against me.

"God," I moaned, wrapping my leg around him and digging my heel into his thigh.

"I know." He exhaled heavily into my mouth. Looking down at my leg and cupping my ass with his hand, he gave it a rough squeeze and murmured, "Have I told you how fucking hot those shoes are? What are you trying to do to me with those wicked little bows?"

"Well, there's another bow somewhere else but you'll need some luck finding it."

He pulled away. "Get in the fucking car," he said, his voice rumbling deep in his throat as he yanked the door open.

I glared at him, willing rational thought to penetrate my clouded brain. What should I do? What did I want? Could I just let him have my body like this again? I was so overwhelmed, I was trembling. Rational thought was quickly abandoning me as I felt his hand run up my neck and into my hair.

Gripping it tightly he jerked my head toward him and stared into my eyes. "Now."

The decision was made, and once again I wrapped

his tie around my wrist, pulling him into the backseat. Once the door closed behind him, he wasted no time going for the ties on the front of my dress. I groaned as I felt him part the material and run his hands across my bare skin. Pushing me back to lie on the cool leather and kneeling between my legs, he placed his palm between my breasts, slowly moving down my abdomen to the lace garter belt. His fingers traced the delicate ribbons to the edge of my stockings and back up again, moving to run across the edge of my panties. The muscles of my abdomen clenched with every movement and I tried to control my breathing. Fingering the tiny white bows, he looked up at me and said, "Luck has nothing to do with it."

I pulled him to me by his shirt and slid my tongue into his mouth, groaning as his palm pressed against me. Our lips searched; our kisses grew long and deep, gaining urgency with every inch of skin uncovered. I pulled his shirt from his pants and explored the smooth skin over his ribs, the sharp definition of muscle at his hips, and the soft trail of hair urging me down his navel and lower.

Wanting to tease him the way he was teasing me, I ran my fingers across his belt and to the hard shape of him beneath his pants.

He groaned into my mouth. "You don't know what you're doing to me."

"Tell me," I whispered back. I was using his words against him, and just knowing the tables were turned for the moment spurred me on. "Tell me and I'll give you what you want."

He moaned and bit his lip, his forehead pressed against mine as he shivered. "I want you to fuck me."

His hands were shaking as he gripped my new panties in his fist, and as insane as it was, I wanted him to rip them. The raw passion between us was unlike anything I'd ever experienced; I didn't want him holding back. Without a word, he tore them from me, the pain of the fabric pulling across my skin only adding to the pleasure.

I pulled my leg forward and pushed him back and off me. Sitting up, I shoved him against the seat back and straddled his lap. I grabbed his shirt and yanked it open, sending the buttons scattering along the seat.

I was lost to everything but him and this. The feel of the air against my skin, the ragged sounds of our breathing, the heat of his kiss, and the thought of what lay ahead. With frantic hands I undid his belt and pants, and with his help managed to get them down his legs. The tip of his cock grazed my entrance and I closed my eyes, slowly sliding down over him.

"Oh, God," I groaned, the sensation of him inside me only making the bittersweet ache intensify. Lifting my hips, I began to ride him, each movement feeling more intense than the one before. The pain from his rough fingertips on my hips only fueled my lust. His eyes were closed and his moans were muffled against my breast. Moving his lips across my lace bra he pulled one cup down and took my hardened nipple between his teeth. I gripped his hair tightly and elicited a moan from him, his mouth opening around my skin.

"Bite me," I whispered.

He bit down, hard, making me cry out and pull harder on his hair.

My body was so in tune with his, it reacted to his every look and touch and sound. I both hated and loved how he made me feel. I'd never been one to lose control, but when he touched me like this, I happily threw it out the window.

"Do you like feeling my teeth?" he asked, his breath short and jagged. "Do you fantasize about where else I could bite you?"

I pushed on his chest and stared up at him. "You just don't know when to shut your mouth, do you?"

He lifted me off and roughly threw me down onto the seat. Pushing my legs apart he thrust back into me. My car was too small for this, but there was nothing that could have stopped us now. Even with his legs bent awkwardly below him and my arms braced above me to protect my head from the door, it was almost too much.

Pulling himself onto his knees and into a more comfortable position, he picked up one of my legs and placed it over his shoulder, forcing his cock deeper inside me.

"Oh, God, yes."

"Yeah?" He lifted my other leg to rest across his other shoulder. Reaching out, he gripped the door frame and used it for leverage to deepen his thrusts. "Is that how you like it?" The change in angle caused me to gasp, as the most delicious sensations spread throughout my body.

"No." With my hands pushing off the door, I lifted my hips off the seat to meet each motion of his hips. "I like it harder."

"Fuck," he murmured as he turned his head slightly, his open mouth leaving wet kisses up and down my leg. By now our bodies were glistening with sweat, the windows were completely fogged up, and our groans filled the silent space of the car. The dim glow from the garage lights emphasized every carved indentation and muscle of the masterpiece above me. I watched him in awe, his body straining with the effort, his hair mussed and sticking to his damp forehead, the tendons in his neck pulled tight.

Ducking his head between his outstretched arms, he closed his eyes tightly and shook his head. "Oh, God," he panted. "I just . . . I can't stop."

I arched to get closer, needing to find a way to pull him deeper, more completely into me. I'd never wanted to consume another body as rabidly as I did when he was inside me, but even like this, I could never seem to get close enough to the parts of him I wanted to feel. And it was with that thought in my mind that the delicious, ratcheting tension along my skin and in my belly crystallized into an ache so heavy I slipped my legs off his shoulders, pulling all of his weight on top of me and pleading, "Please, please, please," over and over.

I was so close. *So close.*

My hips circled, and his hips answered rough but steady, as savage above as I was underneath. "So fucking close, *please.*"

"Anything," he growled in reply, before bending to bite my lip and growl. "Take fucking *anything.*"

I screamed as I came, my nails digging into his back and the taste of his sweat on my lips.

He swore, his voice deep and hoarse, and with one last powerful thrust he tensed above me.

Exhausted and shaking, he collapsed with his face against my neck. I couldn't resist the urge to run my trembling hands through his damp hair as we lay there panting, his heart racing against my chest. A million thoughts skittered through my mind as the minutes passed.

Slowly, our breathing calmed and I almost thought he'd fallen asleep when he moved his head away.

My sweaty body was instantly chilled as he started getting dressed. I watched him for a moment before sitting up and putting on my dress, feeling heavily ambivalent. More than just physically fulfilling, sex with him was some of the most fun I'd had in a long time.

But he was such an asshole.

"I assume you'll ignore the account. I realize this can't happen again," he said, startling me from my own thoughts. I turned to look at him. He was shrugging on his torn shirt, his eyes fixed straight ahead.

Moments passed before he turned to look at me. "Say something so I know you've heard me."

"Tell Susan I'll be there for dinner, Mr. Ryan. And get the hell out of my car."

Six

The burning in my chest was almost enough to distract me from the mess inside my head. *Almost.*

I increased the incline on the treadmill and pushed myself harder. Feet pounding, muscles on fire, it always worked. That was how I lived my life. There was nothing I couldn't accomplish if I just pushed hard enough: school, career, family, women.

Shit. *Women.*

Disgusted, I shook my head and turned up the volume on my iPod, hoping it would distract me long enough to get some fucking peace.

I should have known it wouldn't work. No matter how hard I tried, she was always there. I closed my eyes and it all came back: hovering over her, feeling her wrapped around me, sweaty, aching, wanting to stop but not being able to. Being inside of her was the most perfect torture. It satiated the hunger I felt at that moment, but like a junkie I found myself consumed by the need for more as soon as it ended. It was terrifying, because in those moments with her, I'd do anything she asked. And that feeling was starting to bleed into moments like this too, when I wasn't even with her and still wanted to be what she needed. Ridiculous.

My earbud was tugged free, and I turned toward the source of the annoyance. "What?" I said, glaring at my brother.

"You keep that up, we're gonna be peeling you off the floor, Ben," he replied. "What'd she do to piss you off this time?"

"Who?"

He rolled his eyes. "Chloe."

I felt my stomach tighten at the sound of her name and focused my attention back on the treadmill. "What makes you think this has anything to do with her?"

"Because I'm not a fucking idiot."

"Nothing's bothering me. And even if something was, why on earth would it have anything to do with her?"

He laughed, shaking his head. "I've never met anyone who gets this kind of reaction out of you. And you know why, don't you?" He had shut off his machine and was now focusing all his attention on me. I'd be lying if I said it wasn't a little unnerving. My brother was perceptive; too perceptive at times. And if there was ever anything I wanted to keep from him, it was this.

I kept my gaze forward as I ran, trying not to meet his eyes. "Enlighten me."

"Because you two are too much alike," he said smugly.

"What?"

Several people turned to see why I was yelling in the middle of the crowded gym. I slammed my hand down on the stop button and turned to face him. "How could you even think that? We are *nothing* alike." I was sweaty, out of breath, and ramped up from running ten miles. But right now, the rise in my blood pressure had nothing to do with my workout.

Taking a long drink from his water bottle, Henry continued to smirk. "Who do you think you're talking to? I've never met two people more alike. First of all . . ." He paused, clearing his throat and bringing his hand up to dramatically tick things off on his fingers. "You're both intelligent, determined, hardworking, and loyal. *And,*" he continued, pointing at me, "she's a firecracker. In fact, she's the first woman in your entire life who can stand up to you and doesn't follow you around like some lost puppy. You hate how much you need that."

Had everyone lost their mind? Sure, she might be some of those things; even I couldn't deny that she was incredibly intelligent. She was a hard worker; I was often surprised at how well she kept up with things. She was definitely determined, although I would describe it more along the lines of pigheaded or stubborn. And there was no question of her loyalty. She could have sold me out a hundred times since we'd started this sick game.

I stood glaring at him as I tried to formulate my response.

"Yeah, well, she's also a raving bitch." *Nice. Very articulate, Bennett.*

Stepping down, I quickly wiped off my machine and made my way across the gym in an effort to escape.

He laughed happily behind me. "See? I knew she was getting to you."

"Fuck off, Henry."

I settled in to do some sit-ups when he stood over me, grinning like a cat that swallowed a canary. "Well, my work is done here," he said, brushing off his hands and looking increasingly pleased with himself. "Guess I'll be heading home."

"Good. Go."

Laughing, he turned to leave. "Oh, but before I forget, Mina wanted me to see if you managed to convince Chloe to make it to dinner."

I nodded, sitting up to fiddle with my shoelaces. "She said she'd be there."

"Am I the only one who thinks it's hilarious that Mom wants to set her up with Joel Cignoli?" There went that feeling in my chest again. Henry and I had grown up with Joel, and he was a pretty decent guy, but something about the thought of the two of them together made me feel like I wanted to punch something. "I mean, Joel is great," he continued. "But Chloe's a bit out of his league, don't you think?" I could feel him staring at me a beat longer. "But hey, good for him if he thinks he stands a chance."

I lay back, began doing sit-ups a bit faster than was necessary.

"See you later, Benny."

"Yeah, later," I mumbled.

———

Sunday night as I lay in bed I replayed the plan in my head. I was thinking about her too much, and differently. I had to be tough and make it a week without touching her. It was like detoxing. Seven days, I could do that. Seven days of not touching her and this thing would be out of my system. I could finally move on with my life. There were just a couple of precautions I had to take.

First, I couldn't be goaded into arguing with her. For some reason, the two of us arguing was like some sick form of foreplay. Second: no more fantasizing about her, ever. That meant no more reliving sexual encounters, no more fantasizing about new ones, and no more picturing her naked or with any of my body parts coming in contact with any of hers.

And for the most part, things seemed to go according to plan. I was in a constant state of discomfort and the week seemed to drag on, but aside from a lot of dirty fantasies, I remained in control. I did my best to stay busy outside the office, but during the times we were forced together, I kept a constant distance, and for the most part we treated each other with the same polite aversion we had before.

But I swear she was trying to break me. Each day it seemed that Miss Mills looked sexier than the day before. Every day there was something about what she wore or did that brought my mind back to the gutter. I'd made a deal with myself that there would be no more lunchtime "sessions." I had to stop this, and imagining her while masturbating—hell, imagining *her* masturbating—wasn't going to help.

Monday she wore her hair down. All I could think about as she sat across from me during a meeting was wrapping it around my hands as she went down on me.

Tuesday she had on a formfitting knee-length skirt and those stockings with the seam up the back. She looked like some sort of hot secretary pinup.

Wednesday she wore a suit. That was unexpectedly worse, because I couldn't get my mind off what it would feel like to slide those pants down her long legs.

Thursday she had on a perfectly ordinary V-neck blouse, but twice when she bent over to pick up my pen I got a good look down her shirt. Only one of those times was on purpose.

By Friday I thought I would explode. I hadn't jacked off once all week and was walking around with the worst case of blue balls known to man.

As I walked into the office Friday morning, I was praying that maybe she would call in sick. Somehow I knew I wouldn't be that lucky. I was horny and in a particularly bad mood, and when I opened the office door I almost had a heart attack. She was bent over watering a plant in a charcoal gray sweater dress and knee-high boots. Every curve of her body was on display. Someone up there really hated me.

"Good morning, Mr. Ryan," she said sweetly, stopping me as I passed her. Something was up. She never said anything sweetly to me. I eyed her suspiciously.

"Good morning, Miss Mills. You seem to be in an exceptionally cordial mood today. Did somebody die?"

The corner of her mouth lifted in a devilish smirk. "Oh, no. I'm just excited about dinner tomorrow, and meeting your friend Joel. Henry's told me all about him. I think we really might have a lot in common."

Son of a bitch. "Oh right. Dinner. I'd completely forgotten. Yes, you and Joel . . . Well, since he's a mama's boy and you're an overbearing shrew, you two should find a pretty solid love connection. I'd love a cup of coffee if you're getting one for yourself." I turned and headed into my office.

It occurred to me that it might not be in my best interest to let her make my coffee. One of these days she was likely to put something in it. Like arsenic.

Before I'd even sat down, she knocked at my door.

"Come in."

She set my coffee down hard enough that some of it spilled on what she knew damn well was a custom-built fifteen-thousand-dollar desk, and turned to look at me.

"Are we having the scheduling meeting this morning?" She was standing near my desk in a pool of sunlight. Shadows draped across her dress, accentuating the curve of her breasts. Fuck, I wanted to pull her tight nipple into my mouth. Was it cold in here? How could she be cold when I was sweating bullets?

I had to get the hell out of here.

"No. I forgot about a meeting downtown this afternoon. So I'll be leaving for the day in about ten minutes. Just e-mail me all the details," I replied quickly, heading for the safety and coverage of my desk chair.

"I wasn't aware of any off-site meeting today," she said skeptically.

"No, you wouldn't have been," I said. "It's personal."

When she didn't respond I chanced a glance up and saw a strange expression on her face. What was that look? She obviously looked mad, but there was something else. Was she . . . was she *jealous*?

"Oh," she answered, chewing on her lower lip. "Is it with someone I know?" She never asked questions about where I was going. "I mean, just in case your father or brother need to get ahold of you."

"Well . . ." I paused, trying to torture her a bit. "In this day and age, if someone needs to get ahold of me, they can call my cell phone. Is there anything else, Miss Mills?"

She hesitated for a moment before lifting her chin and

straightening her shoulders. "Since you won't be here, I was thinking that I'd like to start the weekend early. Maybe do some shopping for tomorrow night."

"No problem. I'll just see you tomorrow." Our gazes locked across the desk, and the electricity in the air was so palpable I could feel my heart rate increase.

"Have a nice *meeting*," she said through clenched teeth, leaving and closing the door behind her.

I was relieved when I heard her leave fifteen minutes later. Deciding it was now safe to go, I gathered up my things and headed out. I was stopped by a man carrying a large flower arrangement.

"Can I help you with something?" I asked.

Looking up from his clipboard he glanced around before answering, "I have a delivery for a Miss Chloe Mills?"

What the—? Who the hell would send her flowers? Was she seeing someone while we were . . . ? I couldn't even finish the thought.

"Miss Mills has gone for lunch. She'll be back in about an hour," I lied. I had to get a look at that card. "I'll sign for those and make sure she gets them." He set the arrangement on her desk.

Signing the clipboard quickly, I handed him a tip and mumbled a good-bye as he left. For three long minutes I stood and stared at the flowers, willing myself to stop being such a pussy and to definitely not look at the card.

Roses. She despised roses. I snickered because whoever sent her these knew nothing about her. Even I knew she didn't like roses. I'd overheard her telling Sara one day about how one of her dates sent her a bouquet. She'd immediately given them away, disliking the pungent scent. Finally, my curiosity got the better of me and I ripped the card away from the arrangement.

Looking forward to dinner,
Joel Cignoli

That foreign sensation slowly spread through my chest again as I crumpled the card in my fist.

Retrieving the flowers from her desk, I walked out the door, locking up behind me, and made my way down the hall to the elevator.

Just as the doors opened I passed a wide chrome garbage can, and without a second thought I dropped the vase and all of its contents inside.

I didn't know what the fuck was going on with me. But I did know there was no way in hell she was going out with Joel Cignoli.

SEVEN

I spent the better part of Saturday running at the lake, trying to get some air, some distance, some clarity to my thoughts. Even so, the hour-long drive to my parents' house gave me plenty of time to return to the tangle of frustrations in my head: Miss Mills, how I hated her, how much I craved her, the flowers Joel sent. Leaning farther back into the seat, I tried to let the soothing sound of the car engine calm me. It wasn't working.

So here were the facts: I felt possessive of her. Not in a romantic sort of way, but in a "hit her over the head, drag her off by the hair, and fuck her" way. Like she was my toy and I was keeping the other boys in the sandbox from playing with her. How sick was that? If she ever heard me admit to that, she would cut off my balls and feed them to me.

Now the question was how to proceed. Obviously Joel was interested. How could he not be? All he had was secondhand information from my family, who obviously adored her, and I'm sure they'd showed him at least one photograph. If that was all I knew about her I'd be interested too. But there was no way he could have an actual conversation with her and still find her appealing.

Unless he just wanted to fuck her . . .

The sound of the leather steering wheel straining under my grip told me I'd be better off not thinking about that.

He wouldn't have agreed to meet her at my parents' home if all he wanted was sex, would he? I considered this. Maybe he really did want to get to know her better. Hell, even I could admit to having been a bit intrigued before we actually spoke. Of course, that hadn't lasted long, and she'd proven to be one of the most aggravating people I'd ever met. Unfortunately for me, she was also the best sex I'd ever had.

Fuck, he'd better never get that far. I wasn't sure I knew where to hide a body around here.

———

I still remembered the first moment I saw her. My parents had come to visit me one Christmas while I was living abroad, and one of my gifts had been a digital photo frame. While going through the photos with my mom, I paused the slideshow at a picture of my parents standing with a beautiful brown-haired girl.

"Who is this with you and Dad?" I asked. Mom told me that her name was Chloe Mills, and that she worked as an assistant for my dad and was all kinds of wonderful. She was probably only twenty in the photograph, but her effortless beauty was arresting.

Over the years her face would pop up in photos that my mom sent to me; company functions, Christmas parties, even parties at the house. Her name was brought up occasionally as my family recounted stories about the general goings-on of work and life.

So when the decision was made that I would come home and take over as COO, my father explained that Chloe was getting her business degree at Northwestern, had a scholarship that required real-world experience, and that mine would be a perfect job for her to shadow for a year. My family loved and trusted her, and the fact that my father and brother had absolutely no reservations about her ability to handle the job spoke volumes. I immediately agreed. I was a bit worried that my appreciation for her appearance would interfere with my ability to be her boss, but I quickly reassured myself that the world was full of beautiful women and it would be easy enough to separate the two.

Oh, how stupid I'd been.

And now I could see all the mistakes I'd made over the last few months, how even from that first day, it was all leading up to this.

To make matters worse, I couldn't seem to seal the deal with anyone lately without thinking of her. Just the thought of the last time I tried was enough to make me wince.

It was a few days before the Window Incident—as I was now referring to it—and I had a charity event to attend. Coming into the office I was stunned to see Miss Mills in an incredibly sexy blue dress I'd never seen before. The minute I saw her I'd wanted to throw her on the desk and fuck her senseless.

All that night with my beautiful blond trophy date by my side I'd been distracted. I knew I was coming to the end of my rope and eventually I was going to snap. If only I'd known how soon that would be.

I tried to prove to myself that Miss Mills wasn't really getting inside my head by going home with the blonde. Stumbling into her apartment, we'd kissed and undressed quickly, but everything felt off. It's not that she wasn't hot and interesting enough, but as I lay her down, it was dark hair I envisioned spread across the pillow. When kissing her breasts, it was soft, full ones—not silicone—I wanted to feel. And even as I rolled on the condom and moved into her, I knew she was just a faceless body I was using for my own selfish needs.

I tried to keep Chloe from my thoughts but was unable to stop the forbidden image of what it would be like to have her under me. Only then did I come hard, quickly rolling off my date and immediately hating myself. Now I was even more disgusted with the memory than when it happened, because I'd let her get into my head and stay there.

If I could make it through tonight, things would get easier. I parked the car and began mentally chanting, *You can do this. You can do this.*

"Mom?" I called out, looking into each room I passed.

"Out here, Bennett," I heard her answer from the back patio.

I opened the French doors and was greeted with my mother's smile as she put the finishing touches on the outdoor table.

I leaned over so she could kiss me. "So why are we eating out here tonight?"

"It's such a lovely evening, and I thought it might make everyone more comfortable than sitting in that stuffy dining room. You don't think anyone will mind, do you?"

"Of course not," I said. "It's beautiful out here. Don't worry."

And it was beautiful. The patio was topped with a massive white pergola, the beams draped in heavy greenery. The centerpiece was a large rectangular table that sat eight; it was covered in a soft ivory tablecloth and my mother's favorite china. Candles and blue flowers overflowed small silver pitchers running the length of the table, and a wrought-iron candelabra flickered overhead.

"You do know that not even I can keep Sofia from tearing this stuff off the table, though, don't you?" I popped a grape into my mouth.

"Oh, she's with Mina's parents tonight. And just as well,"

she said. "If Sofia were here all the attention would be on her."

Shit. With Sofia making faces across from me, I would have had something to distract me from Joel.

"Tonight is about Chloe. And I'm really hoping that she and Joel hit it off." She continued flitting around the patio, lighting candles and making last-minute adjustments, completely unaware of my anguish.

I was screwed. As I was contemplating making a run for it, I heard Henry—on time for once. "Where is everybody?" he yelled, his deep voice echoing through the empty house. Opening the door for my mother, we stepped inside, finding my brother in the kitchen.

"Sooo, Ben," he began, leaning his lanky frame against the counter. "Excited about tonight?"

I waited until Mom left the room again to eye him skeptically. "I guess," I answered, going for casual. "I think Mom made lemon squares. My favorite."

"You're so full of shit. I'm looking forward to watching Cignoli make a play for Chloe in front of everyone. Could make for an entertaining evening, don't you think?" Just as he was pulling a chunk of bread from one of the large loaves on the counter, Mina walked in and swatted his hands away.

"Do you want to send your mother into a fit by ruining the dinner she has planned? You be nice tonight, Henry. No teasing or joking with Chloe. You know she has to be nervous enough about all this. Lord knows she puts up with enough crap from this one," she said, gesturing toward me.

"What are you talking about?" I was growing tired of the overeager Chloe Mills fan club around here. "I haven't done anything to her."

"Bennett." My father stood in the doorway, motioning for me to come with him. I followed him out of the kitchen and into his study. "Please be on your best behavior tonight. I realize you and Chloe don't get along, but this is our home, not your office, and I expect you to treat her with respect."

Clenching my jaw tightly, I nodded in agreement, thinking of all the ways I'd disrespected her in the past few weeks.

While I went down to the washroom, Joel arrived, bringing a bottle of wine and a few variations on his eager greetings: a "You look fantastic!" for Mom, a "How's the baby?" for Mina, and a solid handshake-and-man-hug combination for Henry and Dad.

I lingered down the hall, mentally preparing myself for the night ahead.

We'd been good friends with Joel growing up and throughout school, but I hadn't seen him since coming home. He hadn't changed much. He was a bit shorter than me, with a slim build, jet-black hair, and blue eyes. I suppose some women would consider him attractive.

"Bennett!" Handshake, man hug. "God, man. How long has it been?"

"A long time, Joel. I think since right after high school," I answered, shaking his hand firmly. "How have you been?"

"Great. Things have been really great. How about you? I've seen your pictures in magazines, so I guess you're doing pretty well for yourself." He patted my shoulder amiably.

What a dick.

I gave a small nod and a forced smile in return. Deciding I needed a few more minutes to think, I excused myself and headed up the stairs to my old room.

Just walking through the door I felt calmer. The room had changed little since I was eighteen. Even while I was out of the country, my parents kept it virtually the same as the day I left for college. Sitting on my old bed I thought about how I'd feel if Miss Mills actually became involved with Joel. He really was a nice guy, and though I hated to admit it, there was definitely a chance they might hit it off. But the thought of another man touching her made every muscle in my body clench. I thought back to the moment in the car when I told her I couldn't stop. Even now, with all my false bravado, I didn't know if I could.

Hearing a renewal of greetings and Joel's voice downstairs, I decided it was time to man up and face the music.

As I cleared the final landing, I saw her. Her back was to me . . . and the air left my lungs.

Her dress was white.

Why did it have to be white?

She was wearing some sort of girly summer thing that

stopped right above the knee and showed off her long legs. The top was made of the same material, with little ribbons tying it together at the top of each shoulder. All I could think was how much I would love to pull those ribbons loose and see it all fall around her waist. Or maybe drop to the floor.

Our eyes met across the room and she smiled such a genuine, happy smile that for a second even I believed it. "Hi, Mr. Ryan."

My lips twitched in amusement, watching her play the part in front of my family. "Miss Mills," I replied, nodding. Our gaze never broke, even as my mother called everyone onto the patio for drinks before dinner.

As she passed, I turned my head, speaking in a voice low enough that only she could hear. "Successful shopping trip yesterday?"

Her eyes met mine, that same angelic smile on her face. "Wouldn't you like to know." She brushed by me, and I felt my entire body stiffen. "And by the way, a new line of garter belts came in," she whispered before following everyone else outside.

I stopped and my jaw went slack as my mind raced back to our tryst in the dressing room at La Perla.

Up ahead, Joel leaned in close to her. "I really hope you didn't mind the flowers I sent to your office yesterday. I admit it was a bit much, but I've been looking forward to meeting you." I felt a knot tighten in my gut as Joel's words snapped me out of my dirty daydream.

She turned back to look at me. "Flowers? Did I have flowers delivered?"

I shrugged and shook my head. "I left early, remember?" I walked by on my way outside to make myself a Belvedere vodka gimlet.

As the evening wore on, I couldn't help but keep track of her in my peripheral vision. When dinner finally began, it was apparent that things were going relatively smoothly between her and Joel. She was even flirting with him.

"So Chloe, Mr. and Mrs. Ryan tell me you're from North Dakota?" Joel's voice interrupted yet another fantasy—this one of my fist hitting his jaw. I looked over to see him smiling warmly at her.

"That's right. My dad is a dentist in Bismarck. Never was much of a big-city girl. Even Fargo felt huge to me." A small chuckle escaped my lips, and her eyes shot to mine. "Amused, Mr. Ryan?"

I smirked as I took a sip of my drink, staring at her from above the rim. "I'm sorry, Miss Mills. I just find it fascinating that you don't like the city, and yet you choose the third-largest city in the U.S. for college and . . . everything after."

The look in her eyes told me that under any other circumstances, I would either already be naked with her on top of me, or lying in a pool of my own blood on the rug.

"Actually, Mr. Ryan," she began, the smile returning to her face, "my father remarried, and since my mother was born here, I came to spend some time with her before she passed." She stared at me for a moment and I had to admit I felt a hint of guilt twisting in my chest. It was quickly suppressed when she looked back over at Joel, biting her lip in the innocent way that only she could make look so damn sexy.

Stop flirting with him.

I clenched my fists as they continued to speak to each other. But several minutes later I froze. *Could that be?* I grinned into my cocktail. Yes, that was most definitely her foot creeping up my pant leg. Fucking devious little minx, touching me while carrying on a conversation with a man we both knew could never satisfy her. I watched her lips as they closed around her fork, and my cock hardened as her tongue slowly ran across them to remove the traces of marinade left behind by the fish.

"Wow, top five percent of your class at Northwestern. Nice!" Joel said and then looked over at me. "Bet you're glad to have someone so amazing working under you, huh?"

Chloe coughed slightly, bringing her napkin up from her lap to cover her mouth. I smiled as I quickly glanced over to her and then back to Joel. "Yes, it's absolutely amazing having Miss Mills under me. She always gets the job done."

"Aw, Bennett. That is so sweet of you," my mother

gushed, and I watched Miss Mills' face begin to redden. My smile vanished when I felt her foot at my crotch. Then, ever so slightly, she pressed against my erection. *Holy shit.* Now it was my turn to cough, choking on my gimlet.

"Are you all right, Mr. Ryan?" she asked in feigned concern and I nodded, glaring daggers at her. She shrugged and then looked back over to Joel. "So how about you? Are you from Chicago?"

With the toe of her shoe, she continued to rub gently against me and I tried to keep control of my breathing, keep my expression neutral. As Joel began telling her about his childhood and going to school with us, finally talking about his successful accounting business, I watched her expression morph from one of feigned interest to one of genuine intrigue.

Hell no.

I slid my left hand under the tablecloth and met the skin of her ankle, watching her jump slightly at the contact. I moved my fingertips in light circles, ran my thumb along the arch of her foot, feeling increasingly smug when she had to ask Joel to repeat himself.

But then he mentioned he'd like to meet her for lunch sometime this week. My hand came to cover the top of her foot, pressing it more firmly against my cock.

She smirked.

"You could spare her for a lunch break, couldn't you, Bennett?" Joel asked with a cheerful smile, his arm resting over the back of Chloe's chair. It took everything I had not to reach across the table and rip that arm from his body.

"Oh, speaking of lunch dates, Bennett," Mina interrupted, tapping my arm with her hand. "You remember my friend Megan? You met her last month at the house. Midtwenties, my height, blond hair, blue eyes. Anyway, she asked for your number. You interested?"

I glanced back over to Chloe when I felt the tendons in her foot tighten, and watched her swallow slowly as she waited for my answer. "Sure. You know I prefer blondes. Might make for a nice change of scenery."

I had to restrain from yelling out as her heel dug down and pinned my balls to my chair. Holding them there for a moment, she lifted the napkin from her lap and dabbed at her mouth. "Excuse me, I need to use the ladies' room."

Once she was in the house, my entire family scowled at me.

"Bennett," Dad hissed. "I thought we talked about this."

I grabbed my glass and brought it to my lips. "I don't know what you mean."

"Bennett," my mother added, "I think you should go apologize."

"For what?" I asked, setting down my drink a little too roughly.

"*Ben!*" my father said sharply, leaving no room for argument.

I tossed my napkin onto my plate and pushed away from

the table. I stormed through the house, searching the bathrooms on the first two floors, until finally reaching the third floor, where the bathroom door was closed.

Standing outside, my hand resting on the knob, I debated with myself. If I went in there, what would happen? There was only one thing I was interested in, and it sure as hell wasn't apologizing. I thought about knocking but knew for a fact she wouldn't invite me in. I listened carefully, waiting for any noise or sign of movement from inside. Nothing. Finally, I turned the knob, surprised to find it unlocked.

I'd only been in this bathroom a few times since my mother had remodeled it. It was a beautiful, modern room with a custom-built marble counter and a wide mirror covering one wall. Above the vanity table was a small window that overlooked the patio and grounds below. She was sitting on the padded bench in front of the table, staring out at the sky.

"Here to grovel?" she asked. She took the cap off her lipstick, which she carefully applied to her lips.

"I was sent to check on your delicate petal feelings." I reached behind me to turn the lock on the bathroom door, the audible click ringing in the silent room.

She laughed, meeting my eyes in the mirror. She looked completely composed, but I could see the rise and fall of her chest; she was every bit as worked up as I was.

"I assure you, I'm fine." She put the cap back on her lipstick and shoved it into her purse. She stood and started to move past me to the door. "I'm used to you being a prick. But Joel seems nice. I should get back downstairs."

I put my hand on the door as I leaned closer to her face. "I don't think so." My lips lightly grazed under her ear, and she shuddered with the contact. "You see, he wants something that's mine, and he can't have it."

She glared at me. "What year is it? *Two*? Let me go. I am *not* yours."

"You might think that," I whispered, my lips ghosting along the column of her neck. "But your body," I said, running my hands under her skirt and pressing my hand against the damp lace between her legs, "thinks otherwise."

Her eyes closed and she let out a low moan as my fingers moved in slow circles against her clit. "Screw you."

"Let me," I said into her neck.

She let out a shaky laugh, and I pushed her against the bathroom door. Grabbing each of her hands, I raised them above her head, keeping them captive in my own and bending to kiss her. I felt her struggle weakly in my grip and I shook my head, tightening my hold.

"Let me," I repeated, pressing my hardened cock against her.

"Oh, God," she said as her head tilted to the side, allowing me access to her neck. "We can't do this here."

I ran my lips down and across her collarbone to her shoulder. Shifting both of her wrists into one hand, I reached down and slowly pulled one of the ribbons holding her top together, kissing along the newly exposed skin. Moving to the other side I repeated the action and was rewarded when the bodice slipped down to reveal a white lace strapless bra. *Fuck.* Did this woman own anything that didn't make me nearly come in my pants? I trailed my mouth down to her breasts while my free hand unfastened the clasp. There was no way I was missing the sight of her bare breasts this time. It opened easily and the lace fell away, revealing the vision that filled every one of my filthiest fantasies. As I took one pink nipple into my mouth, she moaned and her knees buckled slightly.

"Shhh," I whispered against her skin.

"More," she said. "Again."

I lifted her and she wrapped her legs around my waist, bringing our bodies together more firmly. I released her hands and she immediately brought them up to my hair and roughly pulled me closer. Fuck, I loved it when she did that. I pushed her against the door but then realized there were too many clothes in the way; I wanted to feel the heat of her skin against my own, wanted to bury myself balls deep in her and keep her pinned to the wall until everyone had long since gone to bed.

She seemed to read my mind as her fingers moved down my sides and began frantically tugging my polo from my pants, lifting it up and over my head.

The sound of laughter outside floated up through the open window, and I felt her tense against me. A long moment passed before her eyes met mine, and it was clear she was struggling with what to say.

"We shouldn't do this," she said finally, shaking her head. "He's waiting for me." She halfheartedly tried to push me away but I held my ground.

"Do you actually want him?" I asked, feeling a wave of possessiveness boil up inside me. She held my gaze but didn't answer.

I set her down and pulled her to the dressing table, stopping to stand just behind her. From where we stood, we had a perfect view of the patio below.

I pulled her bare back to my chest and brought my mouth to her ear. "Do you see him?" I asked, my hands sliding along her breasts. "Look at him." I skimmed my hands down her abdomen, along her skirt and to her thighs. "Does he make you feel like this?" My fingers floated up her thigh and underneath her panties. A low hiss escaped my mouth as I felt the wetness there and pushed inside. "Would he ever make you this wet?"

She groaned and pressed her hips back into me. "No . . ."

"Tell me what you want," I whispered against her shoulder.

"I—I don't know."

"Look at him," I said, my fingers moving in and out of her. "You know what you want."

"I want to feel you inside me." She didn't need to ask me twice. I quickly undid my pants and pushed them down my hips, grinding into her ass before I lifted her skirt and gripped her panties in my hands. "Rip them," she whispered.

I'd never been able to be this raw and primal with any- one before, and it felt so fucking right with her. I yanked hard and her flimsy panties tore easily. I tossed them to the floor, running my hands along her skin and sliding my fingers down her arms to her hands, where I pressed her palms flat on the table in front of us.

She was a fucking gorgeous sight: bent at the waist, skirt pushed up over her hips, perfect ass on display. We both moaned as I lined myself up and slid in deep. Bending over, I placed a kiss and another "Shhh" on her back.

More laughter came from outside. Joel was down there. Joel, who was basically a good guy, but who wanted to take her away from me. The image was enough to make me push into her more forcefully.

Her strangled sounds made me smile, and I rewarded her with an increase in tempo. A twisted part of me felt a sense of vindication seeing Chloe muted by what I did to her.

She was gasping, fingers searching for something to hold on to, and my cock so hard inside her, harder every time she tried to make a sound but couldn't.

Speaking softly against her ear, I asked if she wanted to be fucked. I asked her if she liked my mouth dirty, if she liked to see me filthy like this, taking her so rough she would bruise.

She stuttered out a yes, and when I moved faster and harder, she begged for more.

The bottles and jars on the table were rattling and tipping over with the force of our movements, but I couldn't find it in myself to care. Gripping her hair, I pulled her up so her back was against my chest. "Do you think he can make you feel this way?"

I continued to thrust in and out of her, forcing her to look out the window.

I knew I was slipping. My walls were falling around me but I didn't care. I needed her to think of me tonight as she lay in bed. I wanted her to feel me when she closed her eyes and touched herself, remembering the way I'd fucked her. My free hand ran up her sides to her breast, cupping it and twisting her nipples.

"No," she moaned. "Never like this." Sliding my hand down her side I placed it behind her knee and hitched it up to the table, opening her up wider and allowing my thrusts to deepen.

"Do you feel how perfectly you fit around me?" I groaned into her neck. "You feel so fucking good. When you go downstairs, I want you to remember this. Remember what you do to me."

The sensation was becoming too overwhelming and I knew I was getting close. I was beyond desperate. I craved her like a drug, and this feeling consumed my every waking thought. Taking her hand in mine, I laced our fingers and moved them down her body to her clit, both our hands stroking and teasing. I groaned as I felt myself glide in and out of her.

"Do you feel that?" I whispered into her ear, spreading our fingers so they slipped on either side of me.

She turned her head and whimpered into the skin of my neck. It wasn't enough, and I needed to keep her quiet. Removing my hand from her hair, I gently covered her mouth and placed a kiss against her flushed cheek. She let out a muffled cry, the possible sound of my name, as her body tensed and then tightened all around me.

After her eyes closed and her lips relaxed into a satisfied sigh, I started taking what I needed: faster now, watching in the mirror so I could see how my thrusts made her breasts move.

My climax began to rip through me. Her hand fell from my hair to cover my own mouth and I closed my eyes and let the wave overtake me. My final thrusts were deep and hard as I spilled into her.

I opened my eyes, kissing her palm before removing it from my mouth and laying my forehead against her shoulder. The oblivious voices from below continued to carry up to us. She leaned back into me and we stood there quietly for a few moments.

Slowly, she began to pull away, and I frowned at the loss of contact. I watched as she straightened her skirt, retrieved her bra, and attempted to retie the straps of her top. As I reached down to pull up my pants, I grabbed the torn lace of her underwear, shoving it into my pocket. She was still struggling with her dress and I walked over, brushing her hands away and retying the straps without meeting her gaze.

The room was suddenly too small and we glanced at each other once in an uncomfortable silence. I reached for the knob, wanting to say something, anything, to fix this. How could I ask her to fuck me and only me, and not expect anything else to change? Even I knew asking for that was likely to earn me a swift kick to the nuts. But the language for what I felt when I saw her with Joel wasn't crystallizing fast enough. My mind was blank. Frustrated, I opened the door. We both stopped short at the sight before us.

There, standing outside the doorway, arms folded and eyebrow raised knowingly, was Mina.

Eight

The moment he opened the door and we came face-to-face with Mina, I froze.

"What exactly were you two doing in there?" she asked, her eyes moving between the two of us. A recap of all she could have heard flashed through my head, and I felt a burst of heat spread along my skin.

I chanced a look over to Mr. Ryan as he did the same, then turned back to Mina and shook my head. "Nothing, we needed to talk. That's all." I tried to play it off, but knew the tremor in my voice gave me away.

"Oh, I heard something in there, but it certainly wasn't talking," she said, smirking.

"Don't be ridiculous, Mina. We were discussing an issue at work," he said, trying to move around her.

"In the bathroom?" she asked.

"Yes. You sent me up here to find her. This is where I found her."

She shifted in front of him, blocking his path. "Do

you think I'm stupid? It's no secret that you two don't *discuss* anything; you yell. So, what? Are you two, like, dating now?"

"No!" We both yelled at once, our eyes meeting for a brief moment before quickly darting away.

"So . . . you're just fucking then," she said, and it seemed that neither of us could find the words to reply. The tension in that hallway was so heavy I briefly considered how much damage a jump from a third-story window could do. "For how long?"

"Mina . . ." he began, shaking his head, and for once I actually felt bad about his discomfort. I'd never seen him look like this before. It was as if all this time it really hadn't occurred to him that there could be consequences outside of our own turmoil.

"How long, Bennett? Chloe?" she said, looking between us.

"I—we just—" I started, but *just what*? How could I explain any of this? "We—"

"We made a mistake. It was a mistake." His voice cut through my thoughts and I looked over to him in shock. Why did it bother me so much that he said it? It *was* a mistake, and yet hearing him say that . . . hurt.

I couldn't tear my eyes away as she began to speak. "Mistake or not, it needs to stop now. What if I'd been Susan? And Bennett, you're her boss! Have you forgotten that?" She exhaled deeply. "Look, you two are adults, and I don't know what's going on here, but whatever you do, do *not* let Elliott find out."

A wave of nausea hit me at the idea of Elliott ever finding out about this, at how disappointed he'd be. I couldn't bear that. "That won't be a problem," I said, purposefully avoiding Bennett's gaze. "I intend to learn from my mistake. Excuse me."

I moved past them and toward the stairs, anger and hurt settling like a lead weight deep in my stomach. The strength of my work ethic and motivation had always buoyed me through harder times in my life: breakups, the death of my mother, rough patches with friendships. My value as an employee at RMG was now tinged with self-doubt. Was I making him see me differently because I was fucking him? Now that he'd seemed to register—finally—that if others knew about us it could be bad for him, would he start to question my judgment more globally?

I was smarter than this. It was time I started acting like it.

I composed myself before stepping outside and returning to my seat beside Joel.

"Everything all right?" he asked.

I turned my head, letting myself look at him for a moment. He was really quite cute: neatly combed dark hair, a kind face, and the most beautiful blue eyes I'd ever seen. He was everything I should be looking for. My gaze shot up a moment later as Mr. Ryan returned to the table with Mina, but I quickly looked away.

"Yeah, I'm just not feeling well," I said, turning back to Joel. "I think I might need to call it a night."

"Here," he said, standing to pull out my chair. "I'll walk you to your car."

I said my good-byes, feeling the unfamiliar shape of Joel's palm on the small of my back as we walked into the house. Once in the driveway, he gave me a shy smile and took my hand. "It was really nice meeting you, Chloe. I'd like to call you sometime and maybe have that lunch."

"Let me see your phone," I said. Part of me felt bad for doing this, having been with one man upstairs not even twenty minutes ago, and now giving my number to another. But it was time to move past this, and a lunch date with a nice guy seemed like a good place to start.

His smile widened as I handed him his phone, and he gave me his card in return. Taking my hand, he lifted it to his lips. "I'll call you Monday, then. Hopefully your flowers aren't completely wilted."

"It's the thought that counts," I said, smiling. "Thank you."

He looked so sincere, so happy at the simple possibility of seeing me again, and it occurred to me that

I should be swooning, or giddy. I really just wanted to throw up.

"I should go."

Joel nodded, opening my car door for me. "Of course. I hope you feel better. Drive carefully, and good night, Chloe."

"Good night, Joel."

He closed my door and I started the engine, my eyes straight ahead as I drove away from my boss' family's house.

❧

The next morning at yoga I considered spilling my guts to Julia. I'd felt reasonably certain I could handle things on my own, but after an entire night of staring at the ceiling and completely freaking out, I realized I needed to confide in someone.

There was Sara, and more than anyone Sara would understand how maddening my hot boss could be. But she also worked for Henry and I didn't want to put her in an awkward position by asking her to keep such a huge secret. I knew Mina would be happy to talk if I asked, but there was just something about her being a Ryan, and knowing what she might have heard that left me feeling less than comfortable.

These were the times I really wished my mom were still alive. Just thinking about her brought a wrenching pain to my chest and tears to my eyes. Moving here to spend the last years of her life with her had been the best decision I'd ever made. And even though living so far from my dad and friends was tough at times, I knew everything happened for a reason. I just wished the reason would hurry up and make itself known.

Could I tell Julia? I had to admit I was terrified of what she would think of me. But more than that, I was terrified of saying the words to someone out loud.

"Okay, you keep looking at me," she said. "Either you have something on your mind or I'm the embarrassing and gross kind of sweaty."

I tried to tell her nothing, I tried to brush it off and let her think she was being absurd. But I couldn't. The weight and the pressure of the last few weeks came crashing down and before I could control it, my chin started to tremble and I began bawling like a baby.

"That's what I thought. Come on." She offered me her hand and helped me up and, gathering our belongings on the way, led me out the door.

Twenty minutes, two mimosas, and one emotional breakdown later, I was watching Julia's shocked expression at a table in our favorite restaurant. I told her everything: the panty ripping, my liking the panty ripping, the various locations, the mid-make-out-session-I-hate-yous, Mina catching us, my guilt over feeling like I was betraying Elliott and Susan, Joel, Mr. Ryan's caveman declarations, and finally, my fear that I was in the most unhealthy relationship in the history of the world, with no power at all.

When I looked up to meet her gaze, I winced; she looked like she'd just watched a car wreck.

"Okay, let me make sure I've got this straight."

I nodded waiting for her to continue.

"You're sleeping with your boss."

I cringed slightly. "Well, technically not—"

She threw her hand up to stop me from finishing. "Yeah, yeah. I got that. And this is the same boss you oh-so-lovingly refer to as 'Beautiful Bastard'?"

I sighed heavily and nodded again.

"But you hate him."

"Correct," I mumbled, my eyes shifting away from her. "Hate. Very big hate."

"You don't want to be with him, but you can't stay away."

"God, it sounds even worse to hear someone else say it," I groaned as I buried my face in my hands. "I sound ridiculous."

"But the sexytimes? Are good," she said with a touch of humor in her voice.

"Good doesn't even come close to describing it, Julia. Phenomenal, intense, mind-blowing, multiple-orgasmingly amazing doesn't come close to describing it."

"Is 'orgasmingly' even a word?"

I rubbed my face with my hands and sighed again. "Shut up."

"Well," she replied thoughtfully, clearing her throat. "I guess a small penis isn't his problem, after all . . ."

I let my head fall to my arms on the table. "No. No, it most definitely isn't." I looked up slightly at the sound of her muffled laughter. "Julia! This is not funny!"

"I beg to differ. Even you have to see how insane this is. I mean, of all the people I've ever known, you're the last person I would have ever imagined ending up in this situation. You've always been so serious, with each and every step of your life so planned out. Come on, you've only had a few real boyfriends, all of whom you'd been with for what everyone considered a really silly amount of time before you slept with them. This man must be something else."

"I know there's nothing wrong with having a purely sexual relationship with someone—I can handle that. And I know that I can at times be overly controlled, but it's the fact that I feel I have no control over *myself* when I'm with him. I mean, I don't even like him, and yet . . . I keep going back."

Julia took a sip of her mimosa, and I could practically see the wheels turning as she considered everything I'd told her. "What matters to you?"

I looked up to her, understanding. "My job. My life after this. My sense of value as an employee. Knowing my contribution matters."

"Can you feel good about those things and still fuck him?"

I shrugged, unable to actually untangle my thoughts on the matter. "I don't know. If I felt like everything was separate, maybe. But our only interactions are at work. There isn't any instance where it isn't about both work and sex."

"Then you have to find a way to stop doing this. You need to keep your distance."

"It's not that simple," I retorted, shaking my head and beginning to ramble. "I work for him. It's not as if all instances of being alone with him are easily avoidable. The number of times I've sworn off sex with him and then had sex with him hours later is ridiculous. And on top of that, we have a conference to attend in two weeks. Same hotel, same general vicinity at all times. *Beds!*"

"Chloe, what has gotten into you?" Julia asked in an astonished tone "Do you want this to continue?"

"No! Of course not!"

She eyed me skeptically.

"I mean . . . it's just that I'm different with him. Like, I want things I've never wanted before, and maybe I should let myself want those things. I just wish it was someone else making me want them, someone nice, like Joel for instance. The boss is not very nice."

"Boss man makes you want what? Like spankings and stuff?" Julia responded with a chuckle, but when I looked away I heard her gasp. "Oh my God, he's spanked you?"

My wide eyes shot back to her. "A little louder, Julia. I don't think the guy in the back heard you." As soon as I was sure no one was looking, I smoothed loose tendrils of hair back from my forehead. "Look, I know I need to stop this but I—"

I paused as I felt goose bumps rise along my skin. My breath caught in my throat and I turned slowly to look at the door. It was him, scruffy and dressed down in a black T-shirt and jeans, sneakers and hair in even sexier disarray than usual. I turned back around to face Julia, feeling all the blood drain from my face.

"Chloe, what's wrong? You look like you've just seen a ghost," Julia said, reaching across the table to touch my arm.

I swallowed hard in an attempt to find my voice, then looked at her. "Do you see that man next to the door? The tall, good-looking one?" She raised her head slightly to look and I kicked her under the table. "Don't make yourself obvious! That is my boss."

Julia's eyes widened and her jaw dropped. "Holy

shit," she gasped, and shook her head as she looked him up and down. "You weren't kidding, Chloe. That is one beautiful bastard. I wouldn't kick him out of my bed. Or car. Or dressing room. Or elevator, or—"

"Julia! You're really not being helpful here!"

"Who's the blonde?" she asked, motioning toward them. I turned back to see Mr. Ryan being led to a table with a tall, leggy blonde, his hand on the small of her back. A sharp stab of jealousy pressed into my chest.

"What a *prick*," I hissed. "After his behavior last night? He has got to be kidding me." Just as she was about to respond, Julia's phone rang and she reached for it in her purse. The "Hey baby!" greeting told me it was her fiancé, and this would take awhile.

I glanced again at Mr. Ryan, talking and laughing with the blonde. I couldn't tear my eyes away. He was even more attractive in a relaxed setting: smiling, eyes dancing when he laughed. *Dick!* As if he heard my thoughts, he lifted his head and our eyes locked. I clenched my jaw and turned away, tossing my napkin to the table. I had to get out of here. "I'll be right back, Julia."

She nodded and waved absently, never pausing her conversation. Standing up, I quickly made my way past his table making sure to avoid his eyes. I had just turned the corner and spotted the safety of the ladies' room door when I felt a strong hand on my forearm. "Wait."

That voice sent a jolt through me.

Okay, Chloe, you can do this. Just turn around and look at him and tell him to fuck off. He's an asshole who called you a mistake last night and shows up with some blond bimbo today.

Straightening my shoulders, I turned to face him. *Shit.* He looked even better up close. I'd never seen him looking anything other than perfectly groomed, but he obviously hadn't shaved this morning and I desperately wanted to feel the scratch of his stubble on my cheeks.

Or thighs.

"What the hell do you want?" I spat at him, pulling my arm free from his grasp. Without the benefit of my heels I felt like he towered over me. Looking up at his face, I could see faint circles under his eyes. He looked tired. Well, good. If his nights were half as bad as mine, I was happy.

Running his hands through his hair, he glanced around uncomfortably. "I wanted to talk to you. To explain about last night."

"What's there to explain?" I asked, nodding my head toward the dining room and the blonde still sitting at his table. My chest twisted tightly, painfully. *"Change of scenery.* I get it. I'm actually glad to see you here like this—it helps remind me why this thing between us is a terrible idea. I don't want to be indirectly fucking all of your other women."

"What the hell are you talking about?" he asked, looking back at me. "Are you talking about Emily?"

"Is that her name? Well, you and Emily have a lovely meal, Mr. Ryan." I turned to leave but was once again stopped when he grabbed my arm. "Let. Go."

"Why would you even care?"

Our argument had begun to attract attention from the staff passing through to the kitchen. After a quick glance around, he pulled me into the ladies' room and locked the door.

Fantastic, another bathroom.

I shoved him away when he stepped closer. "What do you think you're doing? And what do you mean, why would I care? You *fucked* me last night, told me all about how I couldn't possibly want to go out with Joel, and now you're here with someone else! I let myself forget you're a manwhore. *Your* behavior is completely expected—I'm pissed at *myself*." I was so angry my nails were practically cutting into the palms of my hands.

"You think I'm here on a *date*?" He exhaled heavily, shaking his head. "This is fucking unbelievable.

Emily is a friend. She runs a charitable organization that Ryan Media supports. That's all. I was supposed to meet her Monday to sign some papers but she had a last-minute flight change and is leaving the country this afternoon. I haven't been with anyone else since the wi—" He paused to rethink his words. "Since we first . . . you know . . ." He finished, motioning vaguely between us.

What?

We stood there, staring at each other as I tried to let his words seep in. He hadn't slept with anyone else. Was that even possible? I knew for a fact that he was a womanizer. I'd personally witnessed his ever-expanding collection of arm candy at corporate events, not to mention the stories swimming around the building. And even if what he was saying was true, it didn't change the fact that he was still my boss, and this whole thing was seriously wrong.

"All those women throwing themselves at you and you haven't nailed even one? Aw, I'm touched." I turned for the door.

"It's not that difficult to believe," he growled, and I could feel his eyes burning into my back.

"You know what, it doesn't matter. It was just a mistake, right?"

"Look, that's what I wanted to talk to you about." He moved closer and his scent—like honey and sage—

washed over me. I suddenly felt trapped, like there wasn't enough oxygen in the tiny room. I needed to get out of here, now. What had Julia said less than five minutes ago? Don't be alone with him? Good advice. I happened to like this particular pair of panties and didn't really want to see them in tatters in his pocket.

Okay, that was a lie.

"Are you seeing Joel again?" he asked from behind me. My hand was on the knob. All I had to do was turn it and I was safe. But I froze, staring at that damn door for what seemed like minutes.

"Does it matter?"

"I thought we covered this last night," he said, his breath warm against my hair.

"Yeah, a lot of things were said last night." His fingertips moved up my arm and slipped the thin strap of my tank top off my shoulder.

"I didn't mean to say this was a mistake," he whispered against my skin. "I just panicked."

"That doesn't mean it's not true." My body instinctively leaned into him, my head tilting slightly allowing him easier access. "We both know it."

"I still shouldn't have said it." He brushed my ponytail over my shoulder and his soft lips moved across my back. "Turn around."

Two words. How was it possible that two simple words could make me question everything? It was one thing for him to press me against a wall or force-fully grab me, but now he was putting everything in my court. Biting my lip hard, I tried to bring myself to turn the handle. My hand actually twitched before it fell to my side in defeat.

I turned and looked up to meet his eyes.

His hand came to rest on my cheek, his thumb brushing across my bottom lip. Our gazes locked, and just when I thought I couldn't wait one more second he pulled me to him, pressing his mouth to mine.

The moment we kissed, my body gave up fighting and I couldn't get close enough. My purse landed on the tile floor at my feet and my hands dove into his hair, pulling him to me. He backed me into the wall and ran his hands down my body, lifting me slightly. He pushed into my yoga pants and cupped my ass.

"Fuck. What are you wearing?" He groaned into my neck, his palms sliding back and forth over the pink satin. Lifting me fully, he wrapped my legs around his waist and pressed me further into the wall. He moaned as I took his earlobe between my teeth.

Pulling one side of my top down, he sucked one of my nipples into his mouth. My head fell back and hit the wall as I felt the scruff of his unshaven face against my breast. A shrill sound broke through my haze and I heard him swear. My phone. Placing me on my feet, he stepped away, his face already back in its usual scowl.

I quickly rearranged my clothing and reached for my purse, grimacing when I saw the picture displayed on the screen.

"Julia," I answered breathlessly.

"Chloe, are you in the bathroom fucking that nice slice of man cake?"

"I'll be there in a second, okay?" I ended the call and shoved the phone back into my bag. I looked up at him, feeling my rational side return after the small interruption. "I should go."

"Look, I—" He was cut off as my phone rang again.

I answered without bothering to look at the screen. "God, Julia! I'm not in here fucking the piece of man cake!"

"Chloe?" Joel's confused voice sounded through the phone.

"Oh . . . hi." *Shit*. This could not be happening to me.

"I'm glad to hear that you're not . . . fucking . . . man cake?" Joel said, laughing tightly.

"Who is it?" Bennett growled.

I pressed my hand to his lips and gave him the dirtiest look I could manage. "Look, I can't really talk right now."

"Yeah, I'm sorry to bother you on a Sunday, but I couldn't stop thinking about you. And I don't want to get anyone in trouble or anything, but right after you left I checked my e-mail and there was a confirmation for delivery of your flowers."

"Really?" I asked, feigning interest. My gaze was locked with Bennett's.

"Well, it seems they were signed for by Bennett Ryan."

NINE

I watched as several expressions passed over her face at once: embarrassment, annoyance, and then . . . curiosity? I could vaguely make out a man's voice on the other end and felt the caveman begin to awaken. Who the hell was calling her?

Suddenly, her eyes narrowed, and a tiny voice inside told me I should be nervous. "Well, thank you so much for letting me know. Yes. Yes, I will. Okay. Yes, I'll call you when I decide. Thanks for calling, Joel."

Joel? *Fucking Cignoli.*

She ended the call and slowly put the phone back into her purse. Looking down, she shook her head, a small laugh escaping before a wicked smile graced her mouth.

"Is there anything you'd like to tell me, Mr. Ryan?" she asked sweetly, and for some reason it made me even more anxious. I racked my brain but couldn't think of anything. *What was she talking about?*

"That was the strangest conversation. It seems that when Joel checked his e-mail this morning, he had a delivery confirmation for my flowers. You'll never guess what it said."

She moved one step toward me, and instinctively I moved one step back. I didn't like where this was going. "It turns out that someone signed for them."

Oh, shit.

"The name on the slip said Bennett Ryan."

Fuuuuuck. Why the hell did I sign my own name? I tried to think of a response but my mind was suddenly blank. Obviously, my silence told her everything she needed to know.

"You son of a bitch! You signed for them and then lied to me?" She landed a hard shove on my chest, and I had a sudden instinct to protect my balls. "Why did you do that?" My back was now against the wall and I was frantically searching for an alternative exit.

"I . . . what?" I babbled. My heart felt like it was going to claw its way out of my chest.

"Seriously! What the hell?"

I needed an answer and I needed it fast. Running my hands through my hair for the hundredth time in the last five minutes, I decided it was probably better to just come clean.

"I don't know, *okay*?" I shouted back. "I just . . . *fuck!*"

She took out her phone and appeared to be texting someone.

"What are you doing?" I asked.

"Not that it's any of your business, but I'm telling Julia to just go on without me. I'm not leaving here until you tell me the truth." She glared at me and I could feel the anger coming off of her in waves. I briefly considered telling Emily what was going on, but she'd seen me follow Chloe; I was pretty sure she'd figured it out by now.

"Well?"

I met her eyes and let out a deep sigh. There was absolutely no way I could explain myself and not sound like I'd lost my mind. "Okay, yes, I signed for them."

She stared at me, her chest heaving and her fists balled so tightly that her knuckles were white. *"And?"*

"And . . . I threw them away." As I stood facing her, I realized that I deserved every bit of her anger. I was being unfair. I was offering her nothing but still standing in the way of someone who could possibly make her happy.

"You are fucking unbelievable," she growled through clenched teeth. I knew she was doing everything she could to keep from lunging across the room and pummeling me. "Explain to me why you would do that."

Here was the part I didn't know how to answer. "Because . . ." I scratched the back of my head. I hated that I'd let myself get into this situation. "Because I don't want you to go out with Joel."

"Of all the asinine, chauvinistic—who in the hell do you think you are? Just because we've had sex does not mean you get to make decisions in my life. We aren't a couple, we aren't dating. Hell, we don't even like each other!" she yelled.

"You think I don't know that? It doesn't make any sense, okay? But when I saw those flowers . . . come on, they were fucking *roses!*"

She looked as if she were ready to have me committed somewhere. "Are you on some sort of medication? What does the fact that they were roses have to do with anything?"

"You hate roses!" When I said this, her face fell, eyes soft and dark. I rambled on. "I just saw them and reacted. I didn't stop and think about it. Just the thought of him touching you . . ." My fists clenched at my sides and my voice trailed off as I tried to regain my composure. I was getting angrier by the second: at myself for being weak and letting my emotions get out of hand, *again,* and at her for having this fucking inexplicable hold on me.

"Okay, look," she said, taking a calming breath. "I'm not saying I agree with what you did, but I understand . . . to a point."

My eyes flew to her in shock.

"I would be lying if I said I haven't been feeling similarly possessive," she said reluctantly.

I couldn't believe what I was hearing. Did she actually just admit to me that she felt this way too?

"But that doesn't change the fact that you lied to me.

You lied right to my face. I might think you're an arrogant asshole most of the time, but you've always been someone I trusted to be honest with me."

I flinched. She was right.

"I'm sorry." My apology hung in the air, and I wasn't sure which of us was more surprised by it.

"Prove it." She looked at me so calmly, not an ounce of emotion visible in her features. What did she mean? Then, it hit me. *Prove it*. We couldn't speak through words, because words only led to trouble. But this? This is what we were, and if she would give me this one chance to make up for what I'd done, I'd take it.

I hated her so much in that moment. I hated that she was right and I was wrong, and I hated that she was forcing me to make a choice. I hated how much I wanted her, most of all.

I closed the distance between us, wrapping my hand around the back of her neck. I pulled her to me, meeting her gaze as I drew her mouth to mine. There was an unspoken challenge there. Neither of us would back down or admit that this—whatever *this* was—was beyond our control.

Or maybe both of us just had.

The moment our lips touched, I was overtaken by a familiar buzz coursing through my body.

My hands fisted deeply into her hair, forcing her head back, to take everything I pressed into her. This might be for her, but I was damn sure going to control it. Pressing my body to hers, I groaned at the way each of her curves fit against me. I wanted this need to go away, to be satisfied and move on; but each time I felt her, it was better than I remembered.

Falling to my knees, I grasped her hips and pulled her closer, my lips moving across the waist of her pants. Lifting her shirt up, I kissed each inch of visible skin, enjoying the tensing of her muscles as I explored. I looked up at her, hooking my fingers into the waistband. Her eyes were closed and she was biting her lower lip. I felt my cock harden in anticipation of what I was about to do.

I pulled her pants down her thighs, goose bumps breaking out over her skin as I trailed my fingers down her legs. Her hands went to my hair and pulled roughly, and I groaned as I looked back up at her. I traced the edge of the delicate satin of her lingerie, stopping at the thin straps on her hips. "These are almost too pretty to ruin," I said, wrapping one strap around each hand.

"Almost." With a quick tug they broke easily, allowing me to pull the pink material away and stuff it into my pocket.

A sense of urgency took over me then, and I quickly freed one of her legs, placing it over my shoulder and kissing along the soft skin of her inner thigh.

"Oh, shit," she said on an exhale, running her hands into my hair. "Oh, shit, please."

As I first nuzzled and then slowly licked along her clit, she gripped my hair tightly, moving her hips against my mouth.

Unintelligible words fell from her lips in a hoarse whisper, and seeing her come undone so completely made me realize she was as helpless against this as I was. She was pissed at me, so pissed that part of her probably wanted to hook her leg around my neck and strangle me, but at least she was letting me give her something that was, in many ways, so much more intimate than simple fucking. I was on my knees, but she was vulnerable and bare.

She was also warm and wet and tasted just as fucking sweet as she looked.

"I could fucking consume you," I whispered, pulling back enough to glance up at her expression. Kissing her hip, I murmured, "This would be so much better if I could spread you out somewhere. A table in a conference room, perhaps."

She tugged on my hair, pulling me back to her with a smile. "This is working just fine for me. Don't you dare stop."

I almost admitted aloud that I couldn't, and I was starting to abhor the thought of even trying but soon was lost in her skin again. I wanted to memorize every curse and plea that escaped her mouth and know that I was the reason for it. I moaned against her, causing her to cry out as she twisted her body closer. Sliding two fingers inside her, I pulled on her hip with the other hand to urge her to find her rhythm with me. She began rolling her hips, slowly at first, pressing into me, and then faster. I could feel her tense: her legs, her abdomen, her hands in my hair.

"So close," she panted, her movements faltering, growing jagged and a little wild, and fuck if I didn't feel a little wild myself. I wanted to bite and suck, bury my fingers inside and completely unravel her. I worried I was growing too rough, but her breaths turned into little pants and tightened into pleas. When I twisted my wrist and pushed in deeper, she cried out, legs shaking as her climax overtook her.

Rubbing her hip, I slowly lowered her leg and watched her feet just in case she decided to kick me after all. I ran a finger across my lip and watched her eyes return to focus.

She pushed me away and quickly righted her clothing, looking down at where I kneeled in front of her. Reality crept back as the various sounds of people dining on the other side of the door combined with the sound of our heavy breathing.

"You're not forgiven," she said and reached down for her purse, unlocking the door and leaving the room without another word.

I stood up slowly and watched the door close behind her, trying to sort out what had just happened. I should have been furious. But I felt the corner of my mouth lift in a smile and I almost laughed at the absurdity of it.

Damn her, she did it again. She was beating me at my own game.

———

My night had been hell. I'd hardly slept or eaten, and I'd suffered a near-constant hard-on since leaving the restaurant yesterday. I knew I was in for it as I headed to work. She was going to do everything she could to torture and punish me for lying to her; the sick thing was . . . I was kind of looking forward to it.

I was surprised to find her desk empty upon my arrival. *Strange,* I thought, she was rarely late. I continued into my office and began getting things in order for the day. Fifteen minutes later, I was distracted from a phone call when I heard the outer door slam. Well, she certainly didn't disappoint; I could hear drawers and files slamming and knew this would make for an interesting day.

At ten fifteen I was interrupted by my intercom. "Mr. Ryan." Her cool voice filled the room and despite her obvious annoyance, I found myself smirking as I pressed the button to respond.

"Yes, Miss Mills?" I answered back, hearing my own grin reflected in my tone.

"We need to be in the conference room in fifteen minutes. You'll need to leave at noon to make the lunch meeting with the president of Kelly Industries at twelve thirty. Stuart will be waiting for you in the garage."

"Are you not accompanying me?" Part of me wondered if she was avoiding being alone with me. I wasn't sure how I felt about that.

"No, sir. Management only." I heard papers rustling as she continued to speak. "Besides, I have arrangements to make for San Diego today."

"I'll be out in a moment," I let my finger slide off the button, standing to adjust my tie and jacket.

When I stepped out of my office, my eyes landed on her immediately. Any doubts I might have had about her making me suffer were confirmed. She was leaning over her desk in a blue silk dress that showcased her long lean legs perfectly. Her hair was piled on her head, and when she turned in my direction, I saw she was wearing her glasses. How was I going to manage to speak coherently with her sitting next to me?

"Are you ready, Mr. Ryan?" Without waiting for an answer, she gathered her things and began walking down the hall. There seemed to be more sway to her hips today. The sassy bitch was taunting me.

Standing in the crowded elevator, our bodies were unintentionally pressed together and I had to stifle a groan. It could have been my imagination but I thought I saw a hint of a smirk as she "accidentally" brushed against my semierect cock. Twice.

For the next two hours, I was in my own personal hell. Every time I looked at her she was doing something to bring me to my knees: sly glances, licking her bottom lip, crossing and uncrossing her legs, or absentmindedly twirling a tendril of hair around her finger. At one point, she dropped her pen and casually placed her hand on my thigh as she bent down to retrieve it from under the table.

At the lunch meeting that followed, I was both grateful for the reprieve from her torment and desperate to get back to it. I nodded and spoke at appropriate times, but I was never really there. Of course my father had noticed every second of my surly, quiet mood. On the drive back to the office, he started in on me.

"For three days, you and Chloe will be together in San Diego *without* the buffer of office doors, and there won't be anyone there to run interference. I expect you to treat her with the utmost respect. And before you get defensive," he added, holding his hands up as he sensed my quick rebuttal, "I've already spoken to Chloe about this."

My eyes widened and flashed to his face. He had talked to Miss Mills about *my* professional conduct?

"Yes, I'm aware that it's not just you," he said, leading us into an empty elevator. "She's assured me that she gives every bit as good as she gets. Why do you think I suggested you as her program mentor in the first place? There wasn't a doubt in my mind that she could hold her own with you."

Henry stood silent next to him, a smug smile stretched across his face. *Asshole.*

I frowned slightly as the realization hit me: she had spoken in my defense. She could have easily made it sound like I was a tyrant, but instead she accepted some of the blame.

"Dad, I'll admit that my relationship with her is unconventional," I began, praying that no one understood how true that statement really was. "But I assure you, it in no way interferes with our ability to conduct business. You have nothing to worry about."

"Good," Dad said when we arrived at my office suite.

We walked in to find Miss Mills on the phone, speaking almost inaudibly. "Well, I'm going to let you go, Dad. I have some things to take care of and I'll let you know as soon as I can. You need to get some sleep, okay?" she said softly. After a brief pause she laughed, but then didn't say anything else for a moment. Neither I nor the two men beside me dared say anything. "I love you too, Daddy."

My stomach tightened at the words, and the way her voice shook when she said them. When she turned around in her chair, she startled to find us standing there. Quickly she began gathering the paperwork on her desk.

"How did the meeting go?"

"It went smoothly, as always," my father said. "You and Sara really do a superb job taking care of things. I don't know what my sons would do without the two of you."

Her eyebrow lifted slightly and I could see her struggling to not gloat in my direction. But then her face transformed into a puzzled expression and I realized I'd been full-on grinning at her, hoping to see some of her trademark sass. I put on the best scowl I could manage as I walked into my office. It only hit me when I closed my door that I hadn't seen her smile once since we'd come back and heard her on the phone.

Ten

My head wasn't in the game. I had a few things to show Mr. Ryan before he left for the day, had to get some documents to legal for signatures, but I felt like I was walking through wet sand, the phone conversation with my dad looping endlessly through my thoughts. As I walked into Mr. Ryan's office, I stared down at the papers in my arms, realizing how many things I'd need to organize today: plane tickets, someone to pick up my mail, maybe even a temp for while I was gone. How long *would* I be gone?

I registered Mr. Ryan was saying something—loudly—in my direction. What was he saying? He came into focus in front of me and I heard the end of his rant, ". . . barely paying attention. Jesus, Miss Mills, do I need to write this down for you?"

"Can we skip this game today?" I asked, tired.

"The . . . what now?"

"This asshole-boss routine."

His eyes widened, brows drawing together. "*Excuse* me?"

"I realize you get your rocks off on being an epic dick to me, and I'll admit that sometimes it's actually kind of sexy, but I'm having a horrible, awful day and would really appreciate it if you would just not speak. To me." I was close to tears, my chest constricting painfully. "Please."

He looked like he'd been blindsided, blinking rapidly as he stared. Finally, he spluttered, "What just happened?"

I swallowed, regretting my tantrum. Things were always better with him when I kept my wits. "I overreacted to being yelled at. I apologize."

He got up and began walking toward me, but at the last minute he stopped and sat down on the corner of his desk, fiddling awkwardly with a crystal paperweight. "No, I mean, why is your day so horrible? What's going on?" His voice was softer than I'd ever heard it outside of sex. Except this time, he wasn't quiet to keep a secret; he was quiet because he seemed genuinely concerned.

I didn't want to talk to him about this because part of me expected him to mock me. But an even larger part was beginning to suspect that he wouldn't. "My dad has to have some tests. He's having trouble eating."

Mr. Ryan's face fell. "Eating? Is it an ulcer?"

I explained what I knew, that it had started suddenly and an early scan showed a small mass on his esophagus.

"Can you go home?"

I stared at him. "I don't know. Can I?"

He winced, blinked away. "Am I really that big of a jerk?"

"Sometimes." I immediately regretted it, because no, he'd never done anything to make me think he'd keep me from my sick father.

He nodded, swallowing thickly as he stared out the window. "You can take whatever time you need, of course."

"Thank you."

I stared at the floor, waiting for him to continue with the list of the day's tasks. But silence engulfed the room instead. I could see in my peripheral vision that he'd turned back and was watching me.

"Are you okay?" He'd said it so quietly I wasn't even sure I heard him right.

I considered lying, wrapping up this most awkward of conversations. Instead, I said, "Not really."

His hand reached up, dug into his hair. "Close my office door," he said.

I nodded, oddly disappointed to be so quietly dismissed. "I'll bring the notes from legal for—"

"I mean close the door, but stay."

Oh.

Oh.

I turned, walking across the plush carpet in complete silence. His office door closed with a heavy click.

"Lock it."

I turned the lock and felt him move closer until his breath fanned warm across the back of my neck.

"Let me touch you. Let me do something."

He understood. He knew what he could give me—distraction, relief, pleasure in the face of surging panic. I didn't reply because I knew I didn't need to. I'd closed and locked the door after all.

But then I felt his lips, soft and pressing against my shoulder, up my neck. "You smell . . . amazing," he said, untying my dress where it fastened behind my neck. "I always smell like you for hours afterward."

He didn't add whether that was a good thing or a bad thing and I found that I didn't care. I liked that he smelled me even when I'd gone.

With his hands sliding to my hips, he turned me to face him and bent to kiss me in a single, smooth movement. This was different. His mouth was soft, almost asking. There was nothing tentative about the kiss—there was never anything tentative about him—but this kiss almost felt more adoring and less like a battle being lost.

He pushed my dress from my shoulders and it pooled at my feet as he stepped back, giving just enough room to let the cool air of his office wash his heat from my skin.

"You're beautiful."

Before I could process the soft delivery of these new words he threw me a smirk and leaned to kiss me as he grabbed my panties, twisted and ripped them.

This, we knew.

I reached for his pants but he stepped away, shaking his head. He moved his hand between my legs, found smooth, wet skin. His breath grew faster on my cheek and his fingers were somehow careful and hard, his words coming out deep, filthy, telling me I was beautiful, I was so dirty. Telling me I was a tease, and how good I made him feel.

He told me how much he craved the way I sound when I come.

And even when I did, gasping and clutching his shoulders through his suit, all I could think was that I wanted to touch him too. That I wanted to hear him get lost in me the same way. And it terrified me.

He withdrew his fingers, sweeping across my sensitive clit when he did, and eliciting an involuntary shudder.

"Sorry, sorry," he whispered in response, kissing my jaw, my chin, my—

"Don't." I said, turning my mouth away from his. The sudden intimacy he offered, on top of everything else today, was too bewildering, too much.

His forehead rested against mine for a few beats before he nodded, once. It wrecked me, suddenly, realizing that I'd always assumed he held the power and I held none, but in this moment I knew that I could have as much power over him as I wanted. I just had to be brave enough to take it.

"I'll be leaving town this weekend. I don't know how long I'll be gone."

"Well, then get back to work while you're here, Miss Mills."

ELEVEN

When Thursday morning dawned, I knew we needed to have some sort of discussion. I would be away from the office all day Friday, so today was our last day together before she left town. She'd been meeting with her advisor all morning, and I felt myself getting more and more anxious about . . . everything. I was pretty sure the interaction in my office the day before revealed to us both that she was slowly taking more and more of me. I wanted to be with her almost all of the time, and not just naked and wild. I just wanted to be *near* her, and my own need for self-preservation had been plaguing me all week.

What had she said? *I don't want to want this. This isn't good for me.* Only when Mina discovered us had I truly understood what Chloe meant. I'd hated my desire for her because it was the first time in my life I was unable to push something out of my head and focus on work, but no one—not even my family—would really blame me for being attracted to Chloe. In contrast, she would forever be tainted with the reputation of being the woman who slept her way to the top. For someone as brilliant and driven as she was, that association would be a constant—and painful—thorn in her side.

She was right to put distance between us. This pull we felt when we were together was entirely unhealthy. Nothing good could come from it, and I decided once again to use our time apart to regain my focus. When I entered my office after lunch I was surprised to find her seated at her desk busily working on the computer.

"I didn't know you would be in this afternoon," I said, trying to keep any emotion from my voice.

"Yes, I had some last-minute arrangements to handle for San Diego, and I still needed to discuss my absence with you," she said, never looking up from her computer monitor.

"Would you like to step into my office, then?"

"No," she said quickly. "I think we can handle this out here." Peeking up at me with a sly look she motioned to the chair opposite her. "Would you like to have a seat, Mr. Ryan?"

Ahhh, home-court advantage. I sat down across from her.

"I know you'll be out tomorrow, so there's no reason for me to be here. I realize you don't like having an assistant, but I've arranged for you to have a temp while I'm gone for two weeks, and I've already given Sara a detailed list of your schedule and the things you'll need. I doubt there will be any problems, but just in case, she's promised to keep an eye on you." She raised a brow in challenge and I rolled my eyes in return.

She continued, "You have my numbers, including the number of my father's home in Bismarck, if you need anything." She began going through a list in front of her, and I noticed how cool and efficient she was. It's not that I wasn't already aware of these things, but somehow it seemed a bit more apparent to me right now. Our eyes met and she continued, "I'll get into California a few hours before you, so I'll just plan on picking you up at the airport."

We continued to stare at each other for a few moments, and I was almost positive that our thoughts were the same: San Diego would be a colossal test.

The atmosphere in the room began to shift slowly, the silence saying more than words ever could. I clenched my jaw tightly as I noticed that her breathing had picked up. It took every bit of willpower I had to not walk around the desk and kiss her.

"Have a nice trip, Miss Mills," I said, pleased that my voice betrayed none of my inner turmoil. I stood and lingered for a moment, adding, "So, I'll meet you in San Diego then."

"Yes."

I nodded and walked into my office, shutting the door behind me. I didn't see her for the rest of the day and our terse good-bye for once felt completely wrong.

———

All weekend I thought about what it would be like to have her gone for two weeks. On the one hand, it would be nice to enjoy a full day at work without the distraction. On the other, I wondered if it would feel odd not having her there. She'd been a near constant in my life for almost a year, and regardless of our differences, it had become comforting to have her around.

Sara entered my office on Monday at nine o'clock sharp, smiling brightly as she approached me. She was followed by an attractive, twenty-something brunette who was introduced as Kelsey, my new temporary assistant. She looked up at me with a somewhat timid smile, and I saw Sara place a reassuring hand on her shoulder.

I decided that I would use this as an opportunity. I would prove to everyone that my reputation was simply a result of working with someone as headstrong as Miss Mills.

"It's very nice to meet you, Kelsey," I said, smiling widely and offering her my hand to shake. She looked at me strangely, with a sort of glazed expression.

"It's nice to meet you too, sir," she said as she glanced back at Sara. Sara looked down at my hand quizzically and back up to me before speaking to Kelsey.

"Okay. Well, we've already gone over everything that Chloe left. Here's your desk." She led the temp over to Miss Mills' chair.

A strange feeling crept over me at the image of someone else sitting there. I felt my smile falter and I turned to Sara. "If she needs anything she'll let you know. I'll be in my office."

Kelsey quit before lunch. Apparently I came off "a bit gruff" when she managed to start a small fire in the break room microwave. The last I saw of her, she was in tears and sprinting out my door, wailing something about a hostile work environment.

The second temp, a young man named Isaac, came in around two o'clock. Isaac seemed highly intelligent, and I looked forward to working with someone other than an emotional female. I found myself smiling at the sudden turn of events. Unfortunately, I spoke too soon.

Every time I passed Isaac at his computer he was online, looking at captioned pictures of cats or watching a music video. He would quickly minimize the window, but unfortunately for Isaac I wasn't a complete idiot. I diplomatically asked him to not bother returning the next day.

The third was no better. Her name was Jill; she talked too much, her clothing was too tight, and the way she gnawed on the cap of her pen made her look like an animal trying to free itself from a trap. It was nothing like the way Miss Mills would pensively hold the end of her pen between her teeth when she was deep in thought. That was subtle and sexy; this was nothing short of obscene. Unacceptable. She was gone by Tuesday afternoon.

The week continued on in much the same way. I went

through five different assistants. I heard the booming laugh of my brother in the hall outside my office on more than one occasion. *Jackass.* He didn't even work on this floor. I began to feel that people were enjoying my misery a bit too much and maybe even saw it as a case of reaping what I sowed.

Although I had absolutely no doubt that Miss Mills had already been informed of my temp nightmares by Sara, I received several texts from her throughout the first week, checking on how things were going. I began looking forward to them, even checking my phone periodically to see if I might have missed an alert. I hated to admit it, but at this point I would have traded my car just to have her and her harpy disposition back.

Besides missing her body, which I did desperately, I also missed the fire between us. She knew I was a bastard, and she put up with it. I had no idea why, but she did. I felt my respect for her professionalism grow during that first week apart.

When the second week went by without a single text from her, I found myself wondering what she was doing and with whom she was doing it. I wondered briefly if she'd had any more phone calls with Joel. I was pretty sure they hadn't seen each other again, and she and I had managed to reach a precarious cease-fire regarding the flower incident. Still, I wondered if he'd ever called to follow up and whether he would try to begin something when she was home.

Home. Was she at home now, with her father? Or did

she think of Chicago as home? For the first time, it occurred to me that if her father was very sick, she might decide to move back to North Dakota to be with him.

Fuck.

I started packing for my flight on Sunday night and heard my phone chirp from the bed next to my suitcase. I felt a small thrill reading her name on the screen.

Pick you up tomorrow 11:30. Terminal B near arrival screens. Text when you land.

I paused for a moment as it sank in that we would be together tomorrow.

I will. Thanks.

You're welcome. Everything go ok?

I was a bit taken aback that she had asked about the rest of my week. We were in such uncharted territory here. While working, we texted and e-mailed frequently, but it was usually restricted to simple yes or no answers. Never anything personal. Was it possible she'd had a similarly frustrating week?

Great. You? How is your dad?

I laughed as I pushed send; this situation kept getting stranger. Less than a minute later I received another one.

He's doing fine. I've missed him but am excited to come home.

Home. I noted her word choice and swallowed; my chest was suddenly too tight.

See you tomorrow.

Setting the alarm on my phone, I placed it on the night-stand and sat next to my luggage on the bed. I would see her in less than twelve hours.

And I wasn't entirely sure how I felt about that.

Twelve

Just as I'd hoped, the flight to San Diego had given me time to think. I felt loved and rested after my visit with my dad. After his appointment with the gastroenterologist put us both at ease that the tumor was benign, we'd spent time together talking and reminiscing about Mom, even planning a trip for him to come out to Chicago.

By the time he kissed me good-bye, I felt as prepared as possible considering the situation. I was nervous as hell to face Mr. Ryan again, but I'd given myself my best pep talk. I'd done some online shopping and had a suitcase full of new power panties. I'd thought long and hard about my options, and I was pretty sure I had a plan.

The first step was to admit that this problem was more than just the temptation of proximity. Being a thousand miles apart had done nothing to calm my need. I'd dreamed of him nearly every night, waking each morning frustrated and lonely. I spent far too much time thinking about what he was doing, wondering if he was as confused as me, and trying to glean every bit of information I could from Sara about how things were going back home.

Sara and I had an interesting conversation when she'd called and informed me of the status of my replacement. I'd laughed hysterically hearing about the revolving door of temps. Of course Bennett was having a hard time keeping anyone around. He was an asshole.

I was used to his mood swings and gruff attitude; professionally our relationship ran like clockwork. It was the personal side that was a nightmare. Almost everyone knew it; they just didn't know the extent of the situation.

I thought back often to our last day together. Something in our relationship was shifting, and I wasn't sure how I felt about it. No matter how many times we said it would never happen again, it would. I was terrified that this man, who was all wrong for me, had more control over my body than I did, no matter how much I tried to convince myself otherwise.

I didn't want to be the woman who sacrificed her ambitions for a man.

Standing in the arrival area, I gave myself one last pep talk. I could do this. Oh, God, I hoped I could do this. The butterflies in my stomach were working overtime and I briefly worried I might throw up.

His plane had been delayed in Chicago and it was after six thirty before he finally touched down in San Diego. While the time on the plane out had been good for thinking, the seven extra hours waiting afterward had only reignited my nerves.

I stood on my tiptoes trying to get a better view through the crowd, but didn't see him. Looking down at my phone, I reread his text again.

Just landed—see you in a few.

There was nothing sentimental about the text, but it made my stomach flip anyway. Our messages last night had been the same. It wasn't that we said anything special: I'd simply asked how the rest of his week had gone. That wouldn't be considered unusual in any other relationship, but it was totally new for us. Maybe there was a chance we could actually get past the constant animosity and actually be, what—*friends*?

With my stomach in knots, I paced back and forth, willing my mind to switch gears and my heart rate to calm. Without thinking, I stopped midstep and turned toward the oncoming crowd, searching through the sea of unknown faces. My breath caught in my throat when a head of familiar hair appeared above the others.

Get ahold of yourself, Chloe. Jesus.

I tried once more to get my body under control

and looked up again. *Fuck. I am so screwed.* There he was, looking better than I'd ever seen him. How the hell does someone get better looking in nine days, and coming off of an airplane no less?

He stood nearly a head taller than anyone around him, the kind of tall that stands out in a crowd, and I gave thanks to the universe for that. His dark hair was a nightmare as usual; no doubt he'd had his hands in it a hundred times during the last hour. He wore dark slacks, a charcoal blazer, and a white dress shirt that was unbuttoned at the neck. He looked tired and had a bit of stubble on his face, but that wasn't what had my heart beating a mile a minute. He'd been looking down at the ground, but the moment our eyes met, his face split into the most genuinely happy smile I'd ever seen. Before I could stop it, I felt my own smile explode, wide and giddy.

He stopped in front of me, a slightly tenser look taking over his features, while both of us waited for the other to say something.

"Hi," I said awkwardly, trying to ease some of the tension between us. Every part of me wanted to pull him into the ladies' room, but somehow I doubted that was the proper way to great your boss. Not that that had ever mattered before.

"Um, hi," he answered, his brow furrowed slightly.

Fuck, snap out of it, Chloe! We both turned, head-

185

ing toward the baggage claim, and I felt goose bumps spread across my skin just being near him.

"How was your flight?" I asked, knowing how much he hated flying commercial airlines, even if it was first class. This was so ridiculous. I wished he would just say something asinine so I could go back to yelling at him.

He thought about it for a moment before answering, "It was pleasant enough, once we actually got off the ground. I don't like how crowded the planes are." We stopped and waited, surrounded by bustling people, but the only thing I noticed was the tension building between us, and every inch of space between our bodies. "And your father's health?" he asked a moment later.

I nodded. "Benign. Thanks for asking."

"Of course."

Minutes passed in uncomfortable silence and I was more than a bit relieved when I saw his luggage slide down the conveyor belt. We both reached for it at the same time and our hands touched briefly on the handle. Pulling back, I glanced up to find he was watching me.

My stomach dropped at the familiar look of hunger in his eyes. We both muttered apologies and I looked away, but not before noticing the slight smirk on his face. Fortunately, it was time to pick up the rental car, and we headed to the parking garage.

He looked pleased as we approached the luxury rental, a Benz SLS AMG. He loved to drive—well, he loved to drive fast—and I always made a point of ordering something fun for him when he needed a car.

"Very nice, Miss Mills," he said, his hand sliding along the hood. "Remind me to think about giving you a raise."

I felt the familiar desire to punch him spread through my body and it calmed me. Everything was so much clearer when he was being an outright douche.

Pressing the button to release the trunk I gave him a reproachful look and stepped aside for him to put his things away. He took off his jacket and handed it to me. I shoved it into the trunk.

"Careful," he admonished.

"I'm not a bellhop. Put your own damn coat away."

He laughed and bent to lift his suitcase. "Christ, I'd just wanted you to hold it for a moment."

"Oh." With cheeks flushed at my overreaction, I reached in and grabbed the coat, smoothing it over my arm. "Sorry."

"Why do you always assume I'm being a jerk?"

"Because you usually are?"

With another laugh, he hoisted the suitcase into the trunk. "You must have missed me a lot."

I started to answer but got distracted instead watching the muscles of his back tighten his shirt as he placed his luggage in the trunk next to mine. Up close, I saw that the dress shirt had a subtle gray print and was tailored to fit his broad shoulders and narrow waist without any extra fabric bunching anywhere. His pants were dark gray and crisply pressed. I was pretty sure he'd never done his own laundry—and damn, who would blame him when tailored, dry-cleaned clothes made him so completely fuckable?

Stop. Stop!

He closed the trunk with a slam, breaking me out of my daze, and I placed the keys in his waiting hand. He walked over and opened my door, waiting for me to be seated before closing it behind me. *Yeah, you're a real gentleman,* I thought.

We drove in silence, the only sound provided by the purr of the engine and the GPS calling out directions to the hotel. I busied myself going over our schedule, trying to ignore the man next to me.

I wanted to look at him, to study his face. I wanted to reach out and touch the slight stubble on his jaw, to tell him to pull over and touch me.

All these thoughts ran through my mind, making it impossible to concentrate on the papers in front of me. The time apart hadn't lessened his hold over me at all. If anything it made it stronger. I wanted to ask him how the last two weeks had been. I actually wanted to know how he was.

With a sigh, I closed the folder in my lap and turned to look out the window.

We must have passed ocean and navy ships and people on the streets, but I didn't see a thing. The only thing on my mind was what was inside the car. I felt every movement, every breath. His fingers tapped along the steering wheel. The leather squeaked when he shifted in his seat. His scent filled the closed space and made it impossible to remember why I needed to resist. He completely surrounded me.

I needed to be strong and be my own person, to prove that I controlled my path in life, but every part of me ached to feel him. I needed to regroup at the hotel before this conference, but with him so close, all my best intentions got away from me.

"Are you okay, Miss Mills?" The sound of his voice startled me and I turned to meet his hazel eyes, my stomach fluttering at the intensity behind them. How had I forgotten how long his lashes were?

"We're here." He motioned to the hotel, and I was surprised to see I hadn't even noticed. "Is everything all right?"

"Yeah," I answered quickly. "Just been a long day."

"Hmm," he murmured, continuing to look at me. I saw his gaze flicker to my mouth, and *God*, I wanted him to kiss me. I missed the command of his mouth on mine, as if there were nothing in the world he wanted more than to taste me. And sometimes, I suspected that might actually be true.

As if drawn to him, I leaned forward in my seat. A hum of electricity buzzed between us, and his gaze flickered back to my eyes. He leaned in to meet me, and I could feel his hot breath against my mouth.

Suddenly my door opened and I jumped back into my seat, shocked to see the valet standing there expectantly, hand outstretched. I stepped out of the car, inhaling the air that wasn't permeated by his intoxicating scent. The valet took the bags, and Mr. Ryan excused himself to take a phone call while I checked us in.

The hotel was packed with fellow conference attendees, and I saw several familiar faces. I had made plans to meet up with a group of other students in my program sometime on the trip. I waved to a woman I recognized; it would be great to get out with some friends while we were here. The last thing I needed was to sit alone in my hotel room and fantasize about the man down the hall.

After receiving our keys and seeing that the bellhop would take our bags to our rooms, I headed to the lounge in search of Mr. Ryan. The welcome reception was in full swing, and when I scanned the large room I found him standing next to a tall brunette. They stood close together, his head bent slightly as he listened to her.

His head blocked her face from my view, and my eyes narrowed when I noticed her hand reach up and grip his forearm. She laughed at something he'd said and he pulled away slightly, allowing me a better look.

She was beautiful, with shoulder-length, straight dark hair. As I watched, she placed something in his hand and folded his fingers around it. A strange look crossed his face as he bent his head to examine the object in his palm.

You have got to be kidding me. Did she—did she just give him her room key?

I watched for a moment more, and then something inside me snapped as he continued to stare at the key as if he was considering pocketing it. The thought of him looking at someone else with the same intensity, the thought of him *wanting* someone else at all, made my stomach twist with anger. Before I could stop myself, I was moving across the room until I stood beside them.

I placed my hand on his forearm, and he blinked over to me, a surprised, questioning expression on his face. "Bennett, are you ready to head upstairs?" I asked quietly.

His eyes widened and his mouth opened in shock. I'd never seen him look so utterly at a loss for words.

And then I realized: I'd never said his name before.

"Bennett?" I asked once more, and something flickered across his face. Slowly, the corner of his mouth lifted into a smile and our eyes locked for a moment.

Turning back to her, he smiled indulgently and spoke in a voice so smooth it sent a tremor through me. "Excuse us," he said, discreetly placing her key back in her hand. "As you can see, I didn't come here alone."

The bright pulse of victory in my chest completely overshadowed the horror I should have been feeling. He pressed his warm hand to the small of my back as he led us out of the lounge and down the hall. But the closer we got to the elevators, the more my elation was replaced with something else. I began to panic as I realized how irrationally I had acted.

The reminder of our constant cat-and-mouse game exhausted me. How many times a year did he travel? And how often would he get a room key pressed into his palm? Would I be there every time to pull him back? If I wasn't, would he happily skip upstairs with someone else?

And, truly, who the fuck did I think I could be to him? I shouldn't care!

My heart was racing, the sound of my blood rushing in my ears. Three other couples joined us in the elevator, and I prayed I could make it to my room before I exploded. I couldn't believe what I'd just done. I glanced up to see him wearing a triumphant smirk.

I took a deep breath and tried to remind myself

that this was exactly why I needed to stay away. What happened down there was completely out of character for me, and completely unprofessional of both of us in such a public work setting. I wanted to scream at him, to hurt him and enrage him like he had me, but it was getting harder and harder to find the will.

We rode up in tense silence, until the last couple stepped out, leaving us alone. I closed my eyes, just trying to breathe, but of course all I could smell was him. I didn't want him with someone else, and that feeling was so overwhelming that it took my breath away. And it was terrifying, because if I was to be honest, he could break my heart.

He could break me.

The elevator stopped and with a quiet ding, the doors opened at our floor.

"Chloe?" he prompted, his hand pressed to my back.

I turned, rushing out of the elevator.

"Where are you going?" he shouted after me. I heard his footsteps and knew there was going to be trouble. "Chloe, wait!"

I couldn't outrun him forever. I wasn't even sure I wanted to anymore.

THIRTEEN

A million thoughts ran through my mind in that second. We couldn't keep doing this. Either this would continue or it had to stop. *Now.* It was interfering with my business, my sleep, my head—my fucking life.

But no matter how much I tried to kid myself, I knew what I wanted. I couldn't let her leave.

She practically sprinted down the hall but I chased after her. "You can't pull something like that and then expect me to just let you walk away!"

"The hell I can't!" she yelled over her shoulder. She reached her room and fumbled with her key before shoving it into the slot.

I reached the door just as she got it open, meeting her eyes briefly before she ran in and tried to force it closed. My hand shot out, pushing it open so violently that it crashed into the wall behind it.

"What the *fuck* do you think you're doing?" she yelled. She stepped into the bathroom opposite the door and spun around to face me.

"Will you quit running from me?" I followed her, my voice echoing in the small space. "If this is about that woman downstairs—"

She looked impossibly more furious at my words and took a step toward me. "Don't you dare go there. I have never acted like a jealous girlfriend." She shook her head in disgust before turning to the counter and rummaging through her purse.

I stared at her she grew more and more frustrated. What else could this be about? I was completely bewildered. Her anger usually had me slammed against something and half naked by now. Here, she seemed genuinely upset. "You think I would be interested in any random woman who puts her room key in my hand? What the hell kind of man do you think I am?"

She slammed a brush on the counter, looking up at me furiously. "Are you serious right now? I know you've done this before. Just sex, no strings attached—I'm sure you get room keys all the time."

I started to reply, because in all honesty I had been in relationships that were strictly about the sex, but this thing with Chloe hadn't been *just* sex for a while now.

But she cut me off. "I've never done anything close to this and I don't know how to navigate it anymore," she said, her voice getting louder with each word. "But when I'm with you, it's like nothing else matters. This . . . this *thing*," she continued, gesturing between us, "this isn't me! It's like I turn into a different person when I'm with you, and I *hate* it. I can't do it, Bennett. I don't like who I'm becoming. I work hard. I care about my job. I'm smart. None of that would matter if people knew what was happening between us. Go find someone else."

"I already told you, I haven't been with anyone since we started this."

"That doesn't mean you won't take a room key if it's put in your hand. What would you have done if I hadn't been there?"

Without hesitation, I said, "Handed it back."

But she just laughed, clearly disbelieving. "Look. This whole thing exhausts me right now. I just want to take a shower and go to bed."

It was nearly impossible to imagine walking away from her and leaving this unresolved, but she'd already moved away and was turning on the shower. Just as I reached the door to the hall, I glanced back to where she stood, already surrounded by steam, watching me leave. And fuck if she didn't look as conflicted as I felt.

Without thinking I crossed the room, gripped her face between my hands, and pulled her to me. When our lips met, she made a strangled sound of surrender, immediately digging her hands into my hair. I kissed her harder, claiming her sounds as my own, making her lips mine, her taste all mine.

"Let's call a truce for one night," I said, pressing three

small kisses on her lips, one on each side and a lingering one in the middle, in the heart of her mouth "Give me all of you for one night, no holding back. Please, Chloe, I'll leave you alone after that but I haven't seen you in almost two weeks and . . . I just need tonight."

She stared at me for several painful beats, clearly struggling. And then, with a quiet, pleading sound, she reached up and pulled me to her, standing on her toes to get as close as she could.

My lips were rough and unyielding but she didn't move away, pressing her curves into me. I was lost to everything but her. We bumped into a wall, the counter, the shower door, shifting and pulling in our desperation. The room was completely filled with steam now, and nothing seemed real. I could smell, taste, and feel her, but none of it was enough.

Our kisses grew deeper, our touches wilder. I grabbed her ass, her thighs, slid my hands up and over her breasts, needing every part of her in my palms simultaneously. She pushed me back against the wall and a rush of warmth cascaded across my shoulder and down my chest, bringing me out of my haze. With our clothes still on, we had backed into the shower. We were getting soaked.

We didn't care.

Her hands roamed my body frantically, yanking my shirt from my pants. With shaky hands she unbuttoned it, tearing off some buttons in her haste before sliding the wet fabric from my shoulders and tossing it outside the shower door.

The wet silk of her dress clung to her, accentuating every curve. I traced the fabric along her breasts, feeling her tight nipples underneath. She moaned and brought her hand to rest on mine, guiding my movements.

"Tell me what you want." My voice was rough with need. "Tell me the things you want me to do to you."

"I don't know," she whispered into my mouth. "I just want to see you come apart."

I wanted to tell her that she was witnessing it now, and in all honesty she'd been watching it happen for weeks, but words fell away as I skimmed my hands down her sides and up under her dress. We teased and bit at each other's mouths, the sound of the shower drowning out our moans. I slipped my hands into her panties and felt her warmth against my fingers.

Needing to see more of her, I removed my fingers and slid them up to the hem of her dress. In one movement I pulled it up and over her head and stopped dead in my tracks at the sight of what lay underneath. *Sweet Jesus.* She was trying to kill me.

I took a step back, leaning against the shower wall for support. She stood before me, soaking wet in white lace panties that tied on the side with a satin bow. Her nipples were hard and visible beneath the matching bra, and I couldn't stop myself from reaching out to touch them.

"Fuck, you are so beautiful," I said, running my fingertips along her taut breasts. A visible shiver ran through her and my hand traveled upward, across her collarbone, along her neck, and finally to her jaw.

We could fuck right here, wet and slippery against the tile, and maybe we would later, but right now I wanted to take my time. My heart sped up at the thought that we had an entire night ahead of us. No rushing out or hiding. No bitter fighting and guilt. We had one whole night alone and I was going to spend the entire time with her . . . in a bed.

I reached behind her and turned off the shower. She pushed against me, pressing her body further into mine. I cradled her face in my hands and kissed her deeply, my tongue sliding easily against hers. Her hips rocked against me and I pushed the shower door open, holding on to her as we stepped out.

I couldn't seem to stop touching her skin: down her back, over the gentle curve of her backside, back up again along her sides to her breasts. I needed to feel, to taste every inch of her skin.

Our kiss never broke as we made our way out of the bathroom, stumbling clumsily while we desperately tore at our remaining clothes. I kicked off my wet shoes as I backed her into the bedroom, her hands raking along my stomach as she reached for my belt. Guiding her, I was quickly free of my pants and boxers. In a rush, I kicked them to the side, where they landed in a wet pile.

I traced along her ribs with my knuckles before sliding to

the clasp of her bra, releasing it and practically ripping it off her body. Pulling her closer, I groaned into her mouth as her hard nipples grazed my chest. The tips of her wet hair tickled my hands as they roamed her naked back, felt electric against my skin.

The room was dark, the only illumination coming from the small sliver of light that crept out from the bathroom door and the moon in the night sky. The back of her knees hit the bed and my hands ran down to the last piece of clothing between us. My mouth moved from her lips, down her neck, and across her breasts and torso. I placed soft biting kisses across her stomach and finally to the white lace that hid the rest of her from view.

Sliding to my knees in front of her, I looked up and met her eyes. Her hands were in my hair, running her fingers through the messy, wet strands.

Reaching out, I took one delicate satin ribbon between my fingers and pulled, watching it slide off her hip. A look of confusion crossed her face as I continued running my fingers along the lace edge to the other side and did the same. The fabric fell from her body undamaged until she was completely naked before me. I might not have destroyed them, but she could be damn sure I planned to take these pretties with me.

She laughed, seeming to read my mind.

I guided her back so that she sat on the edge of the bed

and, still kneeling in front of her, I spread her legs. Running my hands down along the silky skin of her calves, I planted kisses along her thighs and between her legs. Her taste slid around my mouth and inside my head, erasing everything else. Fuck, what this woman did to me.

Pushing her back to lie across the sheets I finally moved up to join her, running my lips and tongue along her body, her hands still tangling in my hair, guiding where she wanted me most. I slipped my thumb into her mouth, needing her sucking on me somewhere, needing my own mouth on her breasts, her ribs, her jaw.

Her sighs and moans filled the room and mingled with my own. I was harder than I could ever remember being, and I wanted to bury myself in her over and over again. I reached her mouth and dragged my wet thumb across her cheek when she pulled me down to her, every inch of our naked bodies aligned.

We kissed frantically, hands seeking and grasping as we tried to get as close as possible. Our hips rocked together, my cock sliding against her soaking heat. Each pass along her clit elicited a moan. With one tiny move, I could be deep inside.

And I wanted that more than anything, but I needed to hear something from her first. When she'd said my name downstairs, it had set something off inside me. I didn't un-derstand it yet, didn't know if it meant something I wasn't completely ready to explore, but I knew I needed her to say it, to hear it was me she wanted. I needed to know that for tonight, she was mine.

"I am fucking dying to be inside you right now," I whispered into her ear. Her breath caught and a deep moan escaped her lips. "Is that what you want?"

"Yes," she whimpered, her voice pleading and her hips rocked higher off the bed in search of me. My tip grazed her entrance and I clenched my jaw, wanting to prolong this. Her heels ran up and down my legs, finally locking around my waist. I took each of her hands and placed them above her head, entwining our fingers.

"Please, Bennett," she begged. "I'm losing my mind."

I lowered my head so our foreheads touched and I finally pushed deep inside her.

"Oh, fuck," she moaned.

"Say it again." I was becoming breathless as I began to move in and out of her.

"Bennett—*fuck*."

I wanted to hear it again and again. I pulled myself up on my knees and began thrusting into her more steadily, both of our hands still entwined.

"I can't get enough of this." I was getting close and I needed to hold out. I'd been away from her too long, and nothing I'd fantasized about while she was away compared to this.

"I want you like this every day," I growled against her damp skin. "Like this, and bent over my desk. On your knees sucking my dick."

"Why?" she hissed between clenched teeth. "Why do I love it when you talk to me like that? You're such a *prick*."

I lowered myself onto her again, laughing into her neck.

We moved together effortlessly, sweat-slicked skin sliding against skin. With each thrust she raised her hips to meet me, her legs around my waist pulling me deeper. I was so lost in her that time seemed to stop. Our hands were still tightly clasped above her head and she began gripping tighter. She was getting close, her cries becoming louder and my name leaving her lips over and over, pushing me closer to the edge.

"Give it up." My voice was ragged with the desperation I felt. I was so close but I wanted to wait for her. "Let go, Chloe, come all over me."

"Oh, God, Bennett," she moaned. "Say something else." *Fuck. My girl got off on dirty talk.* "Please."

"You're so fucking slippery and hot. When you get close," I panted, "your skin flushes everywhere and your voice gets hoarse. And there is nothing more fucking perfect than your face when you come."

She squeezed me harder with her legs and I felt her breath hitch, felt her tighten around me.

"Your fucking bee-stung lips go all soft and open when

you pant for me, your eyes begging me to make it good and, fuck, nothing is better than the sound you make when you're finally there."

That was all it took. I deepened my strokes, lifting her off the bed with every thrust. I was teetering on the edge now, and when she cried out my name, I couldn't hold back any longer.

She muffled her screams against my neck as I felt her let go, clenching wildly beneath me—nothing in the world felt as good as this, letting the rush build inside and crash over us, together—and I let go too.

Afterward, I moved my face close to hers, our noses touching, breath coming out hard and fast. My mouth was dry, my muscles ached, and I was exhausted. I loosened her grip on my hands and rubbed her fingers gently, trying to bring some of the circulation back.

"Holy shit," I said. Everything felt different, but completely undefined. Rolling off her, I closed my eyes, trying to block out the tangle of thoughts.

Beside me, she shivered.

"Cold?" I asked.

"No," she answered, shaking her head. "Just really overwhelmed."

I pulled her to me and reached down, dragging the blankets over us. I didn't want to leave, but I wasn't sure if I was welcome to stay either. "Me too."

The silence stretched between us as did the minutes,

and I wondered if she'd fallen asleep. I shifted slightly and was surprised to hear her voice. "Don't go," she said into the darkness. I bent, kissed the top of her head, and inhaled her sweet, familiar scent.

"I'm not going anywhere."

———

Fuck, that felt good.

Something warm and wet enveloped my dick again and I groaned loudly. *Best. Dream. Ever.* Dream Chloe moaned, sending a vibration along my dick and straight through me.

"Chloe." I heard my own voice and jerked slightly. I'd dreamed of her hundreds of times but this seemed so real. The warmth disappeared and I frowned. *Don't wake up, Ben. Don't fucking wake up from this.*

"Say it again." A soft, throaty voice broke into my consciousness and I forced myself to open my eyes. The room was dark and I was lying in a strange bed. The warmth was back and my eyes flew to my lap, where a beautiful dark head of hair moved between my open legs. She sucked my cock back into her mouth.

In a rush, the entire night came back to me, the haze of sleep rapidly disappearing.

"Chloe?" There was no way I could be lucky enough for this to be real.

She must have gotten up sometime in the night to shut off the bathroom light; the room was so dark I could barely make her out. My hands drifted out to find her, my fingers tracing her lips around my cock.

She bobbed her mouth up and down on me, her tongue swirling and her teeth raking lightly against my shaft with each movement. Her hand slipped to my balls and I moaned loudly as she rolled them gently in her palm.

The feeling was so intense, the realization of my dreams and reality coming together, that I didn't know how long I could last. She moved slightly, her finger lightly rubbing a spot just below, and a long hiss escaped my clenched teeth. No one had ever done that to me. I almost wanted to stop her, but the feeling was so incredible I was helpless to move.

While my eyes adjusted to the light, I ran my fingers through her hair and across her face and jaw. She closed her eyes and increased the suction, bringing me closer and closer to the edge. The combination of her mouth on my dick and her finger pressing against me was unreal, but I wanted her up with me, that mouth on my mouth, sucking my lips while I buried myself in her.

Sitting up, I pulled her into my lap, wrapping her legs around my hips. Our naked chests pressed together, I took her face in my hands, looking into her eyes. "That is the best wake-up call I've ever gotten."

She laughed a little, licking her lips to a delicious shine. Reaching down I placed my cock at her entrance and lifted her slightly. In one smooth motion I was deep inside her.

Her forehead fell to my shoulder and she rocked her hips forward, taking me further inside.

Being with her in a bed was unreal. She was leisurely riding me, grinding in tiny movements. She kissed along every inch of the right side of my neck, sucking and pulling at my skin. Short utterances punctuated every circuit of her hips.

". . . like being on top of you," she breathed. "Feel how deep you are? Feel that?"

"Yeah."

"Want faster?"

I shook my head, absolutely lost. "No. God, no."

For a while, she stayed slow, tiny circles, teeth all up and down my neck. But then she shifted closer, whispering, "I'm gonna come, Bennett," and instead of releasing a string of curse words to describe what hearing that did to me, I bit her shoulder, sucked a bruise into her skin.

Working me harder now, she began to talk. Words I could barely process. Words about my body inside her, her need for me. Words about my taste and how wet she was. Words about wanting me to come, *needing* me to come.

With each swivel of her hips, the pressure began to build. I gripped her tighter, fearing briefly that I would leave bruises every time I moved my hands, and quickened my thrusts. She moaned and writhed above me and just when I thought I couldn't hold out anymore, she called my name again and I felt her begin to spasm around me. The intensity of her orgasm brought on my own, and I moved my face to her neck, pressing a loud groan into her skin.

She collapsed against me and I lowered us both to the bed. We were sweaty and panting and utterly exhausted, and she looked fucking perfect.

I pulled her to me, her back pressed against my chest, and wrapped my arms around her, entangling my legs with hers. She mumbled something I couldn't make out but was asleep before I could ask her.

Something had shifted tonight, and my last thought as my eyes closed was that there would be plenty of time to talk tomorrow. But as the early morning sunlight began to creep under the dark curtain, I realized with an uneasy feeling that tomorrow was already here.

Fourteen

Consciousness fluttered on the edge of my sleep-filled mind, and I tried to force it away. I didn't want to wake up. I was warm and comfortable and content.

Vague visions of my dream passed behind my closed eyes as I snuggled into the warmest, best-smelling blanket I'd ever slept in. It snuggled back.

Something warm pressed against me, and my eyes fluttered open to see a head of familiar messy hair inches from my face. A hundred images flashed through my mind in that second as the reality of last night came crashing down on my muddled brain.

Holy shit.

It was real.

My heart rate quickened as I lifted my head slightly to see the beautiful man wrapped around me. His head lay on my chest, his perfect mouth parted slightly, releasing puffs of warm air across my bare breasts. His long body lay flush against mine, our legs tangled together and his strong arms wrapped tightly around my torso.

He stayed.

The intimacy of our position hit with a crushing force that actually took my breath away. He didn't just stay, he *clung* to me.

I struggled to find my breath and not panic. I was keenly aware of each inch of where our skin touched. I felt the powerful thump of his heartbeat against my chest. His cock was pressed against my thigh, semihard in his sleep. My fingers burned to touch him. My lips ached to press against his hair. It was too much. He was too much.

Something changed last night and I wasn't sure I was ready to deal with it. I didn't know what that change entailed, but it was there. In every move, every touch, every word, and every kiss, we had been together. Nobody had ever made me feel that way, as if my body were made to fit his.

I'd been with other men, but with him I felt as if I was being carried away by a hidden undertow, completely unable to change the course. I closed my eyes, trying to quell the sense of panic that was building. I didn't regret what happened. It was—as always—intense and easily the best sex I'd ever had. I just needed a few minutes alone before I could face him.

Placing one hand into his hair and the other on his

back, I managed to roll him off me. He began to stir and I froze, holding him close and silently willing him to go back to sleep. He mumbled my name before his breathing evened out again, and I slipped out from underneath him.

I watched him sleep for a moment, the panic receding somewhat, and was once again struck by just how gorgeous he was. Stilled by sleep, his features were tranquil and peaceful, and so very different from any expression he ever wore around me. A thick curl had fallen down across his forehead, and my fingers itched to brush it back. Long lashes, perfect cheekbones, full pouty lips, and a stubble-covered jaw.

Christ on a cracker, he's pretty.

I started to make my way to the bathroom but caught my reflection in the mirror over the bedroom vanity.

Wow. Freshly fucked. That was definitely how I looked.

Leaning in, I examined the small red scrapes that were scattered along my neck, shoulders, breasts, and stomach. A small bite mark was visible on the underside of my left breast, a hickey on my shoulder. Glancing down, I ran my fingers along the red marks on my inner thigh. My nipples hardened as I recalled the feeling of his unshaven face brushing along my skin.

My hair was a wild and tangled mess, and I bit my

lip as I remembered his hands twisted in it. The way he pulled me first into his kiss and then onto his cock . . .

Not helping.

I was jolted out of my thoughts by a voice thick with sleep. "Awake and freaking out already?"

Turning, I caught a glimpse of his naked body as he twisted in the sheets and sat up before pulling them over his hips and leaving his torso bare. I didn't think I would ever get tired of looking at—and feeling—his broad, muscular chest, washboard abs, and tantalizing happy trail that led to the most gloriously hung man ever seen. When my eyes—finally—reached his face, I scowled at his lopsided grin.

"Caught you looking," he murmured, rubbing a hand over his jaw.

I wasn't sure whether to smile or roll my eyes. Seeing him rumpled and vulnerable in his half-awake state was disorienting. We never bothered to close the heaviest drapes last night, and now sunlight streamed in, blindingly bright against the tangle of white linens. He looked so different—still my asshole boss, but also someone else now: a man, in my bed, looking like he was ready for round . . . four? Five? I couldn't keep track.

And as his eyes raked over every inch of me, I remembered that I too was completely naked. In this moment, his expression was as intense as his touch. I briefly wondered, if he continued to look at me like that, would my skin ignite? Would I feel his touch on my flesh the same as when he put his hands on me?

I fixed my expression into something I hoped camouflaged that I was mentally cataloging every inch of his skin and bent over to retrieve his white undershirt off the floor. It had been in front of the air conditioner all night and was a little cold but, thankfully, mostly dry. When I slipped the soft cotton over my head, I inhaled the sagey scent of his skin and then emerged, catching his dark stare.

His tongue darted out to wet his lips. "Come here," he growled quietly.

I moved to the bed, intending to sit beside him, but he pulled me so I straddled his thighs, and said, "Tell me what you're thinking."

He wanted me to condense a million thoughts into a single sentence? The man was insane.

So I opened my mouth and let the first thought out: "You said you haven't been with anyone since we were first . . . together." I stared at his collarbone so I wouldn't have to look him in the eye. "Is that true?"

Finally, I looked up.

He nodded and slipped his fingers beneath the undershirt, running his hands slowly from my hips to my waist.

"Why?" I asked.

He closed his eyes, shook his head once. "I haven't wanted anyone else."

I wasn't sure how to interpret that. Did he mean he hadn't met anyone he wanted but was open to it? "Are you usually monogamous if you're sleeping with someone?"

He shrugged. "If that's the expectation."

Bennett kissed along my shoulder, to my collarbone and up my neck. I reached around him, grabbing the complimentary bottle of water on the nightstand and taking a sip before handing it to him. He finished it in a few long swallows.

"Thirsty?"

"I was. Feeling a little hungry now."

"Not surprising, we haven't eaten in like—" I stopped as he wiggled his eyebrows and grinned.

I rolled my eyes, but they fell closed as he leaned forward and kissed me once, sweetly, on the lips.

"Is monogamy the expectation here?" I asked.

"After what happened last night, I think you need to tell me."

I didn't know how to answer that. I wasn't even sure I could be with him like this, let alone be monogamous about it. The idea of how that would work made my head spin. Would we actually be . . . friendly? Would he say, "Good morning," and mean it? Would he feel safe criticizing my work?

He spread his fingers over my lower back, pressing me into his side and pulling me out of my rambling thoughts. "Never take this off," he whispered.

"Deal." I leaned back to give his mouth better access to my throat. "I'll wear this and nothing else down to the poster session this morning."

His laugh was low and playful. "Like hell you will."

"What time is it?" I asked, trying to see behind him to the clock.

"Don't give a shit." His fingertips found my breast, and slipped back and forth over the soft underside.

But in the process of leaning away from him, I'd exposed the skin just above his hip. *What the hell?*

Was that a *tattoo*?

"What is—?" I could barely form the words. Pushing him away slightly, I looked up to meet his eyes before returning them to the mark. Right below his hipbone was a string of black ink, words written in what I guessed was French. How the hell had I missed that? I thought back briefly to all the times we'd been together. We'd always been rushed, or in the dark, or in only a state of semiundress.

"It's a tattoo," he said, bemused, pulling back a bit and trailing his fingers over my navel.

"I know it's a tattoo, but . . . what does it say?" *Mr. Serious Business had a fucking tattoo.* Another piece of the man I thought I knew fell away.

"It says, 'Je ne regrette rien.'"

My eyes flew to his, my blood heating at the sound of his voice dissolving into a perfect French accent. "What did you say?"

He definitely smirked. "Je ne regrette rien." He spoke each word slowly, emphasizing every syllable. It had to be the sexiest fucking thing I'd ever heard. Between that and the tattoo and the fact that he was completely naked under me, I was going to spontaneously combust.

"Isn't that a song?"

He nodded. "It's a song, yes." Laughing quietly he said, "You might think I'd regret that one drunken night in Paris, thousands of miles from home, without a single friend in the city, I decide to go get a tattoo. But no, I don't even regret that."

"Say it again," I whispered.

He moved closer, hips rolling against mine, his breath hot in my ear, and whispered it again. "Je ne regrette rien. Do you understand?"

I nodded. "Say something else." My breasts were heaving with each labored breath, my sensitive nipples grazing against the cotton of his shirt.

Bending slightly, he kissed my ear, saying, "Je suis à toi." His voice was strained and gravelly as he held himself up for me and I put us both out of our misery, sinking down over him with a groan, and loving the depth of this position again. He whispered a single, profane syllable over and over, staring up at me. Instead of clutching my hips, his hands fisted the shirt at my sides.

It was so easy, so natural between us, that it somehow just added to the space of uneasiness that I couldn't seem to shake. Instead of focusing on that, I focused on his quiet grunts into my mouth. I focused on the way he sat us up abruptly and sucked on my breasts through his shirt, exposing the pink beneath. I got lost in his urgent fingers on my hips and thighs, his forehead pressed to my collarbone as he got closer. I got lost in the feel of his thighs under me, his hips moving faster and harder to meet every one of my movements.

Flipping me over, he spread his hand flat on my chest, hips stilling. "Your heart is *pounding*. Tell me how fucking good this feels."

Instinctively, I relaxed when I looked up at his cocky grin. Did he know I needed some reminder of who we'd been less than a day ago? "You're doing that talking thing again. Stop."

His smile widened. "You love my talking. You especially love it when it coincides with my dick being in you."

I rolled my eyes. "What gave that away? The orgasms? The way I ask you for it? Good sleuthing."

He winked, pulling my foot up to his shoulder and kissing the inside of my ankle.

"Have you always been this way?" I asked, tugging uselessly on his hips. I hated to admit it, but I wanted him moving. When he was still, it teased, it was sore, it felt incomplete. When he moved I just wanted time to freeze. "I pity the females whose discarded egos litter the path."

Bennett shook his head, leaning over me and propping himself up on his hands. Mercifully, he started moving, hips shifting forward and up, pushing deep into me. My eyes rolled closed. He hit the perfect spot again and again and again.

"Look at me," he whispered.

I looked up, watched the sweat bead on his brow, his lips part as he stared at my mouth. Shoulder muscles bunched as he moved, his torso shone with a thin layer of sweat, and I watched where he moved in and out of me. I'm not sure what I said when he pulled almost all the way out and then pushed hard back into me, but it was quiet and filthy and instantly forgotten as he pounded into me. "*You* make me feel cocky. It's the way you react to me that makes me feel like a fucking god. How can you not see that?"

I didn't answer, and clearly he didn't expect me to, his gaze and the fingers of one hand drifting down my neck and over my breasts. He found a particularly sensitive spot and I gasped.

"It looks like someone bit you here," he said, his thumb sweeping across his bite mark. "Did you like it?"

I swallowed, pushing up into him. "Yes."

"Fucking wicked girl."

My hands slid over his shoulders and down his chest, across his abs and to the muscles of his hips, my thumb running back and forth over his tattoo. "I like this too."

His movements grew jagged and forceful. "Oh, fuck, Chloe . . . I can't . . . I won't last long." Hearing his voice so desperate and out of control only intensified my need for him. I closed my eyes, focusing on the delicious feeling beginning to spread throughout my body. I was so close, teetering right on the edge. Reaching between us, my fingers found my clit and I began to rub it slowly.

Tilting his head, he looked down at my hand and swore. "Oh, fuck." His voice was desperate, his breath coming out in deep pants. "Touch yourself, just like that. Let me fucking see you." His words were all I needed, and with one last brush of my fingers, I felt my orgasm overtake me.

I came hard, clenching around him, the nails of my free hand digging into his back. He cried out, his body seizing as he came inside me. My whole body shook in the aftermath, tiny tremors continuing even as my orgasm faded. I clung to him as he stilled, his body sinking against mine. He kissed my shoulder and my neck before placing a single kiss to my lips. Our eyes met briefly, and then he rolled off me.

"Christ, woman," he said, exhaling a heavy breath, forcing a laugh. "You're going to kill me."

We rolled to our sides in unison, heads on our pillows, and when our eyes met, I couldn't look away. I lost every hope I ever had that the next time would be less powerful, or that our connection would somehow melt away if we just got it out of our systems. This one night with a "truce" didn't dim anything. I already wanted to move closer, kiss the stubble on his jaw, and pull him back over me. As I gazed at him, it became clear to me that when this ended, it would fucking hurt.

Fear gripped my heart and the panic from last night returned, bringing an uncomfortable silence with it. I sat up, pulling the sheets with me and up to my chin. "Oh, shit."

His hand shot out, wrapping around my arm. "Chloe, I can't—"

"We probably need to get ready," I interrupted before he finished that sentence. It could be the beginning of a million forms of heartbreak. "We have a poster session in twenty minutes."

He looked confused for a moment before speaking. "I don't have any dry clothes in here. I don't even know where my room is."

I fought a blush as I remembered how quickly everything had happened last night. "Right. I'll use your key to go get you something."

I showered quickly and wrapped a thick towel around myself, wishing that I would've had the sense to bring one of the hotel bathrobes in here with me. With a deep breath I opened the door and stepped out.

He was sitting on the bed, and his eyes rose to meet mine as I entered the room.

"I just need . . ." I trailed off, motioning to my bag. He nodded but made no move to speak. I was usually never self-conscious about my body. But standing here in nothing but a towel, knowing that he was watching me, I felt uncharacteristically shy.

I grabbed a few things and rushed by him, not stopping until I was once again safely behind the bathroom door. I dressed faster than I thought possible, deciding I would pull my hair back and finish the rest later. Grabbing the key cards from the counter, I returned to the bedroom.

He hadn't moved. Sitting on the edge of the bed

with his elbows resting on his thighs, he appeared lost in thought. What was he thinking? All morning I'd been a nervous wreck, my emotions shifting wildly from one extreme to the other, but he seemed so calm. So *sure*. But what was he sure of? What had he decided?

"Do you have anything in particular you want me to bring you?"

When he lifted his head, he looked slightly surprised, as if the thought hadn't occurred to him. "Um . . . I just have a few meetings this afternoon, right?" I nodded. "Whatever you pick will be fine."

It only took me a second to locate his room; it was right next door. Great. Now I could imagine him in a bed just through the wall from mine. His bags were already there, and I paused briefly, realizing I would have to go through his luggage.

Lifting the largest one and placing it on the bed, I opened it. His scent hit me and caused a heavy pang of desire to wash through me. I began looking through the neatly packed items.

Everything about him was so tidy and organized, and it made me wonder what his home looked like. I'd never thought about it much, but I suddenly wondered if I would ever see it, if I would ever see his bed.

I paused as I realized that I wanted to. Would he want me to?

It struck me that I was stalling and I continued

searching through his clothes before finally settling on a charcoal Helmut Lang suit, white dress shirt, black silk tie, boxers, socks, and shoes.

Putting everything back where it belonged, I gathered up his clothing and headed for my room. I was unable to stifle my nervous laughter as I walked into the hall, shaking my head over the sheer absurdity of the situation. Thankfully, I managed to compose myself as I reached my door. I made it two steps inside before I froze.

He stood in front of the open window, awash in morning sunlight. Each beautiful line of his chiseled form was accentuated in perfect detail by the shadows cast across his body. A towel hung indecently low on his hips, and there, poking out just above it, was the tattoo.

"See something you like?"

I reluctantly returned my attention to his face. "I—"

My eyes drifted back down to his hip as if pulled by a magnet.

"I said, did you see something you like?" He crossed the room, stopping just in front of me.

"I heard you," I said, glaring. "And no, just lost in thought."

"And what exactly where you thinking?" He reached out, moving a piece of my damp hair behind my ear. Just that simple touch caused my stomach to jump.

"That we have a schedule to keep."

He moved a step closer. "Why don't I believe you?"

"Because you're self-absorbed?" I suggested, meeting his gaze.

He quirked an eyebrow and watched me for a moment before taking his clothing from my hands and placing it on the bed. Before I could move, he pulled the towel from his hips and tossed it to the side. *Sweet mother of God.* If there was a finer specimen of man on this earth, I'd pay big money to see it.

Picking up his boxers, he began to step into them before he stopped, looking at me. "Didn't you just say we had a schedule to keep?" he questioned, eyeing me humorously. "Unless, of course, you see something you like."

Son of a—

I narrowed my eyes and turned quickly, returning to the bathroom to finish getting ready. As I dried my hair, I couldn't get past the unsettling feeling that he was trying to say something more important than "Look at my naked body some more."

Before I could even untangle my own emotions I was trying to guess at his. Was I worried he would want to leave or stay?

When I returned to the bedroom, he was already dressed and waiting, looking out the large window. He turned, walked to me, and placed his warm hands on my face, staring at me intently. "I need you to listen to me."

I swallowed. "Okay."

"I don't want to walk out that door and lose what we found in this room."

His simple words rocked me. He wasn't declaring, he wasn't promising, but he said exactly what I'd needed to hear. We might not know what was happening, but we wouldn't leave it unfinished.

Letting out a shaky breath I brought my hands to his chest. "I don't either, but I also don't want your career to swallow mine."

"I don't want that either."

I nodded, feeling like words tangled my thoughts and I was unable to think of anything articulate to add.

"Okay then," he said, looking me up and down. "Let's go."

FIFTEEN

The theme of the conference this year was The Next Generation of Marketing Strategy, and as a way to embrace the new generation, the organizers had scheduled a poster session for students getting their degrees. Most students from Chloe's program were here, standing straight and eager beside their poster boards. In fact, presentation at this venue was considered a requirement for Chloe's scholarship, but I had applied for an exception for her given the size and confidential nature of the Papadakis account, her primary project. No other student here was managing a million-dollar deal.

The scholarship board had been happy to grant the exception, practically drooling over the prospect of putting Chloe's success story in their program brochure once the design was completed, signed, and released publicly.

But although she had no presentation at the meeting, she insisted on walking through every aisle and looking at every poster. Given that I was apparently incapable of being more than four fucking feet away from her and didn't have a meeting until ten, I followed her around the entire time, counting posters (576) and staring at her ass (perky, fun to spank, currently wrapped in black wool).

She'd mentioned in the elevator that her best friend, Julia, provided a majority of the wardrobe I loved/hated. This morning's selection of a fitted pencil skirt and deep blue blouse was now also on my list. I tried a couple of times to convince Chloe that we needed to go back to the room to get something, but she'd only raised an eyebrow and asked, "Get something? Or get *some*?"

I'd ignored her, but now I wished I'd admitted I needed one more round before conferencing. I wondered if she'd have gone for it.

"Would you have gone back to the room?" I asked into her ear as she carefully read an undergraduate poster on a rebranding idea for some small cellular company. Graphs were *taped* to the poster board, for crying out loud.

"Shhh."

"Chloe, you're not going to learn anything from this poster. Let's go get a cup of coffee and maybe a blow job in the bathroom."

"Your father told me it was impossible to predict where I'd get my best ideas, and to read everything I could find. Besides, these are my student colleagues."

I waited, toying with a cuff link, but she apparently wasn't going to address the latter part of what I'd said. "My dad doesn't know what he's talking about."

She laughed, appropriately. Dad had been on every top-twenty-five list of CEOs practically since before I was born.

"It doesn't have to be a blow job. I could fuck you against a wall," I whispered, clearing my throat and looking around to be sure no one was near enough to hear. "Or I could lay you down on the floor, spread you wide, and make you come against my tongue."

She shivered, smiled at the student near the next poster, and walked closer to read it. The man held his hand out to me. "Excuse me, but are you Bennett Ryan?"

I nodded, distracted as I shook his hand, watching Chloe move farther away.

The aisle we were in was practically deserted but for the students standing near the posters. Even they had begun to wander off to more interesting areas of the room, where larger companies—conference sponsors, mostly—had put together shiny, trademark-filled posters in the interest of getting the inaugural student-led session off the ground successfully. Chloe bent and wrote something on her note-pad: *Rebranding for Jenkins Financial?*

I stared at her hand and then up at her face, fixed in a thoughtful expression. The Jenkins Financial account wasn't one of hers. It wasn't even one I handled. It was a small account, occasionally half-ass managed by one of the junior executives. Did she actually know how much it was struggling with the dinosaur marketing campaign we had?

Before I could ask, she turned and moved on to the next

poster, and I was mesmerized with Chloe at work. I'd never let myself watch her so openly—the surreptitious stalking I had done only told me she was brilliant and driven, but I never realized the breadth of her company knowledge before.

I wanted to compliment her somehow, but the words got tangled in my head, and a strange defensiveness surged in my chest, as if to praise her work would somehow break strategy. "Your penmanship has improved."

She smiled up at me, clicking the end of her pen. "Fuck off."

My dick twitched in my pants. "You're wasting my time here."

"Then why don't you go glad-hand some executives over in the reception hall? They have breakfast there. Those little chocolate muffins you pretend not to like?"

"Because it's not what I feel like eating."

A small grin pulled at her lips. She watched my face as another student introduced herself to me.

"I've followed your career ever since I can remember," the woman said, breathless. "I heard you speak here last year."

I smiled, shook her hand as briefly as I could without appearing rude. "Thanks for saying hello."

We moved to the end of the aisle and I wrapped my hand around Chloe's elbow. "I have one more hour until I have a meeting. Do you have any idea what you do to me?"

Finally, she looked up. Her pupils were so large her eyes turned nearly black, and she licked her lips into a wet, decadent pout. "I suppose I need you to take me upstairs so you can show me."

———

Chloe was still looking for a new pair of panties when I was already five minutes late to my one o'clock. It was with Ed Gugliotti, a marketing executive for a smaller Minneapolis firm. We used Ed's firm to subcontract smaller jobs, and had a more significant project we were thinking of passing off to him to see how they handled it. As I zipped my pants, I reminded myself that Ed was himself pathologically late.

Except this time he wasn't. He was already waiting for me in one of the hotel meeting rooms, two of his junior people sitting beside him, eager smiles in place.

I hated being late.

"Ed," I said, greeting him with a handshake. He introduced me to his team, Daniel and Sam. They shook my hand in turn, but by the time I got to Sam, his attention was behind me, at the door.

Chloe had walked in, hair down now, looking wildly beautiful but professional, miraculously hiding the fact that she'd just had a screaming orgasm atop the desk in her hotel room.

Gugliotti and his men watched in rapt silence as she walked over, pulled out a chair, and sat down beside me, turning to give me a small smile. Her lips were red and swollen, and a faint red mark bloomed on her jaw. Stubble burn.

Too right.

I cleared my throat until everyone finally looked back at me. "Let's get started."

It was a simple meeting, and the kind of thing I'd done a thousand times. I described the account in the most general, nonconfidential terms, and of course Gugliotti told me he thought his team could come up with something great. After meeting the men he'd assign to it, I agreed. We planned to meet again the following day, when I would present the account in its entirety and officially hand it over. The meeting was over in less than fifteen minutes, giving me time before my two o'clock. I looked over at Chloe and raised an eyebrow in silent question.

"Food," she said with a laugh. "Let's get some food."

―――――

The rest of the afternoon had been productive, but I'd been entirely on autopilot, and if someone had asked me specifics about the meetings, it would've taken me a good long time to remember any details. Thank God for Chloe and her obsessive note taking. I'd been approached by many colleagues, had likely clasped a hundred hands over the afternoon, but the only touch I remembered was hers.

She distracted me endlessly, and what bothered me was that it was different here than usual. It was work, but it was a completely new world, one where we could pretend our circumstances were whatever we wanted them to be. The itch to be near her was even greater than it was when I had to keep my distance. Looking back to the evening keynote speaker at the podium, I tried unsuccessfully once again to redirect my thoughts to something productive. I was sitting up front, I had given the keynote last year at this very conference, and yet I somehow couldn't find a way to engage.

I saw her shift in my peripheral vision and instinctively I looked across the table at her. When our eyes met, every other sound blended together, floating around me but never breaking into my consciousness. Without thinking, I leaned toward her, she leaned toward me, and a tiny grin flickered across her mouth.

I thought about this morning, and how transparent she'd been in her panic. By contrast, I'd felt strangely calm, as if everything we'd done had been leading to that precise moment when we could both see how easy it was to just *be*.

A cell phone ringing somewhere behind me broke me from my trance, causing me to look away. Quickly sitting back in my chair, I was shocked to see how far forward I'd actually been leaning. I looked around and stopped dead as a pair of unfamiliar eyes met mine.

This stranger had no idea who we were, or that Chloe worked for me; he'd only glanced at us and quickly looked away. But in that moment, every bit of guilt I'd been suppressing hit me. Everyone knew who I was, no one here knew her, and if it ever got out that we were fucking, the judgment of an entire community would follow her around for the rest of her career.

A quick glance back at Chloe told me she could see panic written all over my face. I spent the rest of the lecture staring forward, not giving her another glance.

———

"Are you okay?" she asked in the elevator, breaking the heavy silence that had accompanied us for fourteen floors.

"Yeah, just . . ." I scratched the back of my neck and avoided her eyes. "Just thinking."

"I'm going out with some friends tonight."

"That sounds like a good idea."

"You have dinner with Stevenson and Newberry at seven. I think they're meeting you at that sushi place you like in the Gaslamp."

"I know," I said, relaxing as we fell into the familiar details of work. "What's their assistant's name again? She always comes."

"Andrew."

I looked over at her, confused. "That's a touch manlier than I was expecting."

"They have a new assistant."

How on earth did she know that?

She smiled. "He was sitting next to me at the keynote and asked if I'd be at the dinner tonight."

I wondered if his was the pair of unfamiliar eyes that caught me staring at Chloe, and he asked because of the way I looked at her. I stuttered out a few sounds before she interrupted me. "I told him I had other plans."

My unease returned. I wanted her with me tonight, and soon she wouldn't be my intern anymore. Could I be her lover then? Could I still be her boss *now*? "Did you want to come?"

She shook her head, looking up at the doors as we reached the thirtieth floor. "I think I should probably go do my own thing."

━━━━━

The short drive back from the restaurant was quiet and lonely, with only my jumbled thoughts to keep me company. I made my way through the large lobby to the elevator, and robotically moved to Chloe's room before remembering I wasn't actually staying with her. I couldn't remember which room was mine and tried three on the floor before giving up and checking back in at the reception desk. When I returned, I realized my room was just next to hers.

It was a mirror image of her room, but completely different in all of the ways that couldn't be seen. This shower hadn't washed away our pretenses last night; we hadn't slept together, curled around each other in this bed. These walls hadn't been filled with the sounds of her coming apart beneath me. This desk wasn't broken from a late-morning quickie.

I checked my phone and saw that I had two missed calls from my brother. *Great.* Normally, I would have already spoken to my father and brother several times, telling them about meetings or potential clients I'd met. So far, I hadn't talked to either of them once. I'd been afraid they would see right through me and know that my head was not in the game this week.

It was after eleven and I wondered if she was still with her friends, or was she back already? Maybe she was lying there awake, obsessing about all of the same things I was. Without thinking, I reached for the phone and dialed her room. It rang four times before a generic voice mail answered. I hung up and tried her cell.

She answered on the first ring. "Mr. Ryan?"

I winced. She was with other students. Of course she wouldn't call me Bennett now. "Hi. I . . . um, was just making sure you had a way to get back to the hotel."

Her laugh came through the line, muted by the sound of voices and the pulsing of loud music all around her. "There are about seventy cabs waiting outside. I'll just grab one of those when we're done."

"When will that be?"

"When Melissa finishes this drink and probably another. And when Kim decides she's done dancing with every filthy manwhore here. So you can expect me back sometime between now and tomorrow morning at eight."

"Are you being a wiseass?" I asked, feeling a grin spread across my face.

"Yes."

"Fine," I said, exhaling heavily. "Just text me when you get back safe."

She was quiet for a beat and then said, "I will."

I hung up and dropped my phone on the bed beside me, staring at the floor for probably an hour. I didn't even know what to do with myself.

Finally, I got up and walked back downstairs.

———

I was still in the lobby when she came back at two in the morning, cheeks bright and smile firmly in place as she dropped her phone into her purse. My phone buzzed in my hand and I glanced down.

I'm back safe.

I watched her walk past the reception desk and directly toward where I sat near the bank of elevators. She stopped when she saw me, bleary-eyed, in my rumpled suit. I was sure my hair was a fucking joke because I'd been worried sick. I suddenly had no idea what I was doing waiting for her like an anxious spouse. I only knew I couldn't be the one to decide we wouldn't work, because deep down, I wanted to figure it out.

"Bennett?" she said, glancing at her friend, who waved and walked to the elevator. I didn't give a damn what the friend was thinking, but I could feel her stare on us until she got into the elevator.

Chloe was wearing a tiny black dress and heels I wanted to petition become a uniform until her internship ended. Thin straps crisscrossed all the way from her pink-painted toes midway up her shins. I wanted to peel the dress from her body and fuck her into the couch, gripping those heels for leverage.

"Hey," I mumbled, mesmerized by the miles and miles of bare leg in front of me.

She walked closer, stopping just a few inches away. "What are you doing down here?"

"Waiting."

I struggled to hide how she affected me, how my present thoughts could barely be torn from the fantasy of my fists in her hair, the way my thumbs could completely cover her small, pink nipples, or how her clit was the softest part of any body I'd ever touched. I wanted to taste her from her toes to her earlobes, telling her every thought I had on the way.

"Are you drunk?"

I shook my head. *Not the way you mean.* "Someone saw me looking at you earlier."

"I know." She reached up, ran her fingers through my hair. "At the keynote. I saw your face."

"I panicked."

Chloe didn't say anything in response to that; she just laughed, a soft husky sound.

"I'm not worried about how it looks for me. I'm worried about how it looks for you," I said.

I heard her sharp inhale, felt her fingers tighten in my hair. When I looked up at her face, she looked bewildered.

How could she not know how infatuated I'd become? I was sure she could see it every time I looked at her. As always, I wanted to grip her from behind, spank her when she made a sound. Pull her hair when I came. Bite her breast again. Drag my teeth over her spine. Pinch the back of her thigh and then smooth it over with the softest touch.

But I also wanted to watch her sleep, and then watch her wake up and see me, and gauge her feelings from that first, unfiltered reaction.

I was starting to see that this wasn't just sex, and it wasn't just working something out of my system. Sex was just the fastest route to the deeper possession I needed. I was falling in love with her, and falling too fast and hard to easily find any footing.

It was scary as fuck.

I decided to give her the truth.

"I need another night."

She sucked in a breath and stared, and only then did it occur to me that she could be feeling something very different than I was.

"Feel free to say no. I just . . ." I ran a hand through my

hair and looked up at her. "I just would really like to be with you again tonight."

"Greedy, aren't you?"

"You have no idea."

———

Upstairs in her room, between her sheets, and with her body coiled tight and sweet, sucking me in, everything else slipped away. Her scent and noises clouded my brain, made my thrusting erratic and hard. She was drenched—all of her: skin outside and flesh inside, slick and pulling me deeper. Her legs clamped around my hips and she flipped me over with a laugh, riding me with her back arched away and her head thrown back, fingers digging in my abdomen, anchoring herself in me. Her skin shone and I sat up underneath her, needing to feel the slide of her chest over mine as she slithered and slid. I pushed her back again, hovering over her once more this time with her legs on my shoulders and her mouth quivering as she struggled to find words.

Her nails dug into my back and I hissed, telling her "more" and "yes" and wanting her to mark me, to leave something that would still be there tomorrow.

She came once, and then again, and once more, and pulled at her hair, looking wild and untamed. I collapsed on her, incoherently stringing words together as I came, trying to tell her what we both already knew: that whatever happened outside of this room was irrelevant.

Sixteen

We slowly returned from orbit, and with limbs tangled in the sheets, talked for hours about our day, about the meeting with Gugliotti, about his dinner and my night out with friends. We talked about the broken desk, and that I only packed enough underwear for a week, so he couldn't ruin any more.

We talked about everything except the havoc he was wreaking on my heart.

I ran a finger down his chest and he stilled it with his hand, bringing it to his lips and saying, "It's nice to talk to you."

I laughed, pushing his hair off his forehead. "You talk to me every day. And when I say talk, I mean yell. Shout. Slam doors. Pout—"

With his fingertips, he drew spirals over my bare stomach, distracting me. "You know what I mean."

I did. I knew exactly what he meant, and I wanted to find a way to stretch this moment, right there, into eternity. "So tell me something."

He raised his eyes to my face, smiling a little nervously. "What do you want to know?"

"Honestly? I think I want to know everything. But let's start small. Give me the history of Bennett's women."

He ran a long finger across his eyebrow and repeated in a laugh, "Let's start small. *Riiiight.*" He cleared his throat and then looked at me. "A few in high school, some in college, some in grad school. Some after grad school. And then, one long-term relationship when I lived in France."

"Details?" I twisted a strand of his hair around my finger, hoping I wasn't pushing him too much.

But to my surprise, he answered without hesitation. "Her name was Sylvie. She was an attorney at a small firm in Paris. We were together for three years and broke up a few months before I moved home."

"Was that why you moved home?"

A smile tugged at one corner of his mouth. "No."

"Did she break your heart?"

The smile turned into a full-on smirk directed at me. "No, Chloe."

"Did you break hers?" Why was I even asking this? Did I want him to say—yes? I knew he was capable of breaking hearts. I was actually fairly certain he would break mine.

He bent to kiss me then, sucking on my lower lip for

a few moments before whispering, "No. We just didn't work anymore. My romantic life was entirely without drama. Until you."

I laughed. "Happy to change up the pattern."

I could feel his laugh in the vibrations along my skin as he kissed up my neck. "And oh, you do." Long fingers made their way down my stomach, to my hips, and finally, between my legs. "Your turn."

"To have an orgasm? Yes, please."

He circled a lazy finger around my clit before sliding it inside me. He knew my body better than I did. When did that happen?

"No," he murmured. "Your turn to spill your history."

"No way can I think about anything when you're doing that."

With a kiss to my shoulder, he moved his hand back to my stomach, drawing circles there once again.

I pouted but he missed it, watching his fingers on me instead. "God, there have been so many men, where will I ever begin?"

"Chloe," he warned.

"A couple in high school, one in college."

"You've only had sex with three men?"

I pulled back to look at him. "Hello, Einstein. I've had sex with four men."

A cocky grin spread across his face. "Right. And am I the best by an embarrassingly wide margin?"

"Am I?"

His grin disappeared, and he blinked, surprised. "Yes."

It was sincere. It made something inside me melt into a tiny, warm hum. I reached to kiss his chin, trying to hide what that information did to me. "Good."

Kissing along his shoulder, I moaned happily. I loved his taste, loved to inhale that clean, sage smell of his. Digging my fingers into his hair, I tugged him down so I could nibble at his jaw, his neck, his shoulders. He held himself very still, propped over me, very clearly not kissing me back.

The hell?

He inhaled to speak and then closed his mouth again. Somehow I managed to drag my mouth away long enough to ask, "What?"

"I realize you think I'm just a filthy manwhore, but it does actually matter to me."

"What matters to—?"

"I want to hear you to say it."

I stared at him, and he stared back, irises growing a familiar shade of angry brown-green. Mentally rifling through the last few minutes, I tried to understand what he was talking about.

Oh. "Oh. Yes."

His brows pulled together. "Yes, what, Miss Mills?"

Heat pulsed through me. His voice was different when he said that. Sharp. Commanding. Hot as hell. "Yes, you're the best by a very embarrassing margin."

"That's better."

"At least so far."

He rolled on top of me, grabbing my wrists and pinning them above my head. "Don't tease."

"Don't tease? Please," I said, breathless. His cock pressed into my thigh. I wanted it higher. I wanted it pushing inside me. "Teasing is all we do."

As if to prove me wrong, he reached down, grabbing his length and guiding himself into me, pulling my leg around his hip. Holding very still, he stared down at me. His upper lip twitched.

"Please move," I whispered.

"You'd like that?"

"Yes."

"And if I don't?"

I bit my lip, tried to glare at him.

He smiled, growling, "*This* is teasing."

"Please?" I tried to move my hips but he followed my movements so I couldn't gain any friction.

"Chloe, I never *tease* you. I fuck the sense out of you."

I laughed, and his eyes fell closed when I did, my body constricting him even more.

"Not that you have much sense to begin with," he said, biting my neck. "Now tell me how good I make you feel." Something in his voice, some vulnerability or dip in its strength as the sentence ended told me he wasn't playing around.

"No one has ever made me come before. Not with hands or mouth or anything else."

He'd been holding still before, though the telltale signs of strain had been apparent; his shoulders trembled and his breath came out in shallow pants, as if his entire body wanted to explode into a wild tangle in the sheets. But when I said this, he completely froze. "No one?"

"Only you." I stretched to nibble his jaw. "I'd say that puts you a bit ahead of the field."

He exhaled my name as his hips moved back and then forward. And again back and forward. The conversation was done; his mouth found mine, and then my chin, and my jaw, and my ears. His hand moved up my side, to my breast, and finally to my face.

And when I thought we were both lost to the rhythm and I could feel my climax just beyond me, but so close, and I dug both heels into his ass, needing more, and faster, and all of him, he whispered, "I wish I'd known that."

"Why?" I managed, an exhale carrying the sound barely past my lips. *Faster*, my body screamed. *More.* "Would it have changed how big an asshole you were?"

He unwrapped my legs from around him, flipped me over and up onto my knees. "I don't know. I just wish I'd known," he grunted, pushing into me once again. "Jesus. So fucking deep like this."

His movements were so fluid, like dancing, rippling water; like the sliding of the sunlight across a room. The mattress springs groaned beneath us, the force of his thrusts pushing me farther up the bed.

"Almost." I clutched at the sheets, begged him to keep going. "Almost. Harder."

"*Fuck*. I'm so close. Get there." He synchronized every movement with the last, knowing now was the point where he couldn't change a thing. "*Get there.*"

His face, his voice, his scent—each part of him filled my mind as I obediently came apart beneath him.

He thrust roughly; then every muscle froze before he melted against me as he came. "Fuck, fuck, *fuck* . . ." he breathed into my hair before falling quiet, heavy and still on top of me.

The air conditioner turned on with a rattle and then a steady drone. After he caught his breath, Bennett rolled off me, dragging his hand across my sweaty back. "Chloe?"

"Mmm?"

"I want more than just this." His voice was so thick and heavy, I wasn't actually sure he was awake.

I froze, my thoughts exploding in a chaotic mess. "What did you just say?"

He opened his eyes, with apparent effort, and looked at me. "I want to be with you."

Lifting myself on an elbow, I stared down at him, completely unable to pull a single word out of my brain.

"So sleepy." His eyes rolled closed and he threw a heavy arm around me, pulling me down onto him. "Baby, come here." He pressed his face into my neck and mumbled, "It's okay if you don't want it too. I'll take anything you'll give me. Just let me stay here until the morning, okay?"

I was suddenly wide awake, staring at the dark wall and listening to the hum of the air conditioner. I was terrified that this changed everything, and even more terrified that he had no idea what he was saying, and it would change nothing.

"Okay," I whispered into the dark, hearing his breathing slow into a steady, sleeping rhythm.

❧

I rolled over and pulled a pillow against my body, seeking comfort. His scent pulled me out of sleep, but the cool sheets on the other side of the bed told me I was alone. I looked toward the bathroom door, trying to focus on any noise I could hear coming from inside. There wasn't any.

I continued to lie there, clutching his pillow as my eyes began to grow heavier. I wanted to wait for him. I needed the reassurance of his warm body next to mine and the feel of his strong arms wrapped around me. I imagined him holding me, whispering that this was all real and nothing would change in the morning. Before long, my eyes drifted closed and I slipped back into an uneasy sleep.

Sometime later, I awoke again, still alone. Rolling over quickly, I looked at the time: 5:14 a.m.

What? Fumbling in the darkness, I put on the first thing I found and walked to the bathroom.

"Bennett?" No answer. I knocked softly. "Bennett?" A groan and a soft shuffle sounded from the other side of the door.

"Just go away." His voice was hoarse and echoed off the bathroom walls.

"Bennett, are you okay?"

"I'm not feeling well. I'll be fine, go back to bed."

"Is there anything I can get you?" I asked.

"I'm fine. Just please, go back to bed."

"But—"

"Chloe," he groaned, obviously annoyed.

I turned, unsure of what to do, battling an odd, unsettling feeling. Did he even get sick? In just under a year, I'd never seen him with so much as a stuffy nose. It was obvious he didn't want me hovering outside the door, but there was no way I could go back to sleep either.

Walking back to the bed, I straightened the blankets and headed toward the suite's living room. I grabbed a bottle of water from the minibar and sat on the couch.

If he was sick, I mean really sick, there was no way he could make the Gugliotti meeting in a couple of hours.

I switched on the TV and began flipping through the channels. Infomercial. Bad movie. Nick at Nite. Ahh, *Wayne's World*. Sitting back into the couch, I tucked my legs under me and prepared to wait. Halfway through the movie, I heard the water running in the bathroom. I sat up and listened as it was the first sound I'd heard in over an hour. The bathroom door opened and I flew off the couch, grabbing another bottle of water before entering the bedroom.

"Are you feeling better?" I asked.

"Yes. I think I just need to sleep now." He stumbled into bed, burying his face in the pillow with a groan.

"What . . . what was wrong?" I placed the bottle of water down on the bedside table and sat on the edge of the bed next to him.

"It was just my stomach. I think it was the sushi at dinner." His eyes were closed and even in the dim light coming from the other room, I could see that he looked like hell. He turned away from me slightly but I ignored it, placing one hand in his hair and the other on his cheek. His hair was damp and his face was pale and clammy, and despite his initial reaction, he leaned into my touch.

"Why didn't you wake me up?" I asked, brushing a few damp strands away from his forehead.

"Because the last thing I needed was you in there watching me throw up," he replied almost grumpily, and I rolled my eyes, offering him the bottle of water.

"I could have done something. You don't have to be such a man."

"Don't be such a woman. What could you have done? Food poisoning is a pretty lonely business."

"So what should I tell Gugliotti?"

He groaned, rubbing his hands over his face. "*Shit*. What time is it?"

I glanced at the clock. "Just after seven."

"What time is the meeting?"

"Eight."

He started to get up but was easy enough to shove back down into the bed. "No way in hell are you going to that meeting like this! When was the last time you threw up?"

He groaned. "A few minutes ago."

"Exactly. *Gross*. I'll call him to reschedule."

He gripped my arm before I could walk over to the desk and grab my phone. "Chloe. You do it."

My eyebrows inched to my hairline. "Do what?"

He waited.

"The meeting?"

He nodded.

"Without you?"

He nodded again.

"You're sending me to a meeting alone?"

"Miss Mills, you're as sharp as a spoon."

"Fuck off," I said, laughing and pushing him gently. "And I'm not doing it without you."

"Why not? I bet you know the account we're offering as well as I do. Besides, if we reschedule he's just going to take a lavish trip to Chicago and send us the bill. Please, Chloe."

I stared down at him, waiting for him to break into a teasing grin or take it back. But he didn't. And the truth was, I did know the account, and I did know the terms. I could do this.

"Okay," I said, smiling and feeling a surge of hope that we could figure this—us—out after all. "I'm in."

His face grew harder, and he used the voice I had barely heard in days. It sent small waves of hunger through me. "Tell me the plan, Miss Mills."

Nodding, I said, "I need to make sure he's clear on the project parameters and timelines. I'll watch out for overpromising; I know Gugliotti is notorious for that." When Bennett nodded, smiling a little, I continued. "I'll confirm the contract start dates and the milestones."

When I ticked all five of them off on my fingers, his smile grew. "You'll be fine."

I bent and kissed his damp forehead. "I know."

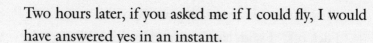

Two hours later, if you asked me if I could fly, I would have answered yes in an instant.

The meeting had gone off perfectly. Mr. Gugliotti, who had initially been peeved to find an intern in the place of a Ryan executive, had softened when he heard the circumstances. And later, he seemed impressed with the level of detail I was able to provide.

He'd even offered me a job. "After you finish with Mr. Ryan, of course," he'd said with a wink, and I carefully demurred.

I wasn't sure I ever wanted to be done with Mr. Ryan.

On the way back from the meeting, I called Susan to find out what Bennett liked when he was sick. Just as I suspected, the last time she'd been able to spoil him with chicken noodle soup and Popsicles, he'd been wearing a retainer. She was delighted to hear from me, and I had to swallow the guilt I felt when she asked if he was behaving. I assured her that all was fine and that he was only suffering from a mild stomach bug and that, of course, I'd have him call. With a small bag of groceries in hand, I walked into the room, stopping in the small kitchen area to drop off the food and take off my tailored wool suit.

Wearing only my slip, I moved into the bedroom, but Bennett wasn't there. The bathroom door was open, and he wasn't there either. It looked as if house-keeping had been in; the linens were crisp and neat, and the floor had been tidied of our piles of discarded clothes. The balcony door was open, letting in a cool breeze. Outside, I found him sitting in a chaise, elbows propped on his knees, his head in his hands. He looked like he'd had a shower and was now dressed in dark jeans and a short-sleeved green T-shirt.

My skin hummed, warming at the sight of him.

"Hey," I said.

He looked up, eyes taking in every curve. "Holy *fuck*. I hope you didn't wear that to the meeting."

"Well, I did," I said, laughing. "But I wore it beneath a very prim navy suit."

"Good," he growled. He pulled me close, wrapping his arms all the way around my waist and pressing his forehead into my stomach. "I missed you."

My chest twisted tightly. What were we *doing*? Was this real or were we playing house for a few days and then returning to normal? I didn't think I could do our normal after this and wasn't sure I could see several steps into the future to how this all played out.

Ask him, Chloe!

He looked up at me, his stare burning hot on my face as he waited for me to say something. "Are you feeling better?" I asked.

Coward.

His face fell but he hid it quickly. "Much," he said. "How did the meeting go?"

Although I was still on a high from the meeting with Gugliotti and was dying to tell him every detail, when he asked this, he removed his arms from my waist and sat back, leaving me feeling cold and hollow. I wanted to hit the rewind button and take us back two minutes to when he told me he'd missed me, and I could answer, "I missed you too." I'd kiss him, and we'd get distracted, and I'd tell him all about Gugliotti a few hours from now.

But instead I gave him every detail of the meeting, how Gugliotti reacted to me, and how I redirected his focus to the project at hand. I recounted every aspect of the discussion in such detail that by the end of my story, Bennett was laughing quietly.

"My, you're wordy."

"I think it went well," I said, stepping closer. *Put your arms around me again.*

But he didn't. He leaned back and gave me a stiff

smile, the detached Beautiful Bastard kind. "You were great, Chloe. I'm not at all surprised."

I wasn't used to this kind of compliment from him. Improved handwriting, great blow job—these were the things he knew how to notice. I was surprised how much his opinion mattered to me. Had it always mattered so much? Would he start to treat me differently if we were lovers instead of fuck buddies? I wasn't actually sure I even wanted him to be softer as a boss, or try to blend lover and mentor. I rather liked the Beautiful Bastard at work, as well as in bed.

But as soon as I thought it, I realized the way we used to interact now felt like a strange, foreign object in the distance, or a pair of shoes that I'd long since outgrown. I was torn between wanting him to say something dickish to jerk me back into reality and wanting him to pull me closer and kiss my breast through my slip.

Again, Chloe. Reason number 750,000 you don't fuck your boss. You turn a well-defined relationship into a mess of blurry boundaries.

"You look so tired," I whispered as I began running fingers through the hair at the nape of his neck.

"I am," he mumbled. "I'm glad I didn't go. I threw up. A lot."

"Thanks for sharing," I laughed. Reluctantly, I pulled away and put my hands on his face. "I brought

Popsicles, ginger ale, gingersnaps, and saltines. Which do you want first?"

He stared at me, completely confused for a beat before blurting, "You called my *mom*?"

❧

I went down to the conference for a few hours in the afternoon so he could sleep some more. He put up a strong front, but I could tell even half of a lime Popsicle made him queasy when he turned a matching shade of green. Besides, at this conference in particular he could barely walk ten steps without being stopped, fawned over, pitched to. Even healthy he wouldn't make it far enough to see anything worth his time anyhow.

When I returned to the room, he was sprawled on the couch in a most un–Beautiful Bastard–like pose, shirtless and with his hand shoved down the front of his boxers. There was something so ordinary about the way he sat, bored, staring at the television. I was grateful for the reminder that this man was, in some ways, just a man. Just another person, moving around the planet, getting his bearings, not spending every second lighting the world's stage on fire.

And buried within that epiphany that Bennett was just Bennett was a sense of wild longing because there was this chance that he was becoming *my* Just Bennett, and for a heartbeat, I wanted that more than I think I'd ever wanted anything.

A woman with freakishly shiny hair flipped her head and grinned at us from the television. I collapsed on the couch next to him. "What are we watching?"

"A shampoo commercial," he answered, pulling his hand out of his shorts to reach for me. I started to tease him about cooties but shut up as soon as he began to massage my fingers. "*Clerks* is on, though."

"That's one of my favorite movies," I said.

"I know. You were quoting it the first day I met you."

"Actually, that was *Clerks II*," I clarified, and then stopped. "Wait, you remember that?"

"Of course I remember that. You sounded like a frat boy and looked like a fucking model. What man could ever forget that?"

"I would have given anything to know what you were thinking right then."

"I was thinking, 'Highly fuckable intern, twelve o'clock. Disengage, soldier. I repeat, *disengage*.'"

I laughed and leaned against his shoulder. "God, that first meeting was miserable."

He didn't say anything but kept running his thumb along my fingers, pressing and soothing. I had never had a hand massage before, and if he'd tried to turn it to oral sex, I might have turned him down just to keep him doing what he was doing.

Wow, that's a total lie. I'd take that mouth between my legs any day of the—

"How do you want it to be, Chloe?" he asked, pulling me out of my internal debate.

"What?"

"When we're back in Chicago."

I stared blankly at him, my pulse sending my blood thrumming in heavy bursts through my veins.

"Us," he clarified, with forced patience. "You and me. Chloe and Bennett. Man and shrew. I realize this isn't simple for you."

"Well, I'm pretty sure I don't want to fight all the time." I bumped his shoulder playfully. "Although I do sort of like that part."

Bennett laughed, but it didn't sound like a completely happy noise. "There's a lot of space that comes after 'not fighting all the time.' Where do you want to be?"

Together. Your girlfriend. Someone who sees the inside of your home and stays there with you sometimes. I started to answer and the words evaporated in my throat.

"I guess that depends on whether it's realistic to think it can be anything."

He dropped my hand and scrubbed his face. The movie came back on and we fell into what I think was the most awkward silence in the history of the world.

Finally, he picked my hand up again and kissed my

palm. "Okay, baby. I can handle just not fighting all the time."

I stared at his fingers wrapped around mine. After what felt like an eternity, I managed, "Sorry. This all feels a little new."

"For me too," he reminded me.

We fell into silence again as we continued to watch the movie, laughing in the same places and slowly shifting until I was practically lying on top of him. Out of the corner of my eye I glanced at the clock on the wall and mentally calculated the hours we had left in San Diego.

Fourteen.

Fourteen hours left of this perfect reality where I could have him whenever I wanted him, and it didn't have to be secret, or dirty, using anger as our only form of foreplay.

"What's your favorite movie?" he asked, rolling me over so he hovered above me. His skin was hot and I wanted to take off my blouse, but I didn't want him to move even an inch, for even a second.

"I like comedies," I began. "There's *Clerks,* but *Tommy Boy, Shaun of the Dead, Hot Fuzz, Clue;* things like that. But I would have to say my all-time favorite movie would probably be *Rear Window.*"

"Because of Jimmy Stewart or Grace Kelly?" he asked, bending to kiss a trail of fire up my neck.

"Both, but probably Grace Kelly."

"I can see that. You have very Grace Kelly–like tendencies about you." His hand came up and smoothed a piece of my hair that had come loose from my ponytail. "I hear Grace Kelly had a filthy mouth too," he added.

"You love my filthy mouth."

"True. But I like it better when it's full," he said, meaningful smirk in place.

"You know, if you would shut up once in a while you'd be damn near perfect."

"But I'd be a *silent* panty ripper, which I think is a lot creepier than the angry-boss panty ripper."

I dissolved into giggles under him and he dug a finger between my ribs, tickling.

"I know you love it," he growled.

"Bennett?" I said, trying to sound nonchalant. "What do you do with them?"

He gave me a dark, teasing look. "I keep them somewhere safe."

"Can I see?"

"No."

"Why?" I asked, narrowing my eyes at him.

"Because you'll try and take them back."

"Why would I want them back? They're all ruined."

He grinned at me but didn't answer.

"Why do you do that anyway?"

He studied me for a moment, obviously considering his answer. Finally, he lifted himself onto his elbow and moved his face to within inches of mine. "For the same reason you like it."

With that, he stood up and pulled me with him into the bedroom.

SEVENTEEN

I had experience with negotiations, holdouts, bargaining. Here I was in the unfamiliar position of having laid all my chips on the table, but when it came to Chloe, I didn't care. I was all in.

"Are you looking forward to being home? You've been gone for almost three weeks."

She shrugged, pulling my boxers down without ceremony and wrapping her warm hand around me with a familiarity that made me ache in new places. "I've had a nice time here, you know."

I deliberated over each button of her blouse, kissing every inch of skin as it came into view. "How much time do we have to play before our flight?"

"Thirteen hours," she said, without looking at a clock. The answer certainly came quickly, and from the way her skin felt when I slid two fingers inside her underwear, I didn't think she was looking forward to leaving this hotel room anytime soon.

I tickled her thighs with my fingers, teased her tongue

with mine, and rubbed myself against her leg until I could feel her arching toward me. Her legs slipped around my waist and she spread her hands against my chest as I reached down and pushed myself inside her, determined to make her come as many times as I could before the sun came up.

For me, there was nothing in the world but her slick skin and the soft air of her moans against my neck. Over and over I moved on her, mute with my need, lost in her. Her hips rolled with mine and her back shifted to press her breasts against me and I wanted to tell her, *"This, what we have, is the most amazing thing I have ever felt. Do you feel it too?"*

But I had no words. I had only instinct and desire and the taste of her on my tongue and the memory of her laugh ringing in my ears. I wanted to keep that sound playing over and over. I wanted to be everything for her: her lover and sparring partner and friend. In this bed, I could be everything.

"I don't know how to do this," she said in a weird moment—on the verge of coming and holding onto me so tight I thought I might bruise. But I knew what she meant because it was painful to be filled so full of this longing and have no fucking idea how it would play out. I wanted her in a way that made me feel like every second I was sated *and* starving—and my brain didn't know what to do with it. So instead of answering her or telling her what I thought we could do, I kissed her neck and put my fingers against the soft skin of her hip, and told her, "I don't either, but I'm not ready to let it go yet."

"It feels so good . . ." She whispered this against my throat and I groaned in quiet agony, patently unable to manage one articulate word in response.

I feared I would howl.

I kissed her.

I pushed her deeper into the mattress.

It went on forever, this splintering ecstasy. Her body rising to meet mine, her mouth wet and hungry, biting and sweet.

———

I woke up when my pillow was yanked out from under my head and Chloe mumbled something incoherent about spinach and hot dogs.

The woman was a sleep-talking, restless bed hog.

I ran a greedy hand over her ass before rolling to look at the clock. It was only a little after five in the morning, but I knew we had to get moving soon to make our eight o'clock flight. As much as I hated to leave our merry little den of sin, I hadn't done any work here and was starting to feel increasingly guilty about the career I'd essentially neglected. For the past decade my career had been my life, and although I was growing more comfortable with the obliterating effect Chloe had on that balance, I had to retrieve my focus.

It was time to get home, put on the Boss Hat, and start taking names.

The early morning sun filtered in and washed her pale skin a gray-blue light. She was curled on her side, facing me, her hair a dark tangle across the pillow behind her. Most of her face was now cuddled into my pillow.

I could understand her hesitance to decide how our relationship would work back in reality. The San Diego bubble had been amazing, in part because it lacked every aspect that made our relationship tricky to begin with: her job at Ryan Media, my role in the family business, her scholarship, our independently sharp attitudes. Although I wanted to push to define this thing between us and set expectations so that I could dive in headfirst, her approach—far more tentative—was probably the right one.

We hadn't bothered to pull the blankets back on the bed after we'd worked them to the floor last night, and I took the chance to stare at her nude body. I could definitely get used to waking up with this woman in my bed.

But unfortunately, we didn't have a leisurely morning ahead of us. I tried to wake her with my hand on her shoulder, then a kiss on her neck, and finally a hard pinch on her ass.

She reached out and smacked my arm *hard* before I'd even pulled it back. I wasn't even sure she was awake. "Asshole."

"We should get up and get going. We need to be at the airport in a little over an hour."

Chloe rolled over and stared up at me, face lined with pillow creases and her eyes unfocused. She didn't bother to cover her body like she had the first morning, but she wasn't all smiles, either. "Okay," she said. She sat up, drank some water, and kissed my shoulder before climbing out of bed.

I watched her naked body as she walked to the bathroom, but not once did she look back at me. I didn't exactly need a morning quickie, but I wouldn't have minded a little spooning, maybe some pillow talk.

Probably shouldn't have pinched her ass, then.

She didn't emerge, and after collecting my things, I knocked on the bathroom door. "I'm heading next door to shower and pack."

She was quiet for a few beats. "Okay."

"Can I get something other than 'okay'?"

Her laugh trailed from the other side of the door. "I believe I said 'asshole' earlier."

I grinned.

But when I reached for the door to leave, she opened the bathroom door and stepped directly into my arms, wrapping herself around me and pressing her face to my neck. She was still naked, and when she glanced up, her eyes seemed a little red.

"Sorry," she said, kissing my jaw before pulling me down for a longer, deeper kiss. "I just get nervous before flying."

She turned and walked back into the bathroom before I could meet her eyes and figure out if she was telling me the truth.

———

The room next door felt eerily spotless, even for a high-end hotel chain. It took no time to pack, no time to shower and dress. But something kept me from going back over to Chloe's room so soon. It was as if she needed some time alone in there, to deal with whatever silent battle she was waging with herself. I could tell she was conflicted, but which way would she come down in the end? Would she decide she wanted to try? Or would she decide it wasn't possible to balance work and us?

When impatience won out over chivalry, I pulled my bag into the hallway and knocked on her door.

She opened it, dressed like a naughty businesswoman pinup, and it took me approximately eight years to move my attention from her legs, up over her breasts, and finally to her face.

"Hey, gorgeous."

She gave me a shaky smile. "Hey."

"Ready to go?" I asked, starting to walk past her to get her bag. The sleeve of my jacket brushed against her bare arm, and before I fully understood what was happening, she had my tie twisted around her fist and my back pressed against the wall, her mouth sliding over mine.

I froze, surprised. "Whoa, hello there," I mumbled against her lips.

With one hand splayed on my chest, she began loosening my tie and groaned into my mouth when she felt my dick grow hard against her. Her nimble fingers had my tie yanked from my collar and on the floor at my feet before I remembered we had a flight to catch.

"Chloe," I said, struggling to pull back from her kisses. "Baby, we don't have time for this."

"I don't care." She was nothing but teeth and lips, suction all down my neck, her hungry hands whipping my belt off, palming my cock.

I cursed under my breath, completely unable to resist the way she gripped me through my pants, her bossy wiggling and tugging on my clothes. "Fuck, Chloe, you're fucking *wild*."

I whipped her around, pressing her back into the wall and shoving my hand up beneath her blouse, roughly pushing the cup of her bra aside. Her greediness was infectious, and my fingers relished the pebbling of her nipples, the firm swell of her breast as she pushed forward into my palm. I reached down and slid her skirt over her hips, shoved her underwear down, and she kicked it aside before I lifted her off the floor.

I needed to be in her, now.

"Tell me you want me," she said, the words coming

out as exhales, only air. She was trembling; her eyes were squeezed closed.

"You have no idea. I want everything you'll give me."

"Tell me we can do this." She shoved my pants and boxers down past my knees and wrapped her legs around my waist, digging the heel of her shoe into my ass. When my dick slipped against her, pushing just inside, I covered her mouth as she let out a small, keening noise. Almost a moan.

Almost a sob.

I pulled back, inspecting her face. Tears ran down her cheeks.

"Chloe?"

"Don't stop," she said, hiccupping, leaning to suck at my neck. Hiding. With one hand, she tried to dig between us and reach for me. It was a weird kind of desperation. We knew frenzied fucking, and we knew covert quickies, but this was something else entirely.

"Stop." I pressed closer, pinning her tightly to the wall. "Baby, what are you doing?"

Finally, she opened her eyes, focusing on my collar. She slipped a button loose, and then one more. "I just need to feel you one more time."

"What are you talking about, 'one more time'?"

She wouldn't look at me, wouldn't say anything.

"Chloe, when we leave this room, we can leave everything here. Or we can take everything we have with us. I believe we can figure it out . . . but do you?"

She nodded, her lip pinned between her teeth so tightly the pink flesh was white. When she released it, it flushed a decadent, tempting red. "I want to."

"I told you, I want more than this. I want to be *with* you. I want to be your lover." I swore, digging my hands into my hair. "I'm falling for you, Chloe."

She bent over, laughing, relief spreading through her body. When she stood, she pulled me close again, pressing her lips to my cheek. "You're serious?"

"Totally serious. I want to be the only guy who fucks you against windows, and also the first person you see in the morning—from where you lie, having stolen my pillow. I'd also like to be the person who gets *you* lime Popsicles when *you've* had bad sushi. We only have a few months left where it's potentially complicated."

With my mouth on hers, and my hands on her face, I think she finally started to understand. "Promise me you'll take me to bed when we get back," she said.

"I promise."

"Your bed."

"Fuck yes, my bed. My bed is huge, with a headboard I can tie you to and spank you silly for being so ridiculous."

And in that moment, we were completely perfect.

In the hall, after one final kiss to her palm, I dropped her hand and led her down to the lobby.

Eighteen

Bennett went to get the car while I checked us out at reception. With one final glance around the lobby, I tried to download every memory of the trip. When I stepped outside I saw Bennett standing near the valet. My heart felt like a wild drum beneath my ribs. I was still reeling. I realized he'd given me so many chances to tell him what I wanted, and I'd just been too unsure of whether we could ever make it work. Apparently, his spine was stronger than mine.

I'm falling for you.

My stomach twisted deliciously.

Mr. Gugliotti spotted Bennett from the sidewalk and moved to him. They shook hands, seemed to exchange pleasantries. I wanted to walk up, join the discussion as a peer, but was worried that I wouldn't be able to contain what was presently happening to my heart, and my feelings for Bennett would show all over my face.

Mr. Gugliotti looked up at me but didn't seem to recognize me out of context. He blinked back to Bennett, nodding at something he said, and that lack of recognition made me hesitate even more. I wasn't someone to be noticed yet. The checkout paperwork, Bennett's to-do list, and his briefcase were all in my hand. I hovered at the periphery: an intern.

Hanging back, I tried to enjoy the last few moments of ocean breeze. Bennett's rich voice carried across the few feet separating us.

"Sounds like you all threw around some good ideas. I'm glad Chloe had the chance to go through the exercise."

Nodding, Mr. Gugliotti said, "Chloe is sharp. It went just fine."

"I'm sure we can telecon soon to start the process of handing it over."

Exercise? Start? Isn't that what I'd done? I had given Gugliotti papers from legal to sign and FedEx back.

"Sounds good. I'll have Annie call to set something up. I'd like to go over the terms with you. I wasn't comfortable signing them quite yet."

"Of course you weren't."

My heart sped up as the spiral of panic and humiliation rose in my veins. It was as if the meeting that took place had been a mere performance for my benefit and the real work would happen between these two men, back in the real world.

Was this entire conference one giant fantasy? I felt ridiculous, remembering the details I'd shared with Bennett. How proud I'd been to have crossed this off his list and taken care of it so he could get better.

"Henry mentioned that Chloe's got a Miller scholarship. That's fantastic. Is she staying on at Ryan Media after she finishes?" Gugliotti asked.

"Not sure yet. She's a great kid. Definitely needs some seasoning, though."

I lost my breath in a rush, as if it'd been pulled out by a vacuum. Bennett had to be kidding. I knew, without Elliott having to tell me (and he had, countless times), that I could have my pick of jobs when I finished. I'd worked at Ryan Media for years, working my ass off to both do my job and get a graduate degree. I knew some of the accounts better than the people managing them. Bennett knew this.

Gugliotti chuckled. "Seasoning or no, I'd snatch her up in a beat. She held her own in there, Bennett."

"Of course she did," Bennett said. "Who do you think trained her? The meeting with you was a great way for her to get her feet wet, so I appreciate it. No doubt she'll be just fine wherever she ends up. When she's ready."

He sounded nothing like either Bennett Ryan I knew. This wasn't the lover I'd just left a moment ago, grateful to and proud of me for capably stepping in for him. And this wasn't even the Beautiful Bastard, begrudgingly parsing out praise. This was someone else entirely. Someone who called me "kid" and acted like he'd done *me* a favor.

I felt my face flame with anger and I stumbled back into the hotel lobby, suddenly feeling like there wasn't enough oxygen, anywhere.

Seasoning? I did *fine*? He'd been my *mentor*? In *what* universe?

I stared at the shoes of people moving in front of me as they came and left through the revolving lobby doors. Why did it feel like my stomach had dropped out, leaving nothing but a hole filled with acid?

I'd been in the business world long enough to know how it works. The people at the top don't get there by sharing credit. They get there through big promises, big claims, and bigger egos.

In my first six months at Ryan Media, I brought in a sixty-million-dollar marketing account.

I managed the hundred-million-dollar L'Oréal skin portfolio.

I designed the latest campaign for Nike.

I made a country bumpkin into a business shark.

I had always felt like he praised me against his will, and there had been something satisfying about proving him wrong, about exceeding his expectations almost to spite him. But now that we'd admitted our feelings had turned into something more, he wanted to rewrite history. He hadn't been a mentor to me; I hadn't needed him to be. He hadn't pushed me to succeed—if anything, before this trip, he'd stood in my way. He'd tried to get me to quit by being a bastard.

I'd fallen for him despite all of this, and now he was throwing me under the bus just to save face for missing a meeting.

My heart splintered into a thousand pieces.

"Chloe?"

I looked up and met his confused expression. "The car is ready. I thought we were meeting outside?"

I blinked, wiped my eye as if I had something in it, and not as if I was about to break down in the lobby of the W.

"Right." I stood, collected my things, and looked up at him. "I forgot."

Of all of the lies I'd ever told him, this was the worst, because he saw it, and from the way his brows pulled together and he stepped closer, eyes anxious and searching, he had no idea why I felt like I needed to lie about something like that.

"You okay, baby?"

I blinked. I'd loved it when he'd called me that twenty minutes ago, but now it felt all wrong. "Just tired."

Again, he knew I was lying, but this time he didn't push it. He placed his hand on my lower back and led me out to the car.

Nineteen

I knew women could get moody out of the blue. I knew a few women who would get wrapped up in thoughts and scenarios and take a single what-if down the road thirty thousand years into the future, getting upset about something they assumed I'd do three days from now.

But that didn't feel like what was going on with Chloe, and she'd never been that kind of woman anyway. I'd seen her mad before. Hell, I'd seen every flavor of mad from her: pissed, irate, hateful, borderline violent.

I'd never seen her hurt.

She buried herself in documents on the short drive to the airport. She excused herself to check in with her father when we were waiting at our gate. On the plane, she fell asleep almost as soon as we were in our seats, ignoring my very clever requests to join the mile-high club. She woke up only long enough to decline lunch, even though I knew she hadn't eaten any breakfast. When she woke up as we began our descent, she stared out the window instead of looking at me.

"Are you going to tell me what's wrong?"

She didn't answer for what felt like forever, and my heart started to race. I tried to figure out all of the moments I could have fucked up. Sex with Chloe in bed. More sex with Chloe. Orgasms for Chloe. She had a lot of orgasms, to be honest. I didn't think it was that. Wake up, shower, basically profess my love. Hotel lobby, Gugliotti, airport.

I paused. The conversation with Gugliotti had left me feeling a little slimy. I'm not sure why I had acted like such a possessive jackass, but there wasn't any denying that Chloe had that effect on me. She'd been amazing at the meeting, I knew she had, but I would be damned if she would take a step down and work for a man like Gugliotti when she finished her degree. He'd probably treat her like a piece of meat and stare at her ass all day.

"I heard what you said." Her voice was so quiet it took me a moment to register that she'd said something, and then another beat to process it. My stomach dropped.

"What I said *when*?"

She smiled, turning to look at me finally, and fuck me: she was crying. "To Gugliotti."

"I sounded possessive. I'm sorry."

"You sounded possessive . . ." she muttered, turning back to the window. "You sounded dismissive—you made me seem naïve! You acted like the meeting was a training exercise. I feel ridiculous for how I described it to you yesterday, thinking it was something more."

I put my hand on her arm, laughing a little. "Guys like Gugliotti have egos. He just needs to feel like the executives are listening to him. You did everything we needed. He just wants me to be the one to hand him the official contract."

"But that's absurd. And you perpetuated it, with me as the pawn."

I blinked, confused. I did exactly what she said. But that's how the game is played, isn't it? "You're my intern."

A sharp laugh escaped her lips and she turned to me again. "Right. Because you've cared all this time how my career progresses."

"Of course I do."

"How would you know I need seasoning? You barely looked at my work before yesterday."

"Patently false." I shook my head, getting a little riled. "I know that because I've watched *everything* you do. I don't want to put pressure on you to do more than you can right now, and that's why I'm maintaining control of the Gugliotti account. But you did a great job in there, and I was very proud of you."

She closed her eyes, and leaned her head back against her seat. "You called me '*kid*.'"

"I did?" I searched my memory and realized she was right. "I guess I just didn't want him to see you as this bombshell businesswoman he could hire away and try to fuck."

"Jesus, Bennett. You are such an asshole! Maybe he wanted to hire me because I can do the job well!"

"I apologize. I'm acting like a possessive boyfriend."

"The possessive boyfriend thing isn't new to me. It's that you're acting like you did me a favor. It's how condescending you're being. I'm not sure now is the best time to engage in more typical boss-intern interactions."

"I told you I think you did an amazing job with him."

She glared at me, her face turning red. "You never would have said that before. You would have said, 'Good. Back to work.' That's it. And to Gugliotti you acted like you have me under your thumb. Before you would have pretended you didn't even know me."

"Do we really need to discuss why I was an asshole before? You weren't exactly Little Miss Sunshine yourself. And why is *now* the time to hash this out?"

"This isn't about you being an asshole before. It's about how you're being *now*. You're compensating. This is exactly why you don't fuck your boss. You were a fine boss before— you let me do my thing and you did yours. Now you're the touchy-feely mentor who calls me 'kid' to the guy I saved your ass with? Unbelievable."

"Chloe—"

"I can deal with you being a giant dick, Bennett. I'm used to it, I *expect* it. It's how we work. Because beneath all the huffing and door slamming, I knew that you respected me. But how you were today—it puts a line there that wasn't there before . . ." She shook her head, glanced back out the window.

"I think you're overreacting."

"Maybe," she said, leaning down to dig her phone out of her purse. "But I've worked my ass off to get where I am— am I risking all that?"

"We can do both, Chloe. For a few more months, we can work together and be together. This? What's happening to-day? Is called growing pains."

"I'm not sure," she said, blinking away and looking past me. "I'm just trying to do the smart thing, Bennett. I never questioned my own worth before, even when I thought *you* did. And then when I believed you saw exactly who I was, and you belittled me . . ." She looked up, eyes pained. "I guess I don't want to start questioning myself now. After everything I've worked for."

The plane landed with a jolt and even still it didn't rattle me as much as what she said. I had led discussions with the heads of some of the largest finance departments in the world. I had taken on executives who thought they could squash me. I could fight with this woman until the world ended and feel like more of a man with every word. But right then, I couldn't find a single thing to say.

———

To say I couldn't sleep that night would be an understate-ment. I could barely even lie down. Every flat surface seemed to have her imprint, and it didn't matter that she'd never been to my place. The mere fact that we talked about it—and that I'd planned for her to come here our first night back—made her ghost as good as permanent.

I called her; she didn't answer. Granted, it was at three in the morning, but I knew she wasn't sleeping either. Her silence was worsened by the fact that I knew she felt what I felt. I knew she was in just as deep as I was. But she thought she shouldn't be.

Tomorrow couldn't come soon enough.

———

I got in at six, before I knew she'd be there. I got us both coffee, updated my calendar to save her some time she could use to catch up after being gone. I faxed the contract to Gugliotti, telling him the version he saw in San Diego was final, and whatever Chloe presented would stand. I gave him two days to return the signature pages.

And then, I waited.

At eight, my father came into my office, Henry close behind. Dad scowled often, but rarely at me. Henry never looked pissed.

But both of them looked like they wanted to murder me.

"What did you do?" Dad dropped a piece of paper on my desk.

Ice dripped into my veins. "What is that?"

"It's Chloe's resignation letter. She dropped it off with Sara this morning."

It was a full minute before I could speak. In that time,

the only sound was my brother saying, "Ben, dude. What happened?"

"I fucked up," I said, finally, pressing the heels of my hands to my eyes.

Dad sat down, face composed. He was sitting in the chair that, not a month ago, Chloe had sat in, spread her legs, and touched herself while I tried to keep it together on the phone.

Christ, how did I let it get to this?

"Tell me what happened." My father's voice got very quiet: a lull between quakes.

I pulled my tie looser around my neck, suffocating under the weight on my chest.

Chloe left me.

"We're together. Or, we were."

Henry shouted, "I knew it!" just as Dad yelled, "You *what?*"

"Not until San Diego," I reassured them quickly. "Before San Diego we were just—"

"Fucking?" Henry offered helpfully, and received a sharp look from Dad.

"Yes. We were just . . ." A spike of pain gouged into my chest. *Her expression when I leaned in to kiss her. Her full bottom lip caught between my teeth. Her laugh against my mouth.* "And as you both know, I was a jerk. She gave back just as good, though," I assured them. "And in San Diego, it became more. *Fuck.*" I reached for the letter before pulling my hand back. "She really resigned?"

My father nodded, his face completely unreadable. It was his superpower, all my life: in the moments when he felt the most, he showed the least.

"This is why we have the office fraternization policy, Ben," he said, softening his tone with my nickname. "I thought you knew better than this."

"I know." I scrubbed my hands over my face and then motioned for Henry to sit down, and told them every detail of what happened with my food poisoning, the meeting with Gugliotti, and how Chloe had covered, capably. I made it clear that we had essentially just decided to be together when I ran into Ed at the hotel.

"You are such a stupid son of a bitch," my brother offered once I'd finished, and what could I do but agree?

After a stern lecture and an assurance that there would be more discussion on all of the ways I fucked up, Dad went to his office to call Chloe to request that she come work for him for the remainder of her internship.

His concern wasn't just for Ryan Media, though if she chose to stay on after she finished her MBA, she could easily become one of the most important members of our strategic marketing team. It was also that she had less than three months left to find a new internship, learn the ropes, and take on a new project to present to the scholarship board. Given their influence on the business school, their feedback would determine whether Chloe would graduate with honors and receive a personal letter of recommendation from the CEO of JT Miller.

It could make or break the beginning of her career.

Henry and I sat in stony silence for the next hour; he glared at me and I stared out the window. I could almost feel how much he wanted to kick my ass. Dad came back into my office and picked up her resignation letter, folding it into neat thirds. I still hadn't been able to look at it. She'd typed it, and for the first time since I met her, I wanted nothing more than to see her ridiculously bad penmanship instead of impersonal black-and-white Times New Roman.

"I told her that this company values her and this family loves her and we wanted her to come back." Dad paused, his eyes turning on me. "She said that was more reason for her to do this on her own."

———

Chicago turned into an alternate universe, one where Billy Sianis never cursed the Cubs, Oprah never existed, and Chloe Mills no longer worked for Ryan Media. She resigned. She walked away from one of the biggest deals in Ryan Media history. She walked away from me.

I pulled the Papadakis file from her desk; the contract was drafted by legal while we were in San Diego, and all it needed was a signature. Chloe could have spent the last two months of her master's perfecting her slide presentation for the scholarship board. Instead, she'd be starting all over somewhere else.

How could she have handled everything I gave her before but have left over *this*? Was it really so important for me to treat her like a peer with a man like Gugliotti that she would sacrifice what we had between us?

With a groan, I suspected that the reason I had to ask that at all was also the reason Chloe left. I thought we could have our relationship and our careers too, but that was because I had already proven myself. She was the intern. All she ever wanted was reassurance from me that her career wouldn't suffer from our recklessness, and I ended up being the one to ensure it did.

I had to admit, I was surprised the office wasn't on fire with the story of what I'd done, but it seemed only Dad and Henry knew. Chloe had always kept our secret. I wondered if Sara knew everything that had happened, whether she was in touch with Chloe.

I soon had an answer. A few days after Chicago changed, Sara walked into my office without knocking. "This situation is complete bullshit."

I looked up at her and put down the file I held in my hands, staring at her just long enough to make her fidget before I spoke. "I want to remind you that *this situation* is not your business."

"As her friend it is."

"As an employee of Ryan Media, and an employee of Henry's, it isn't."

She gazed at me for a long beat and then nodded. "I know. I would never tell anyone, if that's what you mean."

"I mean that, of course. But I also mean your behavior. I won't have you barging into my office without knocking."

She looked contrite but didn't shrink under my stare. I was beginning to see why she and Chloe were such close friends: they were both strong willed bordering on reckless, and fiercely loyal. "Understood."

"May I ask why you're here? Did you see her?"

"Yes."

I waited. I didn't want to press her confidence, but *good lord,* I did want to shake every detail out of her.

"She's been offered a job at Studio Marketing."

I let out a tense breath. A decent firm, if small. An up-and-comer with some good junior executives but a few real assholes at the top. "Who is she reporting to?"

"A guy named Julian."

I closed my eyes to hide my reaction. Troy Julian was on our board, an egomaniac with a penchant for barely legal arm candy. Chloe would know this; what was she thinking?

Think, asshole.

She was probably also thinking that Julian would have the resources to get her a project that she could get worked up substantially enough to present in three months.

"What's her project?"

Sara walked to my door and closed it to keep the information quiet. "Sanders' Pet Chow."

I stood, slamming my hands on my desk. Fury strangled me, and I closed my eyes to get a grip on my temper before taking it out on my brother's assistant. "That's a *tiny* account."

"She's only a master's student, Mr. Ryan. Of *course* it's a tiny account. Only someone in love with her would let her work on a million-dollar, ten-year marketing contract." Without looking back at me, she turned and left my office.

———

Chloe didn't answer her cell, her home phone, or any e-mails I sent to the personal account she had on file. She didn't call, come by, or give any indication that she wanted to talk to me. But when your chest feels like it's been cracked open with a pickax and you're unable to sleep, you do things like look up your intern's apartment address, drive over there on a Saturday at five in the morning, and wait for her to come out.

And when she didn't emerge from the building after almost an entire day, I convinced the security guard that I was her cousin and was worried about her health. He escorted me up and stood behind me as I knocked at her door.

My heart was going to slam its way out of my chest. I heard someone moving around inside, walk to the door. I could practically feel her body just inches from mine, separated by wood. A shadow moved through the peephole. And then, silence.

"Chloe."

She didn't open the door. But she didn't walk away either.

"Baby, please open up. I need to talk to you."

After what felt like an hour, she said, "I can't, Bennett."

I leaned my forehead against the door, pressed my palms flat. A superpower would have come in handy at that moment. Fire hands, or sublimation, or even just the ability to find the right thing to say. Right now, that felt impossible.

"I'm sorry."

Silence.

"Chloe . . . Christ. I get it, okay? Berate me for being a new kind of prick. Tell me to go fuck myself. Do this on your terms—just don't leave."

Silence. She was still right there. I could feel her.

"I miss you. Fuck, do I miss you. A *lot*."

"Bennett, just . . . not now, okay? I can't do this."

Was she crying? I hated not knowing.

"Hey, buddy." The security guard definitely sounded like here was the last place he wanted to be, and I could tell he was pissed I'd lied. "This isn't why you said you wanted up here. She sounds fine. Let's go."

I drove home and proceeded to drink a lot of scotch. For two weeks, I played pool at a seedy bar and ignored my family. I called in sick and only got out of bed to grab an occasional bowl of cereal, or refill my glass, or use the bathroom, whereupon I'd look at my reflection and give myself the finger. I was a sad sack and, having never experienced anything like this before, had no idea how to snap out of it.

Mom came by with some groceries and left them at my doorstep.

Dad left me daily voice mails with updates about work.

Mina brought me more scotch.

Finally, Henry came by with the only known set of spare keys to my house and dumped a pot of cold water on me, then handed me some takeout Chinese. I ate the food while he threatened to tape pictures of Chloe all over my house if I didn't get my shit together and come back to work.

Over the next few weeks, Sara surmised that I was incrementally losing my mind and needed a weekly update. She would keep it professional, telling me how Chloe was faring in her new job with Julian. Her project was coming together well. The folks at Sanders loved her. She pitched the campaign to the executives and got their go-ahead. None of this surprised me. Chloe was better than anyone they had, by a mile.

Occasionally Sara would let something else drop. "She's back at the gym," "She looks better," or, "She cut her hair a little shorter—it looks really cute," or, "We all went out on Saturday. I think she had a good time, but she left early."

Because she had a date? I wondered. And then I discarded the thought. I couldn't imagine seeing someone else. I knew what it had felt like between us, and was fairly sure Chloe wasn't seeing anyone either.

The updates were never enough. Why couldn't Sara pull out her phone and take some covert pictures? I hoped I would run into Chloe at the store, or on the street. I trolled La Perla a few times. But I didn't see her for two months.

One month flies by when you're falling in love with the woman you're using for sex. Two is an eternity when the woman you love leaves you.

So when the eve of her presentation rolled around and I heard from Sara that Chloe was prepared and handling Julian with a fist of fire, but also looked "smaller and less like herself," I finally found my balls.

I sat down at my desk, opening PowerPoint and pulling up the Papadakis plan. Beside me, my desk phone rang. I considered not answering it, wanting to focus on this, and only this.

But it was an unknown local number, and a significant portion of my brain wanted to think it could be Chloe.

"This is Bennett Ryan."

A woman's laugh rang through the line. "Beautiful, you are one Stupid Bastard."

Twenty

Director Cheng and the other members of the scholarship board filed in, greeting me amiably before finding seats. I checked my notes, triple-checked the connection between my laptop and the projector system, and waited for the last few stragglers to make their way into the conference room. Ice clinked in glasses as people poured themselves water. Colleagues spoke to each other in low voices, the occasional louder laugh breaking through the quiet.

Colleagues.

I had never felt so isolated. Mr. Julian hadn't even bothered to show up to the presentation to support me. Big surprise.

This room was so much like another boardroom, in a building seventeen blocks away. I had stood outside Ryan Media Tower earlier that morning, silently thanking everyone inside for making me who I was. And then I walked, counting the blocks and trying to ignore the twisting pain in my chest, knowing that Bennett wouldn't be in the room with me today, stoic, fondling his cuff links, eyes penetrating my calm exterior.

I missed my project. I missed my coworkers. I missed Bennett's ruthless, exacting standards. But mostly, I missed the man he'd become to me. I hated that I'd felt the need to choose one Bennett over the other, and ended up with neither.

An assistant knocked, poking her head in and catching my eye. To Mr. Cheng she said, "I just have a few forms for Chloe to sign first. We'll be right back."

Without question I followed her out the door, shaking my hands at my sides and willing my nerves to disappear. *You can do this, Chloe.* Twenty measly slides detailing a mediocre five-figure marketing campaign for a local pet food company. Piece of cake.

I just had to get through this, and then I could get the hell out of Chicago and start over somewhere hundreds of miles away. For the first time since I moved here, Chicago felt completely alien to me.

Even so, I was still waiting for the thought of leaving to feel like the right decision.

Instead of stopping at the assistant's desk, we moved on down the hall to another conference room. She opened the door and motioned for me to go in ahead of her. But when I walked in, instead of following, she closed the door behind me, leaving me alone.

Or not alone.

She left me with Bennett.

It felt like my stomach evaporated and my chest sank into the hollow space. He stood at the wall of windows at the far side of the room, wearing a navy suit and the deep purple tie I got him for Christmas, holding a thick folder. His eyes were dark and unreadable.

"Hi." His voice broke on the single syllable.

I swallowed, looking away to the wall and begging my emotions to stay bottled up. Being away from Bennett had been hell. More times a day than I could count, I would fantasize about going back to Ryan Media, or watching him walk into my new cubicle *Officer and a Gentleman*–style, or seeing him show up at my door with a La Perla bag hanging from a long, teasing finger.

But I wasn't expecting to see him here, and after not seeing him for so long, even that one crooked syllable almost wrecked me. I'd missed his voice, his snark, his lips, and his hands. I'd missed the way he watched me, the way he waited for me first, the way I could tell he had started to love me.

Bennett was here. And he looked terrible.

He'd lost weight, and although he was neatly dressed and clean-shaven, his clothes hung all wrong on his tall frame. He looked like he hadn't slept in weeks. I knew that feeling. Dark circles were carved beneath his eyes, and gone was the trademark smirk. In its place was a mouth fixed in a flat line. The fire I'd always assumed was just ingrained in his expression was completely extinguished.

"What are you doing here?" I asked.

He lifted a hand and ran it through his hair, completely ruining the pathetic styling job he'd attempted, and my heart twisted at the familiar disarray. "I'm here to tell you that you are a fucking idiot for leaving Ryan Media."

My jaw dropped at his tone, and a familiar surge of adrenaline heated my veins. "I was an idiot about a lot of things. Thanks for coming. Fun reunion." I turned to leave.

"Wait," he said, his voice low and demanding. Old instincts kicked in and I stopped, turning back to him. He'd taken a few steps closer. "We were both idiots, Chloe."

"On that we agree. You're right to say you worked hard to mentor me. I learned my idiocy from the biggest idiot of all. Any good stuff I learned from your father."

That one seemed to hit home and he winced, taking a step back. I'd had a million emotions in the past few months: plenty of anger, some regret, frequent guilt, and a steady hum of self-righteous pride, but I realized what I'd just said wasn't fair, and I immediately regretted it. He *had* pushed me, even if he didn't always mean to, and for that I owed him something.

But as I stood in the cavernous room with him, the silence blooming and spreading like a plague between us, I realized what I'd been completely missing this entire time: *he* gave me the chance to work on the most important projects. *He* brought me along to every meeting. *He* made me write the critical reports, make the difficult calls, handle the delivery of the most sensitive accounting documents.

He'd mentored me—and it had mattered greatly to him.

I swallowed. "I didn't mean that."

"I know. I can see it in your face." He ran his hand across his mouth. "It's partly true, though. I don't deserve credit for how good you are. I suppose I want to take some of it anyway, being an egomaniac. But also because I find you truly inspiring."

The lump that had started in my throat seemed to spread both down and out, clogging my ability to breathe, pressing down against my stomach. I reached for the chair nearest me, repeating, "Why are you here, Bennett?"

"Because if you mess this up, I will personally ensure you never work for a Fortune 500 again."

That was not what I expected, and my anger reignited fresh and hot. "I'm not going to mess this up, you asshole. I'm prepared."

"That's not what I'm saying. I have your Papadakis slides here, and I have handouts here"—he held up a USB drive and a folder—"and if you don't ace this presentation to that board, I will have your ass."

There was no cocky grin, no intentional play on words. But behind what he said, something else began to echo.

Us. This is us.

"Whatever you have there isn't mine." I motioned to the drive. "I didn't prepare the Papadakis slides. I left before I put them together."

He nodded as if I was exceptionally slow. "The contracts were drafted for signature when you resigned. I put these slides together from all of *your* work. This is what you're presenting today, not some marketing campaign for some shitty dog food."

It was humiliating having him throw that back in my face, and I took a few steps closer. "Damn you, Bennett. I worked my ass off for you, and I worked my ass off for Julian. I will work my ass off wherever I go next—whether it's selling pet food or brokering million-dollar campaigns—and I'll be damned if you think you can come in here with this and tell me how to manage my career. You don't control me."

He walked closer. "I don't want to control you."

"Bullshit."

"I want to help you."

"I don't need your help."

"Yes, Chloe, you do. Take it. This is your work." He was close enough to reach out and touch, and took one step closer. Close enough now for me to feel his body heat, smell the way his soap and skin combined into that familiar scent. "Please. You've earned this. It will impress the board more."

A month ago, I'd wanted more than anything to present this account. It had been my life for months. It was mine. I could feel tears forming in my eyes and blinked them back.

"I don't want to be beholden to you."

"This isn't a favor. It's me paying you back. It's me admitting I fucked up. It's me telling you that you've got one of the sharpest business minds I've ever known." His eyes softened, his hand reaching out to push a strand of hair behind my shoulder. "You won't be beholden to me. Unless you want to be . . . in a completely different way."

"I don't think I could work for you again," I said, pushing the words past the wall of heartbreak in my throat. It was taking every ounce of strength I had to not reach out and touch him.

"That isn't what I mean. I'm telling you that I messed up as a boss." He swallowed nervously, taking a deep breath. "And I really messed up as a lover. I need you to take these slides," he said, holding out the USB drive. "And I need you to take me back."

I stared at him. "I need to get back to the board-room."

"No, you don't. They're delayed." He glanced at his watch. "About a minute ago I had Henry call Cheng with some bullshit distraction so I could talk to you alone and tell you A, that you're an idiot and B, that I want another chance with you."

A grin wobbled at the edges of my mouth and I bit down on my lower lip to keep it in check. Bennett's eyes flamed victorious.

"I appreciate what you're doing here," I said care-fully. "I worked hard on that account, and I do feel ownership over it. If you don't mind, I'd like the board to see the details on the Papadakis in the handouts you have. But I'm still going to present the Sanders pitch."

He considered this, eyes moving over my face. A muscle in his jaw twitched, a telltale sign of his impa-tience. "Fine. Pitch it to me here. Convince me you're not committing suicide in there."

Straightening, I said, "The campaign is a play on *Top Chef.* But each episode, or ad, will feature a differ-ent ingredient in their food and will be a challenge to create something high-end gourmet for pets."

Bennett's eyes were veiled, but he smiled sincerely. "That's clever, Chloe."

I beamed at his honesty, savoring this moment. "Not really. That's the joke. Sanders ingredients are basic: good meat. Simple grains. Dogs don't care how fancy their food is. They want meat. On a bone. That tastes good. My dad gave his dogs gourmet chow every day, with brown rice and wheatgrass. I'm not kidding. And as a special gift on their birthday he'd give them a cheap, meaty bone. It's the owner who cares about the greens and the brown rice and all that shit. Not the pets."

His smile broadened.

"It's a way to make fun of ourselves for pampering our pets and embracing that side of us that treats them like cherished family. Sanders' is the meaty-bone chow that you can spoil them with every day. The animal 'judges' will always choose the Sanders recipe."

"You did it."

"A campaign? That's the point."

"Yes, but I knew you could do that. I meant the way you pitched it. You reeled me in, caught me."

I laughed, knowing a Bennett compliment when I saw it. "Thank you."

"Take me back, Chloe. Tell me right now that you will."

A louder laugh burst out, and I rubbed my hands over my face. "Always such a bossy asshole."

"You're going to pretend you don't miss me? You look like hell too, you know. Julia called me last night as I was putting the slides together—"

I gaped at him. "Julia called you?"

"—and told me you were a mess and I had to get my shit together and find you. I told her it was already under way. I was going to do it anyway, but her call made it easier to come here ready to beg."

"Do you even know how to beg?" I asked, grinning outright now.

Bennett licked his lips, dropping his eyes to my mouth. "Probably not. Want to show me?"

"Give it a try. Give me your best grovel."

"With all due respect, I'm going to have to ask you to suck it, Miss Mills."

"Only if you beg."

His eyes widened, and before he could say anything else, I took the Papadakis folder from his hand and left.

❧

I entered the boardroom with Bennett right on my heels. The murmuring voices stopped when we appeared.

I handed Director Cheng the folder, and he sifted

through the handouts of the Papadakis slides. He smiled. "How on earth did you manage to finish two projects?"

I stammered out a few syllables, completely unprepared for his question.

"She's efficient," Bennett said, walking around me and taking a seat at the table. "When she wrapped up the Papadakis account, we suggested she take a short internship elsewhere until she finished her degree. After all, we're hoping she'll be at Ryan Media for the foreseeable future."

I struggled to hide my shock. *What the hell is he talking about?*

"Fantastic," said an older man at the end of the table. "On Papadakis?"

Bennett nodded. "Working under my father. He needs someone to manage this one since it will take up an FTE. Chloe was the obvious choice, if she'll accept."

I swallowed down about five thousand different reactions. The primary one was irritation, for his bringing this up in front of the board. But tangled up with that were also gratitude, excitement, pride. Bennett would be getting an earful after I was finished here.

"Well, let's get started then," Cheng said, leaning back in his chair.

I picked up my laser pointer and walked to the front

of the room, feeling as though the floor were made of Jell-O. Two seats away from the head of the table, Bennett cleared his throat, catching my eye.

I'd need to ask him about that too. Because I was pretty sure that right before I began speaking he mouthed the words "I love you."

Sneaky bastard.

❧

They said my presentation would be one for the brochure, the Web site, the company newsletter.

They had me sign some papers, pose for some photos, shake a lot of hands.

They even offered me a job at JT Miller.

"She's taken," Bennett said, pulling me to the side. He stared down at me, wordless, while everyone eventually filtered out of the room.

"Yeah, about that," I said, trying to sound angry. I was still on a crazy high from the presentation, from the discussion, from the entire day. Having Bennett within kissing distance didn't hurt at all.

"Please don't say no. I sort of stole Dad's thunder. He was going to call you tonight."

"Is he really going to offer me a job?"

"Are you going to take it?"

I shrugged, feeling giddy. "Who knows? Right now I just want to celebrate."

"You were amazing up there." He bent and kissed my cheek.

"Thank you. It was the most fun I've had in weeks."

"The handouts were good, am I right?"

I rolled my eyes. "Yes, but you made one critical error."

His face fell. "What?"

"You admitted that you know how to operate PowerPoint."

With a laugh, he took my laptop bag from me and put it on a chair behind him, stalking closer with a dark smile. "I used to make slides for my boss. I was an intern once too, of course."

Goose bumps broke out along my skin. "Did your boss yell?"

"Occasionally." He ran his index finger up my arm.

"Criticize your handwriting?"

"Constantly." He leaned down, kissed the corner of my mouth.

"Did your boss kiss you?"

"My father has always been more of a handshaker, really."

I laughed, slipping my hands under his jacket so I could wrap my arms around him. "Well, I'm not your intern anymore."

"No, you're my colleague."

I hummed, liking the sound of that.

"And my lover?"

"Yes." My voice shook on the single syllable, and I understood very clearly the meaning of "drowning in relief." I was positive Bennett could feel my heart pounding against him.

He bit my earlobe. "I'll have to find new excuses to get you up to the boardroom and naked against the window."

Steam filled my veins, thick and warm. "You don't need excuses to take me home, though."

Bennett kissed across my cheek and pressed a single, soft kiss to my mouth. "Chloe?"

"Yes, Bennett?"

"This flirting is all well and good, but I mean it when I tell you, I can't have you leaving me again. It almost broke me."

My ribs seemed to squeeze all of the air out of my lungs at the thought. "I don't think I could. I don't want to be away from you again either."

"But you need to give me a chance to fix things when I screw up. You know I'm an ass sometimes."

"Sometimes?"

Growling, he whispered, "And I tear lingerie."

I pushed a curl off his forehead. "And hoard it. Don't forget the creepy hoarding."

"But I love you," he said, looking at me with wide eyes. "And I'm on a first-name basis now with most of the sales staff at La Perla. I did a lot of in-store moping while you were gone. I also have it on good authority that I'm the best sex you've ever had. So, hopefully those things outweigh the bad."

"Sold." I pulled him down to me. "Come here." I slid my mouth over his, nibbling his bottom lip. With my fists gripping his lapels, I turned and pressed him against the window, standing on my toes to get closer, as close as I possibly could.

"So demanding now that you're all official."

"Shut up and kiss me," I laughed into his mouth.

"Yes, boss."

Acknowledgments

Our first declaration of love has to be for Holly Root, our agent, our cheerleader, our adorable ninja, and the baddest badass out there. Remember that time we put on our big-girl pants and told you all of our secrets? You accepted our piglet side with as much enthusiasm as the rest of it. Thank you for letting us tick the *All of the Above* box. You are an amazing human.

The excited-fangirl kind of shoutycaps for Adam Wilson, our editor at Gallery, for immediately getting *BB,* for getting *us,* and for margin notes that had us laughing for (literally) days. Also, we're happy to know at least one guy has read this story. We promise we'll never use "vulva."

To Dawn, for her unwavering friendship and her enthusiasm when we suggested making this into something new. Thank you to Rachel, for carefully beta'ing the original fanfic. Moi, you are an amazing friend, and the best head of Office R&D *BB* could ever ask for. And although a blanket, heartfelt thank-you to the

307

fandom will never suffice, it's the best we can do in this space. Rest assured, the space you can claim in our shared history is much more massive. Your love for this story, even after it's been down for over three years, has kept it very much alive. We hope you enjoyed the reworked book as much as you did the original. May you all have your La Perlas ripped at least once.

Beautiful Bastard prereaders—Martha, Erin, Kellie, Anne, Myra, and Gretchen: reworking this into a book with you all was The Most Fun, and we loved every comment, squee, edit and ::vowel sound:: Your excitement has kept us going even when we suspected we might be insane to do this, and especially when we were sure we were. Thank you for taking time to read every word, even the dirty ones we made you read a hundred times.

But perhaps most of all, we want to acknowledge the support of our families. SisterShoes, Cutest, Ninja, Bear, Blondie, and Dr. Mister Shoes—you give us more than encouragement; you indulge us with *time,* and love us even at the peaks of our silliest obsessions. Thank you for being the best part of every day, and the reason we embarked on this adventure in the first place.

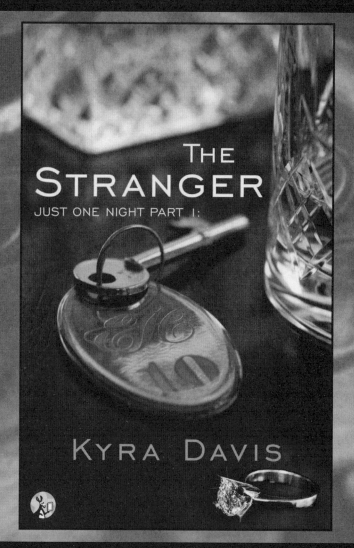